SEVEN SEASONS OF WRATH

A Story Of Penal Servitude

Douglas Coop

This edition published in 2015 by
Andrews UK Limited
www.andrewsuk.com

Copyright © 2015 Douglas Coop

The right of Douglas Coop to be identified as the author of this work has been asserted by him in accordance with the Copyright, Designs and Patents Act 1988

All rights reserved. No part of this publication may be reproduced, stored in or introduced into a retrieval system, or transmitted, in any form, or by any means (electronic, mechanical, photocopying, recording or otherwise) without the prior written permission of the publisher. Any person who does any unauthorised act in relation to this publication may be liable to criminal prosecution and civil claims for damages.

All characters appearing in this work are fictitious. Any resemblance to real persons, living or dead, is purely coincidental.

Contents

Chapter 1	1
Chapter 2	6
Chapter 3	11
Chapter 4	18
Chapter 5	26
Chapter 6	31
Chapter 7	34
Chapter 8	40
Chapter 9	49
Chapter 10	58
Chapter 11	64
Chapter 12	66
Chapter 13	72
Chapter 14	82
Chapter 15	88
Chapter 16	96
Chapter 17	98
Chapter 18	109
Chapter 19	111
Chapter 20	125

Chapter 21	135
Chapter 22	140
Chapter 23	147
Chapter 24	152
Chapter 25	157
Chapter 26	163
Chapter 27	167
Chapter 28	173
Chapter 29	176
Chapter 30	183
Chapter 31	191
Chapter 32	195
Chapter 33	198
Chapter 34	202
Chapter 35	211
Chapter 36	214
Chapter 37	222

To Margaret

Preface

When one reads accounts of the dilapidated state of English jails and the judicial system of the 1830s in England, it becomes possible to visualize the awful conditions of incarceration in those days. Taking these records into account, it is possible to build up a realistic picture of people's lives and the difficulties they must have faced. Since this story is based on true incidents such as jail and hulk records, floggings, the ship fire and famous wreck of the George 111, one can build up a genuine account of the lives of real people.

Visits to relevant sites in Hobart and Launceston, including the remains of Port Arthur Prison and the Cascades Female Factory helped to add perspective. It was a moving experience to stand at the altar of St John's Church and look up at the old prisoners' gallery. The church still retains a painting of the Rev. Thomas Ewing who married George and Elizabeth so long ago.

Enquiries at the Archive Office of Tasmania confirmed both George White and Elizabeth Allen had been transported to Van Diemen's Land for crimes committed in England. They gave me a series of dates, including details of their trials, where they had been imprisoned in England, and the ships used to transport them. They also held records of their behavior while serving penal servitude in Van Diemen's Land, as Tasmania was known in those days. These records also included their physical characteristics. While these facts are simply the bare bones of their lives, they reflect the injustices and miseries suffered by so many of Australasia's early settlers.

Acknowledgements

In the difficult task of creating historical fiction I am especially indebted to the librarians of the Launceston Public Library and to the staff of the Archives Office of Tasmania. The librarians guided me to microfilm and books describing life in London's Newgate prison, and on the prison hulks. For convict experiences during transportation I am indebted in particular to Charles Bateson's Convict Ships, and The Floating Brothel by Sian Rees.

After their arrival in Van Diemen's Land, among the books of relevant interest include The Fatal Shore by Robert Hughes, Convict Women by Kay Daniels, For the Term of his Natural Life by Marcus Clarke.

I am also indebted to Sara Andrews of AUK who guided me through the vicissitudes of publishing a manuscript, and to Victor Crapnell of Art Department Design for the book cover imaging and design. Finally, I want to thank my beloved wife Margaret, who assisted me in every way she could to complete the story.

SEVEN SEASONS OF WRATH

A Story Of Penal Servitude

Chapter 1

The Mill Fire

The long working day at the mill began like every other. In the foundry, young George White kept toiling in the clatter and fumes of large machines as they stamped out metal shapes for household utensils. Like his father before him, he worked in a huge Birmingham mill that emerged during the Industrial Revolution half a century before. While grateful to have employment, the monotony of his repetitive work bored him.

By late afternoon, mists began to shroud the city in a ghostly veil, blurring the buildings and turning them into dim shapes against a colourless sky. As damp air invaded the grimy workshop, George shivered in the increasing chill. He reached for his jacket after glancing across to his foreman, an overbearing fellow, short and stocky, and always watchful for signs of idleness. George had never seen the man's deeply lined face light up with a smile.

He looked across at George and frowned.

'Don't be in such an 'urry to get 'ome, me lad; your day ain't over yet.'

He always takes the worst meaning out of everything, George thought, as he buttoned his jacket. Anyhow, I'm the only one in the workshop able to read and write. I could become a clerk, but how to get started? That's the challenge.

'Get moving, lad, and stop daydreaming,' the foreman shouted, pointing an accusing finger.

George had barely finished buttoning his jacket when he became aware of a pungent smell, and heard a distant shout of 'Fire! Fire!'

Through the open workshop doorway men saw traces of black smoke swirling from an upper window of a storehouse on the other side of the courtyard.

'Gawd! Me father and brothers is in there,' one of George's young workmates cried out.

'And about twenty others, too. We've gotta help,' the foreman called out as he made for the door.

George and the other men in the workshop raced out after him knowing the building stored paint and other inflammable matter. As they reached the burning storehouse, a man lurched from the doorway gasping for breath, and after staggering a few steps collapsed on the cobblestoned courtyard. With some effort he raised himself onto one elbow, and pointing to the door, he rasped out, 'Men... trapped... top floor.'

Moments later a loud explosion in the storehouse alerted the whole mill to the danger. More workers came running. A second explosion followed, blowing out several upper-story windows and showering fragments of glass down onto the gathering crowd. George looked up to see thick black smoke pouring through broken windows, and he caught an occasional glimpse of yellow flames flickering and darting about. He looked with dismay at the fire truck already in the yard. It was simply a handcart supporting a tank containing water and a pump.

'Ain't much use in an upstairs blaze,' one of the crowd cried out in desperation.

'Come on,' yelled the foreman, and plunged into the burning building. With little thought for their own safety, George and a group of workers charged after him. Inside the entrance they passed a large area for loading and unloading goods. Wooden steps on one side led up to a platform where George noticed cans of paint stacked in piles against the wall.

As they hurried past, the foreman gave them a glance before shouting, "'urry, they could blow up anytime.'

Several men hesitated, looked around and began to retreat. Although the hot and dusty air parched his throat with each breath George dismissed the threat, and with several others sped after the foreman.

'Ain't no one down here,' one of them called.

In the absence of smoke in the area they dashed up a nearby flight of stairs to the floor above, and made their way cautiously along the corridor. For a moment the foreman paused, and pointing to a grey haze near the ceiling, shouted, 'Fire's gettin' close now.'

'Better go back,' one of the men suggested. 'P'haps they's all got out.'

'No, keep going,' the foreman yelled.

Amid the irritating smell of smoke and din of the fire raging on the floor above, George could hear sounds of small explosions. As they hurried along the corridore, a man staggered from a side room and collapsed in front of them. The sight of his hair and some of his clothing still smouldering alarmed the would-be rescuers. Part of the man's face seemed to be melting away in the heat, and his eyes stared unblinking. George heard a noise come from the man's throat as he tried to rise, but only his legs moved, scraping across the floor like a dying animal. It added to their awareness of the danger of being burned alive.

The foreman tore off his thick shirt to smother the flames. 'Get 'im out o' here,' he shouted. Two of the rescuers gently lifted the injured man and began to carry him back to the stairs.

For a few moments George lingered to glance into the room in the hope of finding any other survivors. As he peered though the heat haze and dust he made out a figure doubled up against the far wall. He rushed to the man's aid, but found him dead. To his dismay he recognized Jamie Young, a long-time friend and former workmate. His clothes still smouldered in places, and George found his body scorched by heat that seared his limbs rigid, leaving him cemented against the wall. Flames roared in the next room. George put his hand on the wall. It was almost too hot to touch.

He felt the foreman grab his arm, and heard his hoarse voice rasp, 'Get out you fool.'

With heat and fumes making breathing increasingly difficult, George quickly joined the others in the corridor. The group hurried down the stairs, and only just in time before the building shook with another massive explosion that collapsed part of the upper story onto the floor they had left moments before. George heard its timbers give way with muffled thumps. Dust and debris rained down behind them leaving nothing more than a few ribs of wood extending into space where the corridor had been.

Through the roar of flames overhead and the crash of falling beams George heard the warehouse begin to creak and groan. He realized the walls would soon collapse. By now they were close to the door, but the air about them, filling with clouds of dust and irritating yellow smoke, made it almost impossible to see their way ahead. As they groped forwards, George wondered if their silent victim was still conscious, or suffering any pain as they struggled with his limp form over the last few yards before bursting out into the open.

As they emerged, George glimpsed a crowd of mill workers gathered in the courtyard. Astonished bystanders watched as the rescuers laid their drooping figure onto the cobblestones before collapsing next to him. In a state of exhaustion George hardly noticed workers running forward to help and carry them to the safety of a nearby room.

'They's all lucky to get out alive,' he heard somebody say,

George's hands and face felt on fire, and his fellow rescuers suffered widespread burns. Showers of embers had burned through their thin clothing, and red splotches mottled any exposed skin on their back and arms. George was glad he had reached for his thick jacket so recently. Apart from a few superficial burns he suffered no serious harm.

Later he learned, in the turmoil of escaping the fire, some workers managed to get out through a side door. But the majority, working on the upper floor, had no chance of escaping. When the roof collapsed and flames lit up the late afternoon sky, onlookers knew they could do nothing to save either those workers still inside, or the warehouse.

George and his workmates who entered the building were each named a selfless hero. But life had to go on. After a sad day of commemorative church services, work began again as usual at the mill. Even while being congratulated, George heard of others saying he had been more foolhardy than courageous.

The whole incident, especially the death of Jamie, brought back memories of how they had been friends for more than ten years: ever since they were six years old, and both small enough to crawl amongst the machinery to grease moving parts. He remembered how the smell of oil and the clash of metal scared them so much then. Later, they swept floors before graduating to heavier work. It could have been me who died, he thought; through pure chance they sent Jamie to work in the storehouse instead of me.

Later, as he pondered his future, George considered both the fire and the loss of his friend hastened a decision to give up millwork. At night in the darkness of his bedroom he mulled over what he should do next. He knew while his workmates spent what little they earned on tobacco and beer, across the years he had managed to save more than a guinea. It's enough to get me to London and start a better life for myself, he thought. At seventeen I might be young and inexperienced, but I'm literate. I'm sure to find clerical work before the money runs out. I reckon my father and friends will never understand why I want to leave, but I see no future in millwork. Nobody knows how frustrated I feel.

As he moved restlessly about the tiny bedroom he shared with his younger brother, he considered what he should say to his father. Catching sight of his face in the small wall-mirror he stopped to stare. Smiling at his reflection, he continued to look with deep-blue eyes in a gaze that still retained the innocence of youth. Half boy, half man, he felt proud of the dark shading of whiskers that in recent months had begun to cast their shadow on his sallow face, and he instinctively stroked the palm of his hand across his cheek. Despite his average height and build, he stood for some minutes studying his image, pleased with all he saw. At that moment he came to his decision. No point in delay, he thought. Tomorrow I will face my father and tell him bluntly I intend to leave home and make my own way in the world.

Chapter 2

Home Life

The older man stood deep in thought, shoulders hunched and hands thrust into his pockets. For some time he continued to gaze out of the window until suddenly, as if reaching a decision, he turned to face his son.

'I reckon you's very foolish, George. You's got a job for life here at the mill. Why go off to London?'

'Father, I want the chance to better myself.'

'But George, the mill gives you security. You must know that.'

'My future is not here. You remember how mother used to teach me of an evening. Now I'm the only one around who can read and write.'

'I can see you're different from your mates, George. Your mother filled your head with all sorts of learning, but I'm afeared for you. I want the best for you, lad, but I've heard said London be a bad place for young uns.'

George looked at his father, barely into his forties, and saw an old man with failing health, his face, roughly chiseled by lines and creases betraying the hardships and cares of his life.

'I can't stay here, father.' George paused before going on. 'How many mill workers do you see who get injured and can't work? Some we know have even gone blind after working near the furnaces. We pass beggars on the streets every day.'

'But son, we only knows mill work.'

'Now I'm older, father, I can see what others have made of their lives.'

'You're taking a big risk, George.'

'Father, I love you dearly, but I don't want to repeat your life.'

'Well lad, if you must go off to seek your fortune in London I can't stop you,' his father replied. 'But bear two things in mind, son. Stay honest. I've heard tell of the savagery of our English justice system, and know how easy it is to be overtaken by circumstances. And remember; be aware that any girl befriending you in London is sure to have the pox.'

'Don't worry about me, father. I've seen girls on the town as they call them and heard stories of their trade, but I've no interest in them. I see better things ahead.'

His father gave a despondent shrug.

***

George remembered discovering the magic of words when barely four years old. Once again he saw his mother sitting by the window reading her bible. 'What are you doing, Mama?' little George asked as she read. She pointed to words and told him what each one meant. He learned quickly, and she often helped him to copy letters that he learned to assemble into words. Soon she began to read him an occasional phrase, and it delighted her to see how easily he grasped the meaning. In their impoverished circumstances schooling was not available to the family. Still, with his mother's help, George not only learned to read and write, but soon began to master simple arithmetic. As he grew older he read and reread his mother's small collection of well-thumbed books and anything else he could find. Later, in adolescence, he developed an interest in abstract ideas that challenged him.

He felt disappointment when his brother and sisters showed little interest in learning to read. Like most children in the neighbourhood they saw no point in it.

'George, you's a mill worker,' his young brother would gibe. 'What use is reading for the likes o' you?'

'Books are full of interest,' George tried to explain; longing to talk about the exciting things he had read.

'Reading will addle your brain. Us mill workers only needs to know how to write our name,' his brother usually taunted.

When his friends showed little curiosity in the things that fascinated him, George no longer felt comfortable in their company, nor they, he suspected, in his. Little by little he found himself at odds with the climate of illiteracy that ran through the community, and he drifted into his own world of imagination.

Older now, George's thoughts sometimes turned back to times when in his childish imagination he had joined Jason and the Argonauts in seeking the golden fleece, or gamboled in Elysian fields with nymphs and fauns. Now he realized these fables carried messages that could guide him in his daily life.

Like his mother, George took an interest in matters outside their own locality. For a long time he never knew how she came by her knowledge and apparent understanding of affairs well beyond their neighbourhood. When he came to her for help with simple problems she always gave him ready advice, but often challenged him, saying, 'you must learn to be self-reliant. Always insist on being yourself.' At another time she said, 'never imitate others, or you won't reach your full potential.'

He remembered her telling him how in their own lives every day seemed much the same, remarking, 'If you set no goal for yourself, very little changes from year to year, and it's easy to let life waste away.' When they talked of the future, she once said, 'to succeed in life, you must look ahead, or opportunities may be missed.'

While George gave his mother credit for her simple wisdom, he often wondered why she took so much trouble to teach him. He knew it had slowly shaped his mind, but her words roused a restlessness within him: a discontent with his surroundings and a longing for a better life. At night he would lie in bed thinking over what she told him, and already feel equipped to take on the outside world.

In his mid-teens he sensed his mother beginning to lose interest in the things about her. As the weeks passed, he noticed her energy waning, and the slightest exertion left her exhausted. A mild back pain she had barely mentioned now began to bore into her, increasing her suffering. Each evening the family gathered round her bed to talk together for a little while until she tired.

As she languished in his parent's sparsely furnished little bedroom, George could smell the distinct odour of the bedridden, and when he looked at her yellowed and waxen face, he feared she was slowly dying. He remembered her telling him how once, long ago, she had exchanged the boredom of an unfulfilled life of luxury for love of his father, and had revealed to him a secret he had carried with him ever since. Now, seeing his mother lying on a hard bed and covered by a single blanket, George pondered the bitter struggle of her life. As he watched her chest rise and fall he saw her frail body still holding on. And as long as she had breath, she kept saying how sorry she felt to be leaving them in this way.

One evening as they sat round her bed, George became aware of her increasing breathlessness so that she could scarcely turn or move without gasping. But somehow, despite her pain, he noticed a calm envelop her, and she tried to smile with eyes that seemed to see something beyond the present reality. Already the hard lines of suffering had faded from her face, and replaced by a dignified composure in features that no longer responded. Her breathing, almost imperceptible now, became interspersed with occasional shallow gasps until with one last breath followed by an audible sigh she remained quite still. George suddenly felt very much alone.

After her tragic death, life for the family became a constant burden. But their loss seemed to draw them closer rather than drift them apart. Sometimes George still sought his mother in a futile search for guidance. In the quiet of his room he could sense the presence of her spirit all around him, yet she was nowhere.

The family all faced the challenge, working together, cooking and cleaning, at least to their father's satisfaction. George's two sisters soon showed skill in dealing with the plain food, which was all they could afford.

Mary, a skinny eleven, kept up her needlework as best she could, and continued to sell it to the haberdasher. Before long she could bargain for food at the market as well as her mother had done. Her meals were on time, and the family usually complimented her cooking. George had to admit she was smarter than he had given her credit for.

His sister, Emma, a little ragamuffin of nine, soon changed her childish ways. She helped with the housework, and seemed able to acquire wood and other rubbish to keep the stove alight. The rooms never smelled musty, even through the long, damp winters.

His younger brother Alfred, aged thirteen, worked with George and his father at the mill. At home all three co-operated in doing any heavy work round the house: carrying coal, turning the mattresses, or beating dust from mats and blankets.

Ever since George could remember, his father's conversation usually revolved round the simple incidents of daily living. George fancied he must have been quite handsome in his younger days, but he could see a lifetime of millwork had drained his father's vitality, leaving him little passion to embrace the finer things of life. It grieved George to see his father's health deteriorating, and now, as a widower, he would die a lonely old man.

George's mother, careful of her appearance, had a totally different outlook. Small, bright-eyed and efficient, she had gone about her housework quietly and without fuss. Regardless of her long days she always seemed cheerful and enthusiastic. He could tell his parents were a devoted couple despite their difference, and he sometimes wondered what had first brought them together, and how she came to be literate.

Chapter 3

The legacy

A few months before his mother became ill George decided to ask her how she had first met his father.

Her eyes twinkled as she told him. 'It happened years ago during a time of strikes and unrest that troubled the city in those days. Workers and their families were starving, and I sympathized with their plight. Along with other women I bought food to be distributed.'

'Where did you get the food? Were you rich?'

'No George, not rich, but my father was a successful businessman with money to support me. I had a governess, and we lived in a pleasant tree-lined street. I did not need to work.

'So that is how you know enough to teach me.'

'Yes George, but before I met your father I had time to think about the problems of working people. I helped them as best I could during the strikes, but it was against the law. Your grandfather did not know what I did, or he would have stopped me.'

'So how did you meet father?'

'He used to be more active in those days before hard work and ill health wore him down. He was prominent at workers' gatherings, but not one of the ringleaders. I purchased provisions; he collected them from me discreetly and distributed them. It was a satisfying arrangement knowing we were helping others, and our friendship soon grew into something much deeper.'

'It sounds quite romantic,' said George.

'Yes, in those days your father was a fine figure of a man. We met secretly each Sunday. It was exhilarating for us; we were so altruistic, especially me. I was quite prepared to leave the luxury of my home life to be with your father and help the needy.'

'What did grandpa think of father?'

'For a long time I kept it from him. Your grandfather did not want his legacy to go to somebody unable to handle the windfall, and simply waste it. He always hoped I would marry a man with prospects, but the ones I met all seemed so colourless compared to your father.'

'You can't blame grandpa for wanting the best for you, mother. What happened when you told him?'

'He was furious. When we married he told me he disowned me, and never wanted to have anything more to do with me.'

'He must have been very disappointed in you, mother.'

'He was, and probably still is. But he has another big problem. By law, legacies go to the nearest male relative; not to a wife or daughter, and he has no son, but two daughters. My older sister Martha has always been sickly. She may never marry. That is why he hoped I would marry somebody of substance whether the marriage was a happy one or not. Now, when your grandfather dies, as I understand the law, you are legally his next male heir, and in line to inherit his wealth.'

George looked at her open mouthed, and for a few moments seemed lost for words. Finally he burst out saying, 'so this is why you've spent so much time coaching me.'

'Yes George,' she said. 'And I do believe the time has come to introduce you to your grandfather so he can see what a fine young lad you are.'

'Do you think he will accept me?'

'That remains to be seen. Your grandparents have never made any attempt to contact me, but perhaps time has reduced their bitterness. Let us go across next Sunday, a day my father usually rested, and you will meet the relatives you never knew.'

George looked forward to their Sunday trip with anticipation, but not without growing apprehension. Together with his mother they walked closer to the city where she hired a carriage to take them to a better part of town. After clop-clopping their way along quiet tree-lined streets such as George had never seen before, they stopped outside a gleaming white terraced house with steps leading up to a shiny black door graced by a large brass knocker with a lion's head. It was the first time George had seen such luxury and his uneasiness grew.

'In the past, I simply opened the door and went inside,' his mother said. 'Now we must knock and wait.'

After a few moments the door half opened, and George heard a woman's voice say, 'Well, well, look what the cat's brought home. Now you are here, I suppose you had better come in.'

'Hello, Martha,' his mother replied as they came through the doorway and into the hall. 'We've come to speak to father. And I would love to talk to you and mother again.'

'Mother is unwell. She is upstairs resting, and I'm sure she would not want to listen to your troubles.'

Greeted in this unhappy way, George stood awkwardly by, shifting uneasily from one foot to the other. It occurred to him that money did not necessarily buy happiness. We might be poor, he thought, but our family at least respect each other.

Glancing round the hallway he noticed wallpaper with fancy designs, pictures on the walls, and ornaments, -- opulence he had never dreamed of. Viewing his surroundings with awe it seemed incredible to him that perhaps he might inherit it all one day. As they waited, a thickset gentleman in a smoking jacket appeared in the hallway. The moment he spied them George imagined the man's white moustache bristled.

'What do you want of us, Ann? I told you years ago I disowned you. I still stand by my decision. If its money you are after, you had better leave right away.'

'No, father, I am not asking for money. I have come to introduce your grandson, George.'

George could almost feel his grandfather's piercing gaze as the man's eyes ranged from hair to feet, missing nothing in the search. Overcome by shyness, George at first hung his head, but quickly straightened up, and looking into his grandfather's eyes, he smiled.

'Yes, he is fine workman stock. Should do well in the mills.'

'I am sorry to hear you say that, father. I had hoped my family might have shown more compassion for two of their own. I suggest you read the story of the Prodigal Son again. Come along, George, we have wasted our time.'

As they were leaving George turned at the door, and looking back saw his grandfather still standing close by in the hallway, watching them. He gave the elderly man a slight nod, and said the first thing that came to mind, 'Goodbye, Sir, and thank you.' He saw a tear well up and trickle down his grandfather's cheek.

'You didn't give your father any opportunity to relent,' George said when they reached the street.

'I know your grandfather,' his mother replied. 'He is a stubborn man, and after what he said, he would be too proud to change his mind.'

During the journey home George could see his mother looked upset. Her expressionless features and far away look in her eyes suggested she was deep in thought. Nearer home she turned to him saying, 'George, my sister is clearly still single, and looks rather ill. It doesn't surprise me nobody has asked for her hand in marriage. This means you really are the legal heir to your grandfather's estate, unless he has somehow managed to alter his inheritance.'

'What do you intend to do, mother?'

'We must speak to your grandfather's solicitor. I once knew him well; he sometimes attended our dinner parties. It's important he sees you in person.'

'No,' the solicitor said days later. 'I should not be telling you this, but to the best of my knowledge George is still your father's legal beneficiary. I am sorry he does not want to see you again, but he is still deeply hurt and disappointed by your marriage. I am sure he regrets his stance. He is probably waiting to see how George turns out. If he proves to be unsuitable your father may challenge the law of inheritance, or perhaps sell his business.'

'In this uncertain world, can you give me any assurance my son will get his due entitlement? I have schooled him in every way I know. I'm sure he would never squander any material benefit he may gain.'

His mother's command of language impressed George.

'My suggestion is,' the solicitor went on, 'I will prepare a document for you, setting out young George's legal rights as of this date. He should keep it with him in the event of any adverse proceedings in the future. But remember, his grandfather may live for decades yet.'

George left the solicitor's office determined to learn all he could about business and dealings in the outside world. At his mother's suggestion he never spoke of his likely inheritance, even with his own family. She warned him how jealousies can tear families apart. So he kept the solicitor's letter in a safe hiding place in the house, ready if it was ever needed.

Now, the mill fire changed everything for George. When he told his friends he intended to leave home and make his own way nobody shared his hopes and ideas, or encouraged him when he tried to discuss his plans.

'You's a bloody fool, George. There ain't no sense in quitting the mill,' his long-time workmate and neighbour said, when George told him of his intentions.

'But Tom, there must be better things in life.'

'I reckon you's an odd one, George. The mill has always bin good enough for our families. It should be fit for you, too. You used to be one of us. Now, when the lads are down at the pub of a Sunday, talking and laughing, you's got your face in a book. I do believe 'twas your mother did this. All this high falootin' learning's giving you fancy ideas.'

'But I want to make use of my literacy.'

'You's heading for trouble, George,' he answered. 'Don't try and rise above your station.'

These sentiments made him restless. He became tired of the pointless conversations of his friends; always talking about the same things, and tired of the boredom of his workplace. Like Tom, anybody who gave an opinion about him leaving the mill seemed to disapprove. Lately, he noticed his friends seldom looked him in the eye. When he passed housewives gossiping on the street he would notice them pause in their conversation and glance at him askance. From their expressions he sensed them thinking, young George fancies he is too good for the mills. These attitudes made him even more determined to succeed.

He knew others did not share the secret of his inheritance. Ever since his mother told him of it he felt a special duty to keep improving himself to be worthy of the responsibility he hoped to aspire to some day. He knew there must be a world where people discussed interesting ideas and events without being thought pretentious, and he needed something to open the gateway to such a life.

It occurred to him if he wore rough workman's clothing nobody would want to employ him as a clerk, and after some thought, he spent a little of his savings on a white linen shirt. Retiring to the solitude of his bedroom, he shut the door and put on the shirt. Although the mirror was small he studied his new image, and fancied the shirt transformed him from workman to clerk. His spirits rose, and as he continued to look at his reflection, he felt he never wanted to take the shirt off again.

When he arrived at the machine shop on his final day everything looked the same to George except his workmates. The foreman in his dirty overalls watched him as he entered.

'So you's leavin' us, bright boy,' he exclaimed.

George responded with an embarrassed grin, and as he walked to his machine he caught the sullen glances of several of the older men. Once friendly, they looked away when he returned their gaze. None of them spoke. Maybe they imagine I have a low opinion of the work they spend their lives doing here at the mill, he thought. Perhaps they even feel insulted. His young workmates, who usually shared a cheery word with him, remained silent, too.

He looked out the doorway. Across the courtyard the burnt-out shell of the other building stood stark and black in the morning light. He shuddered to think of the awful events it represented, and still so fresh in his mind. I'm glad to be leaving, he thought. But I'll have to prove myself in London if I am to be accepted by my grandfather.

The night before leaving home George laid out his white shirt for the journey, happy in the thought of it offering so much promise. He packed a smart, dark-leather bag with his few possessions: simply a change of clothing, a few toiletries and his well-thumbed bible. This expensive looking bag had special meaning to him. As he grew up, it occurred to him it must have been one his mother used when she left home to live with his father; the one tangible object he had to remind him of his mother's love. He remembered it being the only toy he ever played with as a toddler. In those days his mother would occasionally allow him to open and shut the lid, or put small objects in and out of it.

He retrieved the solicitor's letter from its hiding place and put it with his belongings in the bag. He checked the savings in his money-belt, reminding him he would have to find work quickly before the money ran out. Still, he remained certain his white shirt and stylish suitcase would convince others of his clerical status. Last of all that evening he felt the need of reassurance. Kneeling beside his bed he offered up a small prayer for the family he was leaving, and for his future.

Chapter 4

Departure

The morning of his departure arrived foggy and dismal, the grey, mist-shrouded buildings still shadowy ghosts barely visible by the sombre light of a dull, orange-tinged sun. The humid air seemed to cast a pall of depression across the city, but as George closed the door behind him, a sudden sense of freedom and adventure lifted his spirits almost to bursting point.

Striding along the town's ugly cobblestoned streets, he hoped that never again would he have to live in this miserable working class neighbourhood where everybody was poverty-stricken and everything looked depressing. Once it was all he knew, and he accepted it as normal. Now, after seeing how his grandparents lived, and with a vision of hope for the future, it gave him a sense of satisfaction to be saying farewell to the rows of terraced houses, their walls blackened by years of industrial grime, and all of them damp and dilapidated.

As the town came to life, he passed ragged and poorly fed children playing in the dirt of the streets, and shabby women sweeping clouds of dust from their doorways. Already the streets were filling with faceless hordes of mill workers trudging their way through the cold morning air, their sallow and cheerless features reminding George they belonged to a way of life he had outgrown. But he soon put these thoughts out of his mind. With the world of commerce in front of him, he was eager to meet the challenge.

In less than an hour he reached the coach terminal and checked his name on the waybill. While he waited, two middle-aged women bustled in and sat opposite whispering excitedly together. Pretending disinterest, George noticed one looked older than the other and tended to dominate their conversation while her companion sat primly with hands folded across her lap. He concluded they were on their way to London, their visit involving a pecuniary benefit from an ageing relative. Both wore fashionable bonnets decorated with artificial flowers, and their dark clothes with flowing skirts obscured any underlying shape. He casually observed neither woman wore a wedding ring.

In a little while the clatter of hooves on the cobblestones and the whinnying of horses announced the arrival of the London-bound mail coach. George watched the two women gather their bags and hurry outside. As light rain had begun to fall he gave them time to have their luggage stowed before he picked up his bag and went outside.

While a groom held the reins, four glossy black horses stood in proud formation with heads erect, ears pricked back, and eyes bright, as if in anticipation of their journey. Occasionally one threw its head up and snorted, making the other horses give a little start that would gently rock the well-balanced coach. But in his excitement, George gave them little more than a cursory glance before throwing his bag up to the coachman stacking luggage on the roof, an action he would give much thought to later.

'Going as far as London, lad?' the coachman shouted.

'Yes, all the way.'

'Well, travel inside 'til we pick up more passengers.'

George found the ladies already seated in the brightly painted coach, their hand luggage safe under their seat and a blanket spread across their knees. Opposite them, a rather rotund and bewhiskered gentleman sat in earnest conversation with them. A flowery waistcoat stretched tightly across his paunch belly, and his pallid face presented a large red-tipped nose that suggested a long-term devotion to the port bottle. Two watery blue eyes peered from beneath a pair of bushy eyebrows, and twinkled as he talked to the women. George sat next to him and casually leaned against the side of the cabin.

After a while, he sensed the man studying him with veiled interest. Feeling slightly uncomfortable he turned his head to look out the window, wondering if they all considered him out of place among people of superior rank. Soon the man sat forward, and grasping the head of his silver topped cane with both hands, he turned towards George.

'Off to see the world, young lad?' he asked.

'To work in London, actually.'

'London, eh. Isn't there any clerical work for you in Birmingham?'

So he thinks I'm a clerk, George thought with a surge of pleasure, and glanced down at his white shirt, giving it credit for his new image. Still, he sensed the colour rise in his cheeks. 'The world is bigger than Birmingham, Sir,' he said. 'I hope to find suitable employment in London.'

'So you have all your worldly goods with you, eh?'

At that moment a crack of the whip and a shout from the driver sent the coach lurching into its journey across the bone-juddering cobblestones. Leaving the huddle of mean city streets far behind, the creaking of the coach and regular pounding of hooves on the dirt road became more monotonous as they lumbered their way through the countryside.

The man sat in silence next to George, his body adapting to the sway of the coach. From tine to time George noticed the man's eyelids droop and close for a few moments before waking with a start. He would give an uneasy glance towards the two ladies, perhaps wondering whether he had embarrassed them by snoring. Later he returned to engaging them in casual conversation before turning to George.

'Do you have employment in London?' he asked.

'I have prospects, Sir.'

'London is a difficult place. Employers use people or discard them with little thought for their welfare. Many have more concern for their animals than for the workingman. I do a lot of travelling in my profession,' the man added, ' I can tell you there is never enough work to go round in the big cities. Desperate people are often forced to turn to petty crime to survive.' He glanced across to the two ladies who returned looks of affirmation.

'I certainly have no intention of breaking the law,' replied George, somewhat taken aback. Embarrassed, he remained quiet for a while before turning again to gaze out the window. Still confident London offered many opportunities, he began to think of all the exciting possibilities he hoped lay ahead for him. With the added expectations of a future inheritance, he felt more fortunate than most. After all, he imagined, isn't this how many of the rich and influential people in Birmingham began their path to wealth? Still engrossed in thought, George barely noticed they had left the city mists of Birmingham far behind.

Away from crowded city life, the loneliness of the wayside and its lack of people at first gave George an uneasy feeling of vulnerability, soon to be replaced by peaceful relaxation. At times he noticed farm workers in the fields. They would glance up to watch the coach go by, and then turning, say something to each other before bending to their work.

Here and there their coach passed isolated farmhouses; long, low, stone buildings set back from the roadway, and devoid of any activity, like shapes that had grown out of the ground. At other times they clattered by a cluster of thatched-roof cottages on the outskirts of a small village; homes, George imagined, of the rustics he had seen working in the fields. In these villages he usually caught sight of a blacksmith busy at his forge, or a wheelwright repairing farm wagons and the like. He would see them stop work for a few moments to watch the coach pass, give a wave, or wipe their brow, and go back to work again.

And George took an interest in the many smaller farmyard animals, some of which he had never seen before: ducks and geese waddling awkwardly round the fringe of their pond, or grunting pigs lazing in the morning sun. Further into the countryside, horses grazing in the paddocks would jerk their heads up and peer over fences as the coach lumbered by.

As they made their way through quiet rolling hills and valleys, old churches told a thousand years of history in their ancient stone walls, and George saw an England he had never before considered. How I love this country, he thought.

Later, and well into their journey, the sun retreated behind an ominous sky heavy with a gathering mass of louring grey clouds.

'Looks like we are in for a storm,' the bewhiskered gentleman said.

George noticed the scene about them darkening, and heard the mournful sighs of the wind freshening into frequent gusts.

Soon, a high wind sprang up driving bursts of rain in a furious onslaught against them. When torrents of water lashed the windows of the coach, obscuring any view of the outside world, George noticed the two women passengers becoming uneasy.

Before long, occasional flashes of lightning illuminated the countryside and grew into a barrage that raged closer, lighting up the coach with its flashes. The road turned to mire strewn here and there with broken branches and rocks washed down from the banks. Rivulets of water surged into pools that covered the road in places, concealing hazards, while mud splashed across the coach as it forced its way through the many obstacles. An occasional shout from the driver alerted those in the coach to his increasing difficulty controlling the horses that whinnied and shied in the constant noise and turmoil of the storm.

George shivered in the penetrating cold, and pulled his jacket closer. He noticed the two women becoming frightened, and clinging together with each flash of lightning. Meanwhile, the bewhiskered gentleman busied himself attempting to stop his case sliding from under his seat and across the floor with each judder and sway of the coach.

A shout came from the driver; the coach lurched sideways, and with a loud scraping sound it came to a jarring halt tilted at an angle against a low bank. This unexpected stop sent George sprawling forwards against the two ladies opposite, and already approaching a state of near hysteria. All three slid from their sloping seats in a tangled mass of limbs to land in a heap on the floor. The gentleman somehow managed to grasp his seat to prevent himself being dislodged, but remained puffing, and leaning hard against the side of the cabin.

For some moments George found himself lying astride the younger woman, with one of his hands pressed firmly against the softness of her heaving bosom. She rapidly snatched his hand away and continued to glare at him as if she believed he had done it all on purpose. At first, the older woman lay gasping on the floor, but soon gathered herself, and both women struggled to return to their now slanting seat. All the time they said little while doing their best to regain some decorum and tidy their disheveled appearance.

George hauled himself up the sloping floor to peer through the mud-stained window, but could see very little. Thunder and lighting still raged, and rain beat against the coach as heavily as before, but he could tell their position was not as precarious as he had first thought.

Above the noise of the storm they heard the driver call, 'Has anyone been hurt?'

'Nothing serious,' the gentleman shouted back.

George levered the door open, and saw the rain-drenched coachman wiping mud and debris from his clothes.

'Are you all right, Sir,' George shouted

'Yes,' he answered. 'I was thrown clear when the coach tilted, and landed rather heavily. That's all. Anyhow, the horses be back on their feet.'

'Do you need any assistance?' George asked without thinking.

'Yes, lad, I would be obliged. Thank you for the offer. I could do with help to shift a large rock blocking a front wheel.'

George scrambled out of the coach and into the storm. With the two of them slithering about on the sodden ground, George followed the driver as he inspected the coach. He saw the wheels on one side had sunk into soft earth at the edge of the road, explaining why the coach had such a tilt. As they made their way to the front of the coach, in the half-light, George saw the large rock that had caused their sudden stop. Squelching and slipping in the glutinous mud and driving rain, it required considerable effort from both of them to move it out of the way.

With the obstacle removed, the driver bent down to inspect the damage, and looking up at George, shouted, 'I'm afeared the axle be slightly bent. We'll have to stop at the next town to have it straightened afore going on.'

George stood back and watched as the driver encouraged the horses to slowly edge the coach forward until, with a jolt, it righted itself. By now, shivering with the cold, and his clothes sodden and mud stained, he clambered back into the coach, glad to hear from the others the town of Dunstable was just a short distance ahead.

From the way the two ladies glanced at his damp and muddied clothes George could tell they hardly approved of his presence inside the coach. Still, once on their journey again he began to feel hungry, and from his pocket he extracted a wet parcel that he carefully unwrapped and began to eat several pieces of soggy bread and cheese. From the corner of his eye, he noticed the two ladies sitting opposite him glance at each other with a stony stare, clearly somewhat disgusted by his behavior and appearance. Apparently silenced by the events, even the bewhiskered gentleman remained quiet as the coach crawled on, eased by the driver who did not want to incur any further damage.

When they reached Dunstable the weather showed no sign of lifting. Rain muddied the streets; fog blanketed the buildings, and the few rain-soaked people outdoors hurried about their business as if pursued by ghosts. George felt the coach lurch to a stop and the driver, still limping, opened the coach door.

'You will have to stay here for the night,' he said. 'There be inns nearby, and one or two local houses that take guests.'

George, stiff and shivery in his cold, damp clothes, waited in the coach until the other passengers alighted and collected their luggage, then stepped out into the rain. In the semidarkness of late afternoon, he grabbed his thoroughly wet and mud-stained bag, and ran to the shelter of a nearby inn.

Glad to be out of the downpour, he found the inn almost as gloomy indoors as the weather outside, and wafting through the establishment, he discerned the distinctive reek of an alehouse. Near the entrance a lady he took to be the innkeeper's wife met him. In the dim light he made out a rather short, stout woman with an ample bust that swelled up from the neckline of her dress, and rose and fell with each raspy breath.

After getting his details and taking money for his room she reached for a lighted candle, and in the semidarkness led him along a cold stone-flagged passageway and up a narrow flight of stairs. At the top they followed a dimly lit corridor to reach the door of his room. Inside, on a small table beside the bed George saw a length of greasy candle. Picking it up he lit it from the one she held, and pushed it into its metal holder. Its flame helped to illuminate the gloom with a glow that showed a small room sparsely furnished but clean. A narrow bed with a blanket neatly folded on the mattress stood beside a wall, and nearby a washstand sat under a window that overlooked the street below. Apart from a high-back chair there were no other furnishings.

At that moment George's greatest urge was to change out of his damp clothes and into something dry and warm. Until then he had taken little notice of the wet, mud-stained bag he had hurriedly grabbed in the rain. He picked it up to open it, and although it was similar to the one he owned, to his annoyance he saw it did not belong to him. As it was the only bag remaining, he assumed one of the passengers from the coach must have taken his by mistake. In the hope of finding a clue to the owner he opened it to find it crammed with an assortment of buttons all arranged on display trays. Some were made of brass or bone, others a multitude of colours, while a few were of irregular shape.

Hopeful of locating the coachman, he snatched up the bag and rushed out of the room and along the corridor. Taking the stairs two at a time he burst out of the inn to find the street deserted. The coach had already gone elsewhere for repairs.

He slowly returned to his room knowing that without a change of clothes he would have an uncomfortable night. Climbing out of his wet garments, he wrapped the single blanket round him and lay on the bed, hopeful of retrieving his suitcase in the morning and changing into dry clothes before the coach left. Putting the excitement of the day behind him, he soon drifted into a deep sleep.

Chapter 5

A Twist of Fate

Seemingly oblivious of the pouring rain, the bewhiskered gentleman, Aubrey Jones, stepped from the coach and lent his graceful hand to the two ladies as they emerged to collect their roof luggage already unloaded to the footpath. It was a hurried affair and the ladies were soon on their way. The gentleman immediately turned to collect his own baggage and noticed it lay next to another muddied bag almost identical to one of his own. He presumed it belonged to the young lad presently seated in the coach and politely waiting his turn.

An idea quickly formed in the wily gentleman's mind. Hadn't the youth allowed him to think the bag held all his worldly goods? Perhaps it contained money. As a travelling salesman and occasional actor it was not the first time he had succumbed to temptation. After a quick glance to ensure nobody observed his actions, he picked up George's bag and hurried away leaving his almost identical bag behind.

He paused in the shelter of a building and watched as George sprang from the coach. In the gloom of late afternoon he saw George hastily grab the remaining bag, and hurry away in the pouring rain to an inn along the street. In a happy frame of mind Aubrey Jones made for different lodgings.

In the seclusion of his room he wasted no time in opening George's bag to find it contained little more than an old bible and a change of workman's clothing. Still, it would be enough to bring him a shilling or two in London. As he rummaged through the clothes he came across an envelop with the name *George White* inscribed on the front. He tore it open hoping it contained money, but instead, he extracted a letter couched in beautiful copperplate writing.

He settled back in the room's one comfortable chair, inserted his monocle and proceeded to study the contents. After several minutes he concluded it was a legal document stating George White to be the sole beneficiary of the future estate of one Luke Dunlley, businessman of Birmingham. Could this be a windfall he mused, stroking his whiskers in contemplation: something more valuable than a bag of workman's clothes?

Pouring himself a small glass of port, he continued to sit in thought for some time, pondering what best to do about the document. As he glanced about, his eyes once again alighted on George's bible. A shiver of guilt wracked through him and he paused in thought for a moment. His lucky find might be a prelude to unexpected wealth, but defrauding an estate could lead to the scaffold. That would be a risk, but he convinced himself, if handled well, there should be nothing to fear. He wondered how much Dunlley was worth. He decided to make enquiries.

He would accuse the lad of theft; the authorities would locate his own bag and return it, and George would remain in custody. After a hearty supper he quietly left his lodgings unseen, and in the darkness, disposed of George's bag under a pile of street rubbish. With a sense of accomplishment he pulled his coat closely about him and set out to make a formal complaint at the constabulary.

***

Next morning, soon after first light, George awoke to the sounds of activity in the courtyard below. Feeling cold and uncomfortable, he wondered if the coach had already been repaired. For a few minutes he lingered in bed with little inclination to get up, knowing his clothes would still be damp. At last, in the hope of having his bag returned and changing into dry clothes, he slid out of bed. Shivering in the chill morning air he crossed to the window, lifted the curtain and peered out to see light snow falling, shrouding the street and clinging to buildings. The coach had not returned.

He dressed rapidly but his damp clothes left him feeling miserable. Moreover, he saw his precious white shirt streaked with mud. Catching a glimpse of himself in a small mirror on the wall it perturbed him to see his bedraggled appearance. It left him thinking he had been unwise to leave the coach in pouring rain, even if he had been of help to the coachman.

A loud knocking at the door interrupted his thoughts. He opened it hoping to see somebody standing there holding his bag, but instead, he saw two large men who scrutinized him with a penetrating gaze. When he recognized both were constables of the newly formed civil police, a worried frown crossed his face.

'May we come in?' one of them said with mock politeness. Without waiting for a reply both men entered and closed the door behind them.

'Are you George White who travelled on the Birmingham to London coach yesterday?'

George gave an uneasy nod as he wondered why these two officers of the law should want to question him.

'May we see the bag you collected from the coach yesterday?'

'Certainly, Sir,' replied George. 'But I found the one I collected does not belong to me. One of the other passengers must have taken mine by mistake and left this one. It is full of buttons.'

'Are you blaming another passenger for the blunder?'

'No, Sir, but being last to leave the coach I picked up the only remaining bag, assuming it to be mine.'

'Surely you would have been able to recognize your own bag.'

'It was getting dark, and raining heavily. I grabbed it in a hurry. It looked like mine, but it was wet and splashed with mud. At the time I didn't notice it belonged to somebody else.'

'That was careless of you,' said the officer with a hint of sarcasm. 'When did you discover your mistake?'

'As soon as I arrived up here; I wanted to change into dry clothes, but with a better light in the room I saw the suitcase did not belong to me.'

'Did you try to find the owner?'

'Yes. I ran down to the coachman, but by then the coach had gone. There was nothing more I could do 'til this morning. I am hoping to exchange it with whichever passenger took mine.'

The officers glanced at each other before one said, 'We will return this bag to its rightful owner. Meantime we want you to come with us for further questioning.'

'Will it take long?' George asked. 'The coach will start for London as soon as it has been repaired. I would like to have my bag to change into dry clothes before it leaves.'

When he saw the sullen frowns of the two officers, George realized he could be in serious trouble. Still, he felt confident it would soon be resolved when his bag was returned.

'Come along with us, lad,' one of them said. 'Don't waste time.'

Flanked by an officer on each side of him, they walked a short distance to a large, brick building that George imagined housed the jail. As he trudged along the snow-clad street he kept looking this way and that, hopeful of coming upon the coach. But although the streets were filling with bustling workers, he saw neither coachman nor passengers.

In the chilly atmosphere of the building, officers escorted him to a bleak room with bare walls. High up on one side a barred window admitted a few pale rays of morning light. In the middle of the room he saw several chairs and a large desk on which stood an inkwell and quill pen.

One officer sat down at the desk while the other remained standing beside George. The seated officer reached under the desktop and opened a draw from which he extracted a sheet of paper and placed it in front of him. He signalled George to sit facing him across the table. For a few moments the officer simply stared at him without saying anything. Uncertain how to respond, George returned his gaze.

The officer at the desk leaned forward to speak.

'Mr. Aubrey Jones, the gentleman on the coach, complained to us that one of his bags was missing, believed stolen. He certainly did not take yours by mistake,' the officer began. 'We have already spoken to each of the lady passengers on the coach. Neither had a bag similar to the one you claim was yours, nor does either of them own anything resembling it. In other words we do not believe you ever had a bag of your own.'

'Oh, no! That's not right,' George gasped. Taken aback, his mind went blank.

'In addition', the officer added, 'The two ladies found your behaviour most embarrassing. And, I might say from what they told us, your actions at times were hardly those of an honourable man.'

George could almost feel the colour drain from his face. For a few moments he remained speechless. As he sat looking anxiously from one officer to the other he saw himself condemned in their sight.

'The ladies must have referred to the unfortunate accident when the coach came to a sudden stop and pitched sideways,' he finally stammered. 'It caused me to lose my balance, and I was thrown forward onto them. I can only add my heartfelt apologies for any embarrassment I have caused them.'

'You may be glib of tongue young fellow, but all the evidence is against you,' said the officer. 'We don't believe a young ragamuffin like you would own such an expensive bag, or if you did, you had probably stolen it. We suspect your sole purpose in travelling on the coach was robbery. Under the circumstances, we have no alternative but to arrest you and charge you with robbing the Birmingham coach on its way to London, of a bag containing a quantity of buttons.'

For a few moments George could only stare at his accusers in disbelief. Overcome by the injustice of the accusation, he was about to remonstrate with the two officials when he realized his true predicament. Highway robbery was a hanging offence. He had no alternative but to go along with events, hopeful the truth would come out in court.

The constable stood up abruptly, and going to the door called for guards. Two burley men appeared, each armed with a cudgel.

'Take him to number three,' the officer said.

The men half pushed George along a cold stone corridor. Near the end they unlocked a heavy wooden door, and thrust him headlong into a dark and evil smelling cell holding a group of miserable wretches, some shambling about in leg irons.

Chapter 6

A Plan is hatched

Aubrey Jones woke next morning to the sound of tapping on his door. He tumbled out of bed in his nightshirt, and with slight trepidation slipped the latch and pulled the door ajar.

'Is this your bag, sir?' A constable asked.

'Why, yes,' Aubrey Jones answered, relieved to find his scheme going to plan.

'We found it in the possession of one of the passengers, and we have apprehended him for further questioning.'

'I am most grateful for your assistance,' Aubrey said. 'It is a distressing state of affairs when one's honest livelihood is threatened by the theft of important merchandise. I hope the scoundrel gets his just punishment.' As Aubrey Jones closed the door behind the two officers his confidence grew. Events were going well for him, and he settled to a breakfast of porridge and a large helping of bacon and eggs. An hour later he watched the coachman load his luggage.

'We's all ready to go, 'part from the young lad,' the coachman said as he loaded the last of the bags.

'I do believe he was arrested last night for theft,' Aubrey Jones volunteered.

The coachman stopped, and with a look of astonishment, exclaimed, 'Well I never! 'Tis a shame. Who would have thought a nice young lad like that would do such a thing?'

'Unfortunately the country is full of undesirables. And they are hard to pick,' Aubrey Jones added.

When George did not arrive for the coach, Aubrey journeyed cheerfully on his way to London. He looked back with confidence at the variety of people he had outwitted in the past, and began to make plans to benefit from the solicitor's document that had so unexpectedly come into his hands. Here is easy prey, he thought. I'm sure they will accuse the lad of theft and probably hang him or sentence him to transportation. Even if he mounts a claim, as a convicted felon without documentation, it's unlikely he would succeed.

As soon as he settled into his London lodgings, Aubrey Jones took out George's document. Each time he reread the copperplate writing it reminded him of the serious nature of his plan. At first he kept thinking of his hard life and how thin the pickings, and worried he might be caught and hanged. But after several restless nights, temptation finally convinced him the risk would be worth taking, and he began to feel more settled as he pictured future wealth.

Putting misgivings aside, at the first opportunity he tucked the document into his jacket pocket and set out to visit a forger. This presented no problem as he was already acquainted with several likely names from his days on the stage. These men often forged glowing reports of stage performances before a troupe set out to tour the countryside.

The forger of choice, known as Black Eddie, resided on the top floor of an old Lambeth building away from the more affluent areas of town. After crossing Blackfriars Bridge, Aubrey Jones found his way to the forger's address and climbed the stairs. When he regained his breath he tapped on the door. It opened slightly and a face appeared, its furtive expression changing to one of welcome when the occupant recognized his caller.

'Well, well! If it ain't Aubrey. Is you still on the stage?'

'No Eddie, I've something more important for you to look at.'

The forger studied the document. 'No difficulty in drafting this, Aubrey, 'tis easy to copy copperplate writing,' he said. 'It has all the information I needs, including the solicitor's monogram. You'll have it on identical paper within two weeks.'

'How may I reward you for your services?' Aubrey Jones asked in honeyed tones.

'Since we don't know nothing about Dunlley, or his cash, I reckon we draw up an agreement for you to pay me ten percent o' the inheritance.'

'But that could be worth thousands to you,'

'Take it or leave it,' Black Eddie replied.

Aubrey Jones sighed. After a few moments of contemplation he nodded, muttering, 'I am in your hands, Eddy.' He knew their understanding had no legal binding, but there is honour among thieves and his life could be at risk if he failed to meet his dues. 'Draw up our agreement, Eddie,' he said. 'I'll sign it when I collect the document.'

Aubrey Jones returned to his lodgings in a hopeful mood, but as the days went by his mind began to fill with doubts again. Am I getting in too deep, he wondered? But having gone this far I see no easy way out of the scheme.

He returned as arranged two weeks later.

When he read through the new document he felt reassured. Apart from the substitution of George's name by that of Aubrey Jones, it was a backdated replica of the original. It seemed so real to him he almost felt he was the genuine recipient.

'If you want this to work, Aubrey, you's got lots ahead o' you,' the forger said.

'Never fear, I'll track Dunlley down next time I'm in Birmingham, and find out how much he's worth.'

'Best get something in writing from him too.'

The challenge set Aubrey Jones thinking.

Chapter 7

Blind Justice

George did not stay long in Dunstable. After a meal of foul tasting gruel, armed guards loaded him on to an open wagon with several other miserable-looking felons, and escorted them to Bedford Jail. As he sat confused and depressed on the tray, George pictured yesterday's coach with its passengers, at that moment, going in the opposite direction to London. Barely able to think, he tried to mull over how it had all happened. What should I tell my family he thought? But he decided it best not to worry them by sending word of his predicament. If his suitcase turned up his family need never know. He imagined the authorities would simply apologize and send him on his way, leaving his present plight lingering as a bad dream.

In Bedford's prison yard guards appeared with cutlasses drawn.

'Unload yo'selfs, and get in through that door,' one of them shouted, pointing towards it with his cutlass.

Guards hustled them into a room for a roll call and then along a faggot-lit corridor. Near the end, a guard opened a heavy door, and without a word thrust George into an evil smelling cell. The door clanged shut behind him, and even before he adjusted to the dim light, several convicts surrounded him, eager to snatch his jacket until they found it damp.

'We's got plenty o' time,' one begrimed felon declared. 'Let it dry on 'im first.'

'It costs you money to stay here,' another with a badly pockmarked face said to him in a rather menacing tone. 'We shares everything. So hand over your cash.'

As he stood bewildered, George found himself pushed about to shouts of, 'Hurry up. Hand it over. Come on. Faster.'

Being the first time he had suffered physical manhandling he tried to remain calm and thankful for the few coins in his pocket. While his new cellmates watched in expectation he took out several and threw them up into the air. A wild scramble to find the money followed in the semidarkness. George hoped they would not strip off his shirt and find the belt containing his savings.

One poor emaciated fellow found the effort of locating coins on the filthy floor too much for him and he collapsed in a breathless fit of coughing. It caused him to bring up a mouthful of yellow sputum that he was good enough to spit into a small bucket in one corner.

'Does everybody have to give money?' he asked one of the older men.

'I reckon so,' he said. 'But I do believe 'tis worse if you go to Newgate. They'm calls it the garnish. Be prepared, I says.'

As he became accustomed to his surroundings George noticed a few thin straw pads nailed to sleeping platforms stacked against one wall. Probably full of lice and cockroaches, he thought.

Growing anxiety had his mind spinning, making it difficult to think clearly. I left home and said good-bye just yesterday; it was the happiest day of my life, he mused. Now, sitting despondently on the stone floor of a prison cell he pondered the possibility of being hanged for a crime he did not commit. Each time he thought of it he felt his heart thump, and with little to eat his stomach rumbled. 'When do we get fed?' he asked. The convicts looked at him with amusement.

'Meals be twice a day here.' one emaciated fellow told him.

'We'll get either, peas and barley soup or burgoo, a sort of oatmeal porridge,' another more compassionate felon added. But by the tone of his voice George could tell nobody ever got used to prison fare.

'Why are some of you in leg-irons and others not?' he asked one of the prisoners.

'Leg-irons is for them already convicted: most for theft or assaults. They be waiting to go to Newgate Prison in London. Old Sam over there will most likely end on the gallows.'

George glanced at him, a little birdlike fellow dressed in ill-fitting slops that belied his willowy frame. His eyes kept glancing about the cell missing nothing, and all the while he kept busy talking and laughing with no sign of being bothered by his fate.

'Them as like you without leg-irons goes on trial at the Bedford Court of Assizes,' the man added.

Knowing his innocence, George tried to imagine he was simply going through a bad time before the authorities discovered their mistake. Surely it would only take a few words from the coachman and they would set him free. But what if they never summoned him to give evidence? George could not bring himself to think about that. Still, as the days passed his doubts grew. He trembled and always had a nagging feeling in his gut.

Many of his fellow prisoners reminded him of his old neighbours: good at heart, but victims of poverty and a harsh society. They were friendly enough and he felt at ease with them, although he didn't feel much like talking. While a few of the more hardened prisoners talked about crime, or how to escape the hangman's noose, nobody seemed interested in listening to George and his tale of injustice. 'We're all innocent victims,' one of them assured him.

George still awoke each morning with a fleeting sensation of still being at home in his own bed, but within moments a wretched feeling of the awful reality of his predicament returned to grip him with dark despair. After several miserable days and uncomfortable nights punctuated by the coughing and groaning of prisoners unable to sleep, the door of the cell creaked opened.

'George White,' a guard shouted. 'Get out into the corridor. A court official is here to see you.'

Locking the cell door behind him, he escorted George to the room he had been taken to on his arrival.

'Stand next to the table,' the guard ordered.

As George stood there, another guard ushered in a tall cadaverous-looking man who sat down at a table, and without a glance at George he began to shuffle a few papers. Then, without any introduction, he turned his attention to George who remained standing next to his guard, and not knowing what to expect.

'I'm to defend you in court,' the man said. 'I understand you robbed the Birmingham to London coach. Do you have anything to say in your defence?'

George's hopes rose. Help had arrived. 'I did not rob the coach, Sir,' he exclaimed as vehemently as possible. 'It's all a mistake. It can easily be cleared up.' George outlined the sequence of events, hoping for a sympathetic and helpful response.

But with barely a glance the lawyer replied, 'Courts want quick decisions. They have no patience with those who waste their time in lengthy submissions. I advise you to plead guilty, and be very 'umble about it. If you can produce somebody to give you a good character reference you will probably get only a few months imprisonment. If you have no such friend, I can produce somebody who, at a price, will stand up in court, testify to your unblemished record, and vouch for your excellent character.'

For a few moments George remained speechless. 'But I've done nothing wrong,' he finally blurted out. 'Now you are asking me to perjure myself in court for something I didn't do.'

It occurred to George even if he could pay for such a defence it would leave him penniless, and he would have to return home in disgrace. Seeing himself a convicted felon, he thought, I might never get my mill job back, and have difficulty establishing rights to my legacy. I'd be an object of ridicule to my old workmates and of pity to my family.

'I never stole anything,' he burst out in exasperation. 'I intended to return the bag next morning. The coachman will confirm he stacked my bag.'

The lawyer did not look at him.

By now George had become disillusioned by the man's superficial interest and dismissive attitude, and began to view him afresh. All he saw were scrawny features on a lined and expressionless face with eyes devoid of pity. George realized the lawyer must have dealt with hundreds of lost souls who had committed crimes, most, he imagined, out of desperate necessity rather than from any undercurrent of depravity. Clearly, I can expect little understanding or help from this man, George concluded.

Seeing no way out of his quandary, he had to put his trust in the justice system. Drawing himself up, he exclaimed, 'I will plead not guilty and prove my innocence.'

The lawyer gave a shrug, and the interview was over. Within a few minutes guards led George back to his cell.

'Robbing a coach, eh. They hang you for that,' several of his fellow prisoners assured him. As a highwayman, he gained some respect, if no sympathy from his cellmates.

As weeks went by, and the time of his trial approached, George grew uneasy with nagging doubts. It dawned on him the lawyer probably expected a bribe to ensure he summonsed the coachman. I should have thought of it at the time; it could have been the price of my freedom. It's too late now he realized.

At his trial, guards kept George and the large group of prisoners waiting outside the court. As they stood about in small groups they watched while all the prosecutors and witnesses filed past them to be sworn in by the judge and then be taken to the Grand Jury room.

'I do believe they give their evidence out of public hearing,' one of George's cellmates muttered. And turning to the others, added, 'we'll never know what they be saying about us.'

'It all seems so unfair,' said George, as people continued to file into the public gallery, soon filling it with friends and relatives of the accused and crowds coming for the entertainment. Among them he noticed a group of carefree onlookers going into the courtroom; probably to gossip about stories of crime or the fate of a murderer, he thought. He watched them with contempt.

At last guards escorted the prisoners into the courtroom, and removed a few the Grand Jury had already decided were innocent. The remainder stepped forward one at a time and raised a hand when a clerk called their name.'

'How will you be tried?' the clerk asked.'

'By God and by my country,' each answered.

When all the accused had made this reply, the court assembled a petty jury, a high point in the proceedings. Some of the accused called witnesses to show them in a good light, but George had no such help. He could only stand mutely at the bar.

His appearance in front of Chief Justice Denman was brief and to the point. Key evidence against him centred on the fact his alleged bag had never been found. It led the court to doubt its existence.

Dismayed to find his lawyer had made no attempt to locate the coachman, George had no way to confirm the coachman had stowed his suitcase on top of the coach, nor would the court learn how he had assisted during the storm. It was clear to George his defence lawyer had done nothing to help him.

When the prosecutor read out the crucial testimony of the two single ladies, their damning comments on his character only added to the poor impression of him already gained by the court. With all the findings against him, the verdict was inevitable. The jury went into a huddle and quickly pronounced him guilty.

Once the judge had passed verdicts of guilty on all the accused he retired for lunch, and left those convicted to await sentencing. After a couple of hours he returned and asked each whether they could offer any reason why judgement should not be passed upon them.

'No,' George answered, later wondering if he should have said yes, but concluded this answer would only have led to a longer sentence.

Justice Denman's eyes bored into George. 'You are sentenced to serve seven years transportation to parts beyond the seas, and to such place as His Majesty's Privy Council shall deem fit.'

Trembling with apprehension, George heard the verdict. He knew those words changed his life forever. He had gone to court with a hope of freedom. At least he had escaped the hangman's noose, but how could it be all so unfair? His father's warning of the savagery of the English justice system had come true so swiftly and unexpectedly. Now, as a criminal, all was lost.

Chapter 8

Prison Life

The prison authorities wasted no time. As George left the courtroom, guards, all bearded bullies with drawn swords, confronted him and escorted him into the yard to join others found guilty.

'All you convicts, get into line here,' one of them shouted. 'An' load yo'selfs on that wagon.'

Along with the other prisoners, George quickly scrambled onto the tray with the most wretched bunch of men he had ever seen. Most had been sentenced to transportation: many for ten years, some for life. Overcome by self-pity and misery, George noticed nothing of his surroundings along the short ride back to the jail. The wagon rumbled into the prison yard and stopped.

'Get down an' through that door,' a guard yelled.

Straightaway, jailers emerged to conduct the miserable group of felons into a room to be leg-ironed. George winced as he watched the first man's fetters hammered into place. He heard some of the more emaciated men ahead of him groan out aloud as the blacksmith struck the heavy irons. When his turn came he stood firmly to have the pair of ill-fitting iron fetters clamped in place just above his ankles. Only pride prevented him crying out in pain while the smith riveted the metal.

A heavy chain attached the leg-irons to each other and hung from a thick leather belt that George strapped round his waist. But on taking his first few steps he almost toppled over, as the weight of the irons rooted him to the floor. He found raising the chain made it easier for him to move, and with a little practice he soon learned to keep his balance. Still, the weight of the fetters reduced his walk to a shuffle and he stumbled about until he learned how to manage feeling light-headed.

Whenever he tried to walk during the day the irons irritated his ankles, and in the interminable hours of darkness the pain caused him restless nights, as the metal bit into his flesh whenever he moved. With only fitful bursts of sleep he could never get comfortable on the thin straw bedding. Rats and cockroaches were everywhere; lice caused constant itching, and the overpowering stench of unwashed bodies made existence barely tolerable.

In his cell, George sat angry and dejected, his back against the stonewall, all hope lost. He felt like a man no longer himself. His days as an honest mill worker, and praise for his courage during the mill fire came from another world. Now, trapped in a ruthless justice system he had become a forgotten soul, a felon, and despised by men of good character. He kept thinking seven years of hell, and I did nothing wrong. Even if it had been possible, he felt too ashamed to write to his family. The only thought to bring him any comfort was the hope that one day, if he survived this ordeal, he would inherit his grandfather's estate.

But what had happened to his bag? Why had it never been found? The thought plagued him. He had seen the coachman tie it down and thought it unlikely to have been thrown off during the coach accident. With all day to puzzle, the explanation slowly became clearer. He knew the bag of buttons must belong to Aubrey Jones, and he reasoned this so-called gentleman was a commercial salesman and possibly a rascal well accustomed to travelling about the countryside. George concluded the man must have picked up the wrong bag either by mistake or on purpose, knowing it contained all his possessions and perhaps money. It would have been easy to keep the contents and later claim his own bag with little concern for George.

The longer he thought about it the more he became convinced Aubrey Jones was a thief. His bitterness grew when he realized this self-styled gentleman could be so unprincipled he put another person's life at risk, all for the sake of the few shillings gained by selling the clothes he had stolen.

And he thought of the solicitor's letter. Surely Jones would find it among his clothes, and it worried George to think what the man might make of it. Without the letter his claim on the inheritance could be in jeopardy. Should he write to the solicitor, he wondered. But being a convicted felon he hesitated. Even if he had the means to write the letter he had no way of getting it to its destination.

As week followed week, George continued to languish in his filthy, vermin infested cell. Although one of the convicts had acquired his jacket he was grateful they did not take any of his other clothes, or suspect he wore a moneybelt next to his skin. Several of the older men noticed his misery and began to talk to him.

'Come along lad, don't give up,' one of them said with an encouraging smile. 'Self-pity gets you nowhere.'

The man's support helped to lift George's spirits, and as he slowly accepted his plight his anger lessened. He began to see that pining for his lost freedom had harnessed his mind, and he would find peace only after he ceased to yearn for all he had lost. He decided that whatever the future might hold, he had to keep his spirits up to cope with the humiliation he knew he would have to endure for the next seven years. To rise above his present state he forced himself to keep a jovial turn of mind, and at times even managed a vacuous burst of laughter.

Early one morning just after breakfast he heard the cell door being unlocked and grating open. A jailer entered followed by another who produced a piece of paper, unfolded it and read out a series of names.

'All o' you, get out into the corridor,' he shouted.

When he heard his name called, George emerged to see another guard checking names. The man glared as if suspecting him of some fresh misdemeanor.

'Now all get into line,' he said I a gruff voice.

Again, the guards carefully checked each wretched leg-ironed convict.

'We's agoin' t' chain you all up together, so get moving.'

With the sounds of their fetters echoing along the stone corridor, guards marched them to the room where they had been leg-ironed. Here, the same blacksmith greeted them with a toothless grin of welcome before shackling them all to one long chain. George presumed this must be the beginning of his journey to parts beyond the seas.

Once again, guards inspected the line of chained convicts.

'Now, all you lot get amoving outside,' came the next order.

'I do believe we have to walk in chains to the ship,' the man next to George said.

'But that's about hundred miles away,' George answered with dismay. 'And us in leg irons.'

'I've heard said they's always walked us,' the man replied. 'Folks hear our chains clankin' and see the guards. They laugh and point, and children throw dirt.'

Feeling miserable, and expecting the worst, George shivered as he emerged from the jail to a blustery day. Gusts of wind struck him with icy blasts penetrating his thin clothing and numbing his limbs. He noticed snow on the rooftops, but was glad to find it had stopped snowing. Ashen clouds of the last few days had begun to clear, exposing occasional patches of azure sky. Here and there thin fingers of sunshine broke through, but brought him little warmth. Swatches of snow still lay along the streets, and countless icicles, scintillating like spun glass, hung dripping from the guttering of buildings.

As the line of convicts shuffled into the walled yard George saw bearded jailers standing guard with loaded pistols, and ready to meet the miserable group as they emerged. After a few minutes an open prison wagon drawn by two heavily built horses emerged from an alleyway and stopped beside them.

'Now load yourselfs on the tray.'

Although relieved they did not have to walk after all, George found the rough and uneven boards uncomfortable to sit on, and even more so with their frosty surface. When guards armed with drawn cutlass and pistol climbed on and sat one at each end of the wagon, he heard mutterings that they were on their way to Newgate Prison in London.

As the wagonload of convicts rumbled through the town, the sight of people on the streets and going about their daily lives reminded George he was now a convict and despised by free men. Once again his rage flared, and almost involuntarily, in his despair his foot shot out in anger, thumping the running board on the side of the wagon with a loud crack.

'Got it out of your system now, have you, lad?' said one of the men nearby.

George gave a groan of anguish and continued to ponder his circumstances. He found his fellow convicts poor companions for the journey. They seldom talked among themselves, or showed any interest in their surroundings. Without hope of a better life many appeared indifferent to their fate. George imagined most would have a short life, either though illness or the scaffold. Then he realized he was one of them himself and a sick feeling welled up in his gut.

As they made their way into the countryside George glanced at the man chained next to him, a gaunt fellow with a crippled arm and withered hand. He heard the man had been a successful beggar until his good hand had strayed into a merchant's wallet in the marketplace.

After a while George turned towards him, saying, 'lucky we don't have to walk to London.'

At first the man appeared to ignore the comment and continued to gaze into the distance with expressionless eyes. Then, as if it had finally registered, he muttered in a flat voice, 'I don't care. At least we get two meals a day.'

George fell silent and resigned himself to the long cross-country journey to London, and to the thought that at their slow and lumbering pace it would take them at least two days. During the first morning he was relieved to see the rain-filled clouds clearing to reveal a deep-blue vault of sky arching overhead, with small banks of knurled white clouds lining the crests of distant rolling hills.

As the hours passed George began to feel refreshed by the warmer air of the open countryside. The distant bleat of sheep gave him a semblance of life to the quiet rural setting, and the occasional bark of a dog suggested far off activity in an otherwise peaceful landscape. The clear air with its occasional birdsong brought him the scents of damp earth and foliage. Being city bred, it was a new experience to see the wheeling and turning of birds high above.

In spite of the discomfort of their journey along the country roads it soothed his troubled mind to watch between gaps in the flanking hedgerows for the colourful patchworks of hedged meadows stretching away on either side. Among the ploughed fields, early spring growth had begun to tinge the landscape with a faint greenish tinge, but despite his efforts to be in good heart, now and then, gloomy thoughts would return to remind him of his plight, and fill his mind with melancholy thoughts.

Later in the day a cry interrupted his brooding. 'Whoa,' and the wagoner brought them to a halt outside an old village inn. It gave the horses a few minutes rest, and time to refresh themselves at a horse-trough; a welcome break for the prisoners, too, as the vibrations and lurching of the wagon along uneven roads had left them stiff and sore. One of the guards went into the inn and a few minutes later emerged with a pannikin of water that he handed to the other guard. The man took a long drink, and after wiping his mouth with the back of his fist, handed the container to the nearest convict, refilling it several times as it passed round. Next, he handed a small ration of bread to each of the prisoners. 'You lot be lucky,' he said. 'This don't never happen very often.'

As he relaxed in the late afternoon sunshine, George pictured the inn as a place where for centuries yokels gathered in the evening to talk over their tankard of ale, forgetful of the day's toil. Nearby, and half hidden by ancient trees, he noticed a small stone church fronted by an array of mouldering headstones tilting in irregular rows, and where he supposed the forefathers of the hamlet lay. He could not help feeling the serenity of the place seemed strangely at odds with the cruel justice imposed upon the people.

Soon, the wagon with its cargo of convicts got underway again, and by late afternoon George began to feel a slight chill in the air, but had no way to keep warm. At times the sounds of a cuckoo caught his attention, and as trees began to cast longer shadows he noticed flocks of birds winging their way homewards.

When darkness veiled the landscape, George watched as a large gauzy moon made its entrance above a low range of hills. As their wagon passed through a grove of trees he could sense the eerie patchwork of moonlight kindling a scene of ethereal beauty all around him. In such a spectral setting he recalled stories he had once read about nymphs and fauns playing in the dappled shades of just such a grove, and he could easily imagine their presence. From time to time the distant hoot of an owl, or the song of a nightingale caught his ear, adding to the beauty of nature he sensed all round. But once through the ghostly scene, its influence left him brooding about everything he had lost. Tears of anguish pearled freely down his cheeks, as he mulled over his loss of freedom and revenge for the man who had done this to him. Once again, in his despair, his foot shot out hitting the side of the wagon with a loud crack.

'Just go to sleep, lad,' a voice near him muttered.

In a night of fitful rest, the wagon of convicts continued to bump its slow journey along rutted byways and over ancient bridges of stone spanning little creeks that babbled and chuckled in the quiet night air.

In the morning light, George began to pick out an occasional large manor set back from the road. Some boasted a tree-lined driveway leading up from a lodge at an entrance gate where a porter and his wife might live. Estates of the wealthy, George imagined. It set him wondering am I too ambitious to suppose I could one day live in a house like these, without him realizing the same families had probably resided in these large residences for generations? Nearer London, smaller houses and neat cottages began to replace the large estates, their front gardens coloured by displays of early spring flowers. He watched with interest as small birds, disturbed by their passing, flittered about the branches, eagerly searching for any tidbit that might come their way.

As time passed, he waited with increasing anticipation to get his first glimpse of the city in which he had hoped of building his future. But when they came in sight of London his disappointment grew as their wagon began to make its way between clusters of dirty and dilapidated buildings. Blackened by grime, they flanked a maze of streets that in places seemed to lead off to dark and sinister alleys. George shook his head with growing disillusion, thinking London looked no different from Birmingham. It's definitely not what I've pictured for so long, he thought.

In the smoky atmosphere of the city, the wagonload of miserable convicts had little protection from a biting wind that swirled dirt and powdery snow along the street, and gusted at their open wagon. As they rumbled along, George saw city folk stop to watch the load of chained convicts pass. Ragged urchins appeared, standing in groups laughing and pointing at them.

Later in the afternoon he detected an unpleasant smell that soon increased to a nauseating stench. As the wagon rounded a corner, George saw an imposing but grimy stone building ahead.

'That be Newgate,' one of the convicts said with a grimace. "Tis where the smell comes from.'

Gathered round its ancient entrances, groups of people stood about with many coming and going in and out. By now the convicts began to look around and take more notice of their surroundings. As they got nearer, a wooden structure beside the gateway attracted their attention. Steps on one side led to a platform overhung by a long wooden beam. 'I suppose that's the gallows,' George muttered, pointing in its direction.

'Aye,' the man next to him replied with a nod of his head. 'There'd be hangings there this very morning, cause I do believe the gallows be took away after they cut down the corpses.'

A nearby convict raised himself to his knees, and grabbing the side of the wagon for support, announced in a loud voice, 'I seed hangings here a few year back.' He paused for effect before going on. 'Six poor wretches was brought out onto the platform. Some of 'em was near collapse and 'ad to be 'elped to the rope, but one of 'em even waved and bowed to us crowds. I seed 'em strung up one after t'other, right there in front of us. Several of 'em took a while to die. I watched 'em threshing about at the end of the rope 'til guards came out and 'ung on to their legs to weight 'em down and break their necks. The crowd really enjoyed it. They pay high prices to watch from windows close by.'

'How often do they hang people?' George asked.

'About every six weeks, I do believe,' he replied. 'Hundreds crowd the streets. Gives 'em something to talk about for days. I heard 'em in the taverns talking about how each one died, who 'ad to be 'elped to the rope, and who died game.'

'Gallows is for the lucky ones,' one of the others broke in. 'I've heard said that inside they got worser ways to end your life.' After a few moments, he continued. 'They says prisoners who won't enter a plea in court is squeezed to death in the Press-yard. Heavy weights are used to force the life out of 'em. A guard told me when the weights goes on you can see their eyes pop right out o' their head.'

Not to be outdone, the first, with a wink to the others, turned to George. 'Then, o' course, there's always the whipping post for young highwaymen the likes o' you. Some gets up to several 'undred lashes 'cross their back.'

George could tell that a few of the old hands were picking on him, pulling his leg and trying to scare him. But he was quite prepared to believe all they said about the place.

Chapter 9

Life in Newgate Prison

The wagon rumbled through an arched gateway into a large courtyard where despite the fetid atmosphere of the place, all around he saw crowds of begging prisoners pestering those coming and going on business. Amid the hurly-burly, George noticed several prostitutes plying their trade in the crannies of the building. It reminded him of his father's warning about London girls.

The wagonload of prisoners came to a halt beside a stout wooden door, which like the building seemed coated with the grime of centuries. Several guards armed with drawn cutlasses emerged.

'Get off the wagon and line up,' one of them yelled.

George stretched his stiff limbs and scrambled down in the chain of prisoners. By means of shouts and threats, armed guards herded them through the doorway and along a murky, faggot-lit corridor, bringing the line of convicts to a halt outside a large room. Through the doorway George caught a glimpse of a jailer, a coarse-looking ruffian dressed in a dark leather jerkin and baggy trousers, his short, stout body and awkward movements adding to his ungainly appearance.

'Come in,' he shouted as he gathered up a few papers.

As the convicts shuffled into the room he continued to arrange the papers with grimy hands. Finally, he looked up to give the group a brief sardonic smile that revealed his discoloured teeth. But it seemed to be more out of habit than any show of welcome. His narrow beady eyes gave him a sly and cunning look in features half-hidden behind a dirty white beard, yellowed round the mouth by tobacco stains. His features and attitude warned George to expect a bully of the worst type.

'Line yo'selfs up for a roll call,' he ordered before strutting along the row of chained convicts, scrutinizing each man. George continued to hang his head, careful not to challenge the man by meeting his gaze, but he could sense the jailer's stare.

'Well, well, more scum o' the earth,' he announced with a condescending sneer.

George remembered the old convict's advice and had kept a few coins ready in his pocket, knowing money would be demanded. The order soon came.

'If you want your chain removed, empty your pockets and put everything on the table.' Obviously this jailer had first pickings. George grimaced in disgust for a man who would use his authority to exact everything he could from helpless prisoners.

As George moved past the table in the chain of convicts, it seemed to him most were cowered by the jailer. The man stood by with greedy eyes as each prisoner turned out his pockets and put the contents on the table. The injustice of British Justice unsettled George. Having been tricked out of his freedom by his lawyer's inaction and greed, he watched this bully getting away with robbing helpless prisoners, many driven by hunger to commit crimes no worse. When his turn came, George placed several coins on the table. With an effort he remained silent, but felt tempted to look the jailer in the eye and say, 'you might steal my money, but you will never take my spirit.'

When convinced further menaces would yield nothing more, the jailor produced a large pair of cutters, and handing them to one of the guards, said, 'Strike off the chain, and take care their leg-irons are secure.'

Once again guards unsheathed their cutlasses although the prisoners were plainly too weak or exhausted to offer any resistance.

'Get 'em out of my sight and over to their ward,' he ordered, and guards herded the group out of the door.

With the sounds of their leg-irons clanking and echoing from the stonewalls, the group of convicts made their way through a labyrinth of ill-lit passages, passing rooms swarming with clerks and petty officials going about their business. George noticed seedy-looking solicitors talking to dishevelled prisoners, many hobbled by leg-irons; poor wretches like us, he thought, and probably overwhelmed by debts, or the consequence of petty crime. Further on the group passed an assortment of bewildered women and children milling about, or walking to and fro as if not knowing what to do. George imagined them to be wives or relatives of prisoners. The apparent chaos of Newgate seemed different from the jails he had already experienced.

After some minutes the group came to a halt outside a prison cell. One of the guards produced a key, unlocked the door, and herded them through and onto a stone-flagged floor. Slivers of light from a heavily barred window high up on one stonewall did little to illuminate the gloom in the poorly ventilated cell. Along one wall George noticed a row of about a dozen large hooks each holding a sleeping mat. He heard the door slam shut behind them and the key turn in the lock. Within moments about a dozen dirty, vermin infested occupants gathered round the newcomers.

In the half-light one convict slightly taller than the others took charge, a long white scar across one cheek distorting his surly expression. 'You lot have to pay for your keep in here', he announced in a rather arrogant manner. 'So you all pay up or pay the penalty.'

George, already warned of the garnish, had come prepared for it, and resigned to hand over almost the last of his money hidden in the belt round his waist. He knew after the old hands had ground out as much as possible from the newly arrived prisoners most of the money they collected would have to be handed over to their guards. The prisoners used the remaining funds to purchase such things as candles, extra food, or other small privileges that made life in the cells just that little bit more tolerable.

'Now line up and hand over your cash,' the convict ordered.

George and the others quickly did as directed, and several old hands went along the line taking their contributions. Most of the newcomers knew of the garnish, and had kept as much as they could for the occasion. Those handing over enough were ordered to one side.

But some of George's group had neither money nor goods, having already been imprisoned for months. Some ignorant of the garnish had given their few possessions to the jailer who had their chain removed. Convicts surrounded these unfortunates and soon made them suffer for their lack of contributions. Several of the hardened convicts began to threaten them with dire consequences if they didn't immediately produce more money. Those with little to give were either deprived of some of their food or denied bedding, forcing them to sleep without a blanket on the stone floor.

More out of desperation than defiance, one of the convicts who had no money to give drew himself up. 'You can't get nothing more from me,' he declared,

Another of the new arrivals with little funds joined in to support him, only to be told not to answer back. Some of the old hands began to jostle the two and push them about before forcing them to run a gauntlet between two rows of convicts. The group of newcomers standing nearby watched as the two helpless men suffered numerous blows and kicks until their bodies, already worn down from a life of misery and sickness, remained lying on the floor, injured and bleeding. One of them seemed unconscious the other near to it.

Despite their seedy nature, George felt sympathy for the two men. While his cellmates stood by uneasily, and muttering among themselves, a sense of pity compelled him give what help he could to the injured men. Kneeling down to cradle one man's battered head on his arm, he took out a handkerchief and wiped blood from the man's face and soothed his brow. In a show of gratitude the poor fellow grasped George's arm with his bony and bruised hand. In all the years to come, George never forgot the look of appreciation in the man's eyes; it must have been the first kindly act he had ever experienced.

Through most of that night George heard the other convict groaning. By first light the sounds had become much fainter until they finally ceased. When the cell door opened for their breakfast to be slopped out, guards briefly examined the body and pronounced him dead.

'I do believe he were a bit sick yesterday,' one of the long-term convicts volunteered. 'He must have died from some illness in the night.'

Other convicts joined in clamoring, 'Yes, yes, he looked a bit sick yesterday. We thought he had something wrong with him.'

Although the man's bruises must have been obvious to the guards they simply disregarded them and asked no questions. After a while, two guards brought in a rough stretcher and placed it on the floor next to the dead man.

'You there,' one of the guards shouted, pointing towards two of the more robust convicts. 'Put him on the stretcher and take it all outside.'

The two convicts quickly did as ordered. Between them they lifted the body onto the stretcher, and carried it into the corridor. The door slammed behind them and the lock clicked shut. For several minutes the convicts remained silent in the cell, as if pondering the affair.

Then one of them spoke up, saying, 'I reckon that's the last o' that.'

The comment puzzled George. Clearly this was not the first time the man had witnessed such an incident. George had pictured guards returning either for silence money, or to bully a confession out of his cellmates when the truth would come out. He imagined this would lead to an inquiry by the authorities, and the convicts responsible for the man's death would end their days on the gallows.

While a man had been murdered in his cell, it seemed to George his cellmates expected the authorities would ignore the facts. At the same time, Newgate was full of inmates serving years of incarceration, or even hanged for crimes petty by comparison. He concluded it would probably be too difficult to blame the murder on any particular convicts, especially if all the others claimed they saw no violence. Anyway, an inquiry may have found the guards had been negligent.

George supposed a prison doctor would simply find the dead convict suffered from one or more of the many deadly diseases rampant in the jail, and do nothing further. After all, the wretched prisoner may have been due to hang anyway. It seemed to George that inmates could influence life in Newgate as much as the authorities.

Forced to mingle with such a wide selection of human misery, he soon learned most of those he mixed with had already suffered prolonged incarceration under appalling conditions when, for many, their crime had been simply one of being poor. On the other hand, those convicts with influential friends or independent means usually had better food and warmer clothing.

The authorities never made any attempt to separate prisoners one from the other in their crowded cell. Even the most depraved among them mingled with those accused of minor crimes. When all the inmates lay down to sleep George found little space to move on the floor. Sometimes he lay beside murderous rogues, or disturbed convicts. At other times he slept next to youths aged twelve or less, victims of poverty and neglect, their bodies jammed close to disease-ridden wretches from the London slums. It soon became apparent to George that the more hardened and serious criminals among them suffered the least. Clearly used to these hardships, they knew how to make life easier for themselves at the expense of weaker prisoners. When not contemplating the harsh realities of his situation, George spent his time fending off threats from predatory cellmates, and overcoming a dislike for vermin of all sorts that were everywhere.

One day as Gorge sat idly watching the melancholic scene round him, an evil looking felon with a constant drip on the end of his nose joined him. George had already seen the fellow's persuasive ways, especially with some of his younger and less assertive cellmates. He had never seen the man openly violent, but it intrigued George to watch him acquire small articles such as a ring or a watch quite effortlessly. On one occasion George noticed him comparing footwear with a newly arrived youth. Shortly afterwards he saw the man wearing the youth's shoes.

One morning, George noticed the man quietly working his way across the crowded cell towards him, and finally squatting beside him.

Now he had come to the man's attention George remained alert, wondering if it was his turn to be robbed. But the man seemed quite friendly and began talking about his success as a burglar. At first George thought he simply needed someone to talk to, but soon the man drew a short, dirty-looking knife out of his pocket.

'See this?' he said.

'Yes,' said George, immediately on guard.

'It's my best friend. We's done a lot together.'

'I don't doubt it.'

'Well, I tells you to give me your white shirt.'

'You've already got a shirt,' said George, gruffly.

'Well, hand yours over, I say.'

'You will have trouble taking it from me. I'm more of a match than those weaklings you robbed.'

'You don't understand,' he said. 'This knife could cut you badly afore you knew it. Even a little nick from it could fester. Now take off your shirt like a good lad and give it to me.'

George knew the man meant what he said, and with growing anger he stood up and began to unbutton his shirtsleeves. Outraged, he paused, thinking I'm not only about to lose my white shirt, but I'll reveal my money belt. He looked at the fellow. 'You're a reasonable man,' he said in a quiet voice. 'We should come to an arrangement.'

'What do you mean?'

'Exchange shirts. You will still be better off.'

The fellow bared his discoloured teeth in a sneering laugh. 'You's a rum lad,' he said, and after a few moments of thought, he added, 'but you's made a deal.' Putting his knife on the floor beside him to unbutton his verminous shirt, he began to rise.

At that moment George leapt at him with the full force of his body behind a punch that struck the man's face. Caught off balance, he stumbled backwards and fell to the floor, hitting his head on the flagstones with a crack clearly heard by adjacent bystanders. As he lay there dazed and bleeding, George grabbed the knife. Several onlookers patted him on the back, saying, 'Good for you, lad.'

As his anger subsided, George looked at the man still lying half-stunned. That's the first time I've ever punched anybody, he thought, and I rather enjoyed it. With confidence gained, it occurred to him he could stand up for himself if necessary. As he continued to ponder the event, his mind turned to the time he left home fancying he knew just about everything. But mother was right, he thought, telling me how learning from experience is as important as learning by tuition. I reckon there must still be plenty to learn from these dregs of society.

As the weeks passed, George often tried to talk with his cellmates, usually without much success. In the crowded conditions in their cell most remained prisoners of their own thoughts, and bound up in their own sorry state. On one occasion he asked a fellow of about his own age how he had come to be in Newgate.

'I was too sick to work and starving,' he said. 'I tried to steal some bread, but they easily caught me 'cos I was too weak to run far. At least we get food o' sorts in here.'

Whenever occasional conversations took place among the hardened inmates it usually revolved round crime and boasting of its rewards. After listening to them, George wondered why so many long-term prisoners had first become attracted to its lifestyle, knowing they would eventually be caught and have to pay the penalty. He came across a common background to their introduction to a life of crime. Several he talked to mentioned they had been taught by experienced thieves, and having savoured its rich rewards and freedom from hard manual work, they never wanted to go back to their old days of honesty.

One fellow about George's age, and fairly typical of the others, said, 'I was twelve years old, alone and hungry on the streets, when a kind gentleman took pity on me.'

'Took pity on you?' George asked.

'Yes. For a few days he spent lots o' money buying me cake and fruit such as I had never tasted before. He bought me a fine suit of clothes, and took me to a playhouse where I saw actors, and mixed with the gentry. I told him 'twas a grand life, and he showed me how I could be part of it. I soon learned to steal with the best of 'em, and give him the loot to sell. When I've served me time I'll go back to a life of ease.'

Several others keen to outdo each other with their own stories agreed with the first lad. One said, 'I was coached and well fed, too, but the man got a woman for me. We lived together in luxury, and she sold the goods I stole.'

'We's all gamblers,' another said with a laugh. 'We steal only when the odds is in our favour.' A comment George thought worth remembering.

'After all, lots of honest jobs have a bigger risk of death or injury,' one of them added. Even if we's caught and sentenced to death 'tis still a game o' chance, 'cos most of us can still escape the hangman's noose.'

George learned many of these habitual criminals were not only well acquainted with all the defects in laws surrounding detection and prosecution, but were able to take advantage of its many loopholes to reduce their sentence, or to escape conviction at trial. One pockmarked little man said, 'Even when they hand down a guilty verdict, most can exploit weak points in the law to avoid the death penalty.'

It seemed to George the hardened criminals were the ones who escaped the noose while the naive were hanged. Listening to these conversations gave him a better understanding of those he had to live with, and he felt himself getting more worldly wise because of it.

Chapter 10

The Condemned Sermon

After the first miserable week of incarceration in Newgate, George noticed his ankles becoming more painful whenever he moved about. When he managed to get into better lighting he saw small bloodstains where his fetters bit into the flesh of his legs, but he could do nothing about it. Whatever position he tried, the pain seldom eased and sleeping became even more difficult. The fetid smell of humanity and lack of ventilation in the gloomy cell added to his misery.

He found the food minimal in amount, but enough to keep from starving. He swallowed his breakfasts of warm gruel made from barley and flour with a small amount of bread, but it did little to quell his hunger. The middle of the day always found him waiting for his next meal, which consisted of more bread with soup containing vegetables and a suggestion of beef or pork. Supper was usually the same as breakfast. George always felt hungry.

At first he accepted the bane of Newgate in the expectation of an imminent journey to the colonies. But as he listened to convict tales he soon realized how seldom ships undertook the long and hazardous sea voyage.

'You don't set sail from 'ere,' one of his cellmates told him. 'You goes to a prison 'ulk on the Thames, and you waits there for months afore you're transported. Life on the 'ulks be a curse. They work you hard and flog you if you can't keep up.'

'At least I'm young and still strong enough to do whatever I have to,' George assured him.

'Maybe,' he replied. 'But they do say many a man would commit a petty crime to get himself transported out of squalor here in England an' have a fresh start in the colonies; the only thing stopping 'em is a year or more o' hell on the 'ulks.'

This information did little to cheer George.

One day the door of the cell opened. 'Get out into the corridor, White,' a guard ordered. 'You's agoin' to the other wing to join your friends awaitin' transportation.'

In his new cell George mixed with a different selection of prisoners. Some appeared cheerful and unconcerned for their future, many believing rumours of all the wealth that could be made in the antipodes. He concluded these were not hardened criminals, but mainly men who had fallen on hard times and had resorted to theft. A few reminded him of his old friends at the mill and he felt at ease in their company. Others were subdued and quiet, and more likely to be receivers of stolen goods, or forgers and the like. With all hope gone, they dreaded being sent to the ends of the earth. They only wanted to go back to old associates, and the lifestyle they enjoyed during their times of crime.

Once a day all the inmates of Newgate had to attend a church service in the chapel. George filed in with all those destined for transportation and sat with them on one side of the gallery. Elsewhere round the chapel different classes of prisoners, including women, took their allotted places.

In the centre of the chapel a large black pew for prisoners under the sentence of death always took his attention. On his first day the pew remained empty and he imagined it must be because of the hangings on the morning of his arrival at Newgate. But as the weeks went by, he watched the pew fill with new batches of prisoners condemned to death. Each day they were the last to file into the chapel in full view of the other convicts who showed great sympathy and pity towards them. Their entry always met with hushed whispers and restlessness round the chapel. The service was a daily burden George never became accustomed to. The sight of prisoners condemned to death and sitting so close distressed him, and each day brought him a new ordeal.

At first the demeanour of some of the condemned perplexed George. Boys under the age of fourteen, and old hands knowing they would probably be reprieved, behaved with bravado in front of the assembly, strutting to their places and glorying in the distinction of their danger. Others, uncertain of their future, could be seen trembling or tearful, some stumbling to their places as if in a trance.

As the next few weeks went by, the majority of the condemned had their sentences reprieved and were relocated to the front row of the gallery with those destined for transportation. Here, they sat in full view of those they had left behind on the condemned pew. With all hope lost, those who remained seemed to wilt away under the suspense.

George noticed one of the condemned, a tall, thin man with kindly features and a sad expression that never changed. He thought the man did his best to show a little dignity, and something fatherly about him attracted George's interest. He watched the man each day as he took his place on the black pew, and wondered what crime he had committed.

One morning he noticed the man sitting in front of him among those reprieved. But rather than looking happier his forlorn appearance remained unchanged. George leaned forward and tapped him on the shoulder, saying, 'I'm pleased to see you have escaped the noose.'

With barely a turn of his head, the man said, 'better I did hang.'

George wondered how anybody could think they would be better off dead.

Every six weeks, on the Sunday before the executions, the prison held a special ceremony in the chapel attended by all the convicts, and known as the condemned sermon. They sang special hymns such as 'The Lamentations of a Sinner'; reminding those condemned their executions would take place the following morning at eight o'clock. Part of the burial service followed and performed for the benefit of those condemned.

During his time in Newgate George attended several of these rituals with a feeling of disgust and pity for those whom fate had chosen to die. On each occasion, of the original twenty or more who received the death penalty, most were able by various means to have their sentence commuted to transportation. The unlucky ones were not always the worst of the criminals. As the days passed, George became more and more thankful his sentence had been transportation.

The wretchedness of the ceremony began for George as he watched those condemned to die next morning entering the chapel in front of the assembled inmates. There were uneasy movements from the convicts around the chapel and sounds from the women's gallery. The first to come in was a lad of about his own age, good looking and well built. With features ashen grey, he put on a brave face, glancing up at the women and giving them a wan smile. As he sat down his head drooped, and George saw his limbs trembling. It was known he had stolen goods worth more than five pounds and had nobody to vouch for his otherwise good character.

Another was a middle-aged man. George heard he had tried to salvage his son's failing business with forged letters. Despite months of efforts by friends to save his life, and with some hope of a reprieve, his death sentence finally sealed his fate. He stumbled into the chapel looking pale with apprehension, and collapsed in a heap on the black pew. Others were hardened criminals whose luck had run out. They appeared impassive and resigned to meet their death, although George could see by their strained expressions they did their best to appear calm and indifferent to their fate.

After the convicts sang hymns to the praise and glory of God, and others suitable for the occasion, the preacher went on to read relevant passages in the bible concerning the wages of sin. Then he instructed the young condemned lad to stand up and read from the prayer book, as he was the only literate one among those about to be hanged.

At first the poor lad seemed to be in a trance. He stared blankly at the book as if unable to focus his mind and could not find the place until the preacher reminded him in a loud voice for all to hear, 'the Service of the Dead'. With trembling hands the youth tried to hold the book steady, but shook so much he could barely stumble through the words. George heard an old criminal sitting next to the youth begin to mutter profane oaths, while the man adjacent and newly converted to Christianity mumbled a prayer before raising his hands and start shouting praises to the Lord.

When the youth finished his reading, and quiet had been restored, the preacher began his sermon addressing it to 'those poor fellows awaiting the awful execution of the law'. In it he dwelt on such things as shame, broken hearts, widows and orphans, sorrows, and death tomorrow morning for the benefit of society.

On each occasion George witnessed this diatribe it caused great agitation among those condemned, who finally gave up any pretense of bravery. For the youth, his legs buckled under him during the sermon and with a groan he sank to the floor. The old convict having found religion in his final days, lifted his arms and continued shouting praises to the Lord. A third gave out a high-pitched scream and fell to the floor where he lay jerking in an epileptic fit.

Meantime, George heard noises from the women's gallery where some fainted or had to be removed in a fit of hysterics. Prisoners still awaiting trial became agitated and murmured among themselves, while convicts recently removed from the black pew reacted with emotion; some with tears in their eyes appeared greatly moved.

The whole procedure left George in doubt as to what good there could be in a religious ceremony in which those about to be hanged had to play a part. He wondered if executions ever reduced crime, since clearly it was not always the most guilty who ended their lives on the scaffold. Some in George's cell said the possibility of being hanged never entered their minds when committing crimes. Several even surprised George by saying they were first drawn to a life of crime after watching a public hanging.

On the night before the executions, George and all the inmates, including those about to be hanged, could hear the sounds of workmen erecting the scaffold outside the prison. Dawn was heralded by the mournful sounds of a bell that did not cease tolling out its dirge until all the condemned had passed the agony of death. For the next hour their bodies remained hanging in the street for all to see in the vain hope of its deterrent effects.

Within the prison, most of the convicts remained silent and thoughtful for a few minutes after the bell became silent, no doubt thinking of the last moments of companions so recently among them. But before long, shouts of anger and violent language abusive of the law and the authorities followed the deadly hush.

Once expressed, these outbursts soon died down and life in the prison returned to normal.

On each day of execution there was no service in the chapel, but on the following day all the convicts attended as usual. On this occasion, those who had been reprieved had to give thanks to God for his loving kindness and mercy shown by their deliverance. George wondered what must have been going through their minds as they looked at the black pew that had held companions now dead. He watched as many of the men smiled and winked at one another while the thanksgivings were read. George concluded executions made little lasting impression on many hardened offenders.

Chapter 11
Treachery

Aubrey Jones collected his false document from the forger, certain he would soon find the whereabouts of Luke Dunlley. As a travelling salesman it would be easy. The document said Luke Dunlley of Birmingham, the obvious place to start the search.

He began by spending his evenings in casual conversations with the locals at his Birmingham inn. Here, tidbits of information confirmed Dunlley to be a hardworking and respected businessman, the owner of a wholesale business supplying a wide variety of imported goods to the city's retailers. Rumour had it he also owned three ships. Aubrey Jones began to look forward to future untold wealth, and became even more determined to acquire it all for himself. Now, after several months he was extremely pleased with his efforts, and his doubts about the risky nature of the plan were almost forgotten.

Learning that Luke Dunlley lived in a fine house in a high-class suburb, one sunny afternoon he made a special journey to the tree-lined street to see the property. Overjoyed at the sight, he dallied in the shade of an ageing oak. There, he could not refrain from picturing himself coming and going in and out of the house he imagined would one day belong to him. He believed he would inherit the contents along with the house, and remove any remaining occupants. Their fate was not his problem.

All Jones needed now would be a letter in Dunlley's handwriting. Then the wholesale business and possessions would be as good as his. One night he watched Dunlley leave his office, and saw him to be a man in his sixties, grey headed, but still spry. Aubrey's only problem was to wait for him to pass away. He had to admit this could still be years away.

His next task would be to write a letter to Dunlley that would warrant a reply in his handwriting. Not being exactly a literate person, for several days Aubrey Jones puzzled over what to say. At last he wrote:

Dear Mr Dunlley

As a businesman of repute, I rite to enquire for your co-operation to obtain a contract to emport oranges from the Canary Islands for your distribution to retale markets within the City of Birmingham.

In antisipation of recieving an apointment to discus this matter I am at present residing at the Bush and Hart Inn, a highly reputible establishment in the city.

I have the Honor to remain

Yours faithfuly
K. Brown
Maniger

Aubrey Jones read and reread his letter with satisfaction before entrusting it to a messenger to deliver. Now he simply waited to receive a reply.

Chapter 12

An Early Morning Journey

Unaware of Aubrey Jones scheme to defraud him, George kept his spirits up dreaming of his inheritance and how he might benefit from it after serving his sentence. I'm sure I could take over my grandfather's business and keep it running he would tell himself. And if I come into wealth sooner, the money could work wonders in securing my release. Still, the loss of the solicitor's letter worried him, and he mulled over whether anybody would know where to find him in the event of his grandfather's death? He found too many uncertainties to be sure.

Early one morning the door of his cell opened and a guard called out several names, among them that of George.

'Get outside and line up,' he ordered.

The man beside George looked at him. 'Where does you think we's going this time?' He whispered.

'Who knows,' George answered. 'Maybe to the hulks.'

At that moment another guard arrived with his sword drawn. The two guards moved along the line, inspecting the prisoners, ordering each to call out his name as they passed, and checking the names against a list before counting the party of convicts.

'Now get moving.'

With a rattle of leg-irons the party shuffled along the maze of passageways, retracing the route to the large room George had been taken to on arrival. Here the same grimy jailer waited for them. Another group of miserable leg-ironed convicts had already arrived, among them the sad-faced convict George had spoken to in the chapel.

'The next group o' scum for you, sir,' one of the guards announced.

George ground his teeth.

'Get 'em in 'ere and line 'em up,' the jailer ordered, and at once inspected the new arrivals one at a time.

On this occasion George did not wilt. As the jailer approached he held his head up, and his eyes followed the man's gaze with a defiant stare. The man scowled as he glared back expecting George to slump. It was the jailer who looked away first.

With all correct, he turned to the guards. 'Chain 'em up,' he ordered.

George smiled to himself. He had scored a small victory over the jailer, but wondered where they were going.

Once guards had chained them all together they escorted the hobbled group of twenty convicts outside to the courtyard. In the crisp morning air other guards stood by with drawn cutlasses and pistols at the ready, supervising the dismal group struggling against the discomfort of their leg-irons as they queued in a single long line.

'We must be going to the 'ulks at Woolwich,' one of the convicts muttered.

'Wherever it is, it can't be any worse than Newgate,' George added in an undertone.

'Don't you believe it,' the convict replied.

'The next man to talk will be lashed,' one of the guards roared. 'Now get yo'selfs moving out that gate.'

The line of shuffling convicts did as ordered, crossing the courtyard and passing under the huge stone gateway. As Newgate receded, the stench of the place gradually lessened, but George knew it would take time for the smell to fade from his clothes and from his person.

Even at that early hour they passed people on the streets. As they stumbled along in their chains George noticed well-dressed pedestrians wearing white shirts; no doubt the clerks I hoped to aspire to, he thought. Passers-by turned to stare at all the poor wretches chained together, and at their guards still with cutlasses drawn and pistols at the ready.

How could anybody imagine it necessary to guard shackled convicts so closely, George wondered? We can't escape when we are all chained together, or run away wearing leg-irons. He concluded the show of weapons was an attempt by the authorities to curb crime by drawing attention to the pitiful state of those who broke the law. Expressions told him bystanders were thinking, I'm glad it's them and not me.

George's relief at leaving Newgate changed to despondency when he saw people on the street going about their normal daily lives. It reminded him he never appreciated the freedom he had in Birmingham until he lost it. He wondered if his family knew what had happened to him, or were concerned he had not contacted them in some way since setting out for London. He would have written to his father if he had pen and paper, but he knew there was no way of getting a letter to him.

As George hobbled along city streets lined by fine buildings darkened with grime from years of smoke and fog, an empty feeling of despair soon engulfed him, as if being led to the gallows. He registered little of the city until the group emerged into an open area near a large bridge spanning the Thames. He had never seen such a wide expanse of water, or a river alive with so much activity, and as his interests picked up, his gloomy feelings began to improve.

As the convict party made its way to the quayside, George noticed a fleet of barges coming into sight, drifting from under the bridge, and passing lazily by. He heard a dog barking on one of them, and watched it dashing about, urged on by seagulls swooping and turning above the barge in their never-ending search for scraps of food. While some barges appeared empty apart from one or two people lounging on the decking, he noticed others stacked with boxes, and men moving about as if preparing to off-load the cargo. George saw freedom all around, yet so far from him.

He had never walked as far in heavy leg-irons, and his ankles ached. It was a relief to reach Blackfriars Gate where several longboats waited. Guards with cutlasses drawn sat fore and aft in each of them, while several silent and sullen convicts in leg-irons sat holding the oars. The party of chained convicts remained equally silent and miserable, probably thinking of what might lie ahead for them on the hulks. Guards promptly loaded the longboats with their wretched passengers, and without delay the small flotilla set out downstream in the direction of Woolwich.

The convict whom George had watched during church services at Newgate filed on board and by chance became seated near to him. George noticed the man's pleasant features still tinged with sadness, and he remained withdrawn, seemingly consumed with private thoughts. As he watched the shore line retreating, tears streamed down his cheeks.

George caught the man's eye, and to get his own mind away from his low spirits said, 'I'm George. What's your name?'

The man tried to smile as if he would be more friendly in better circumstances, but he made no reply. After a few moments he looked towards George, and in a quiet voice said, 'Martin.'

'Well Martin, I guess we will have to adjust to life on the hulks,' George replied, and then wondered if his doleful remark only made matters worse for the man. Martin nodded but remained silent.

With the only sound from the longboats coming from the gentle plash of oars, George tried to shake off his foreboding by taking more notice of his surroundings. He found plenty to see with the water and all upon it in constant motion around them. In the morning light they came in sight of many vessels lying at anchor further along the river, some with hands busy scrubbing decks or checking ropes. On another, sailors spread out glistening white sails to dry ready for furling, as if they had just arrived from exotic parts.

George watched men along the bustling and noisy quayside heaving and straining at tackles that took in or unloaded cargoes from the vessels moored there, and saw colliers discharging the coal he knew would soon darken the London air with its fumes. Here and there, and towering above the straggle of blackened buildings lining the shore, an occasional church spire rose up as if to bestow divine blessings upon the busy scene below.

Across the Thames a jumble of narrow streets followed the general course of the river. And as the longboats crept nearer to that side of the river, George noticed people clearly of poorer appearance than the well-dressed clerks they had passed in the city. He watched shabby-looking tradesmen moving about busy with their work, while occasional early morning shoppers with small baskets of produce hurried along or stood in groups discussing their daily lives. They might be poor, George thought, but at least they are free.

Nearer to Woolwich he noticed the buildings were smaller and more dilapidated than those of the city, while across the river a wide expanse of the mist-bound Essex moors loomed sinister and evil. He had been warned of these moors weeks before.

'If you tries to escape from the hulks,' one of his cellmates had confided. 'Don't go through the moors. 'Tis said they be haunted by the spirits of all those lost souls who have been led into the bogs by Jack-o-lanterns and other phantoms.'

Knowing how many people believed in ghosts, hop-goblins, and other phantasms, George was not sure what to make of this warning except to assure his fellow convict he had no intention of trying to escape.

During the journey along the river the convicts spoke hardly a word. From time to time George glanced at the guards and noticed them keeping a careful watch on their cargo of prisoners, although there would be nowhere for any escapee to go except to leap into the water. But shackled by heavy leg-irons and chained together, escape seemed impossible.

Soon the longboats came to Gallion's Reach where for centuries the great man-o-wars of the British navy had been serviced. But the few fighting ships remaining on the river had been converted into floating dungeons, each housing hundreds of convicts many of whom would live and die aboard. George believed it would be from here he would eventually be transported to Australia to serve out his sentence.

After an hour's rowing the longboats reached the lower stretches of the Thames where mist still shrouded the river and the Woolwich shore. Before long, the convicts became aware of an increasing fetid smell reminiscent of Newgate prison. Soon the silhouette of a huge and dilapidated man-o-war loomed out of the haze, its ghostly shape startling George with a sense of foreboding of things to come.

Held by massive rusty anchor chains, and with masts and rigging removed, it had become a mere shell of its former glory. A rough housing replaced the foredeck, and a wooden ladder fixed to the side of the ship gave access to the deck. Although

George knew the hulks were dreaded beyond almost any other punishment, his first disconcerting sight of one made him all the more determined not to allow his natural optimism to be undermined by such a dismal introduction.

Chapter 13

Life on the Hulks

The two longboats did not stop at the prison hulk as George expected. The oarsmen continued to row on in the thickening mist until they reached a smaller merchantman anchored further out. George looked at the narrow wooden ladder attached to its gunwales and considered how to get safely across from the unsteady longboat while wearing leg-irons; a slip into the water would send him straight to the bottom of the river. The order soon came.

'We'll free you from the chain, then climb up the ladder.'

While their longboat rocked and bobbed up and down in the river currents, and scraped against the merchantman, George watched as Martin and several of the more sickly convicts struggled in their ascent. When his turn came he grabbed the ladder and clung to it with all his strength and began to climb. Despite the weight of his fetters he had no difficulty in pulling himself up step by step, but as he scrambled over the bulwark his foot slipped and he sprawled on to the deck. A slash across his shoulders with the birch soon brought him to his feet. As he struggled up he saw his group surrounded by about a dozen bearded guards, ruffians at best, and all with cutlasses drawn.

'All you lot get into line,' one of the guards shouted as the last man struggled over the bulwarks.

The convicts quickly did as ordered.

'We's goin' t' strike off your irons.'

A blacksmith appeared with a hammer and large chisel, and made no attempt to soften the blows. With each stroke George almost cried out with pain. The guards laughed to watch the results. Freed from their weights after months or even years, all the convicts, including George, felt distinctly top heavy.

Disoriented and off balance, they stamped and staggering about the deck as if drunk.

When they had recovered their balance and lined up again, two well-attired officers emerged from the poop deck to inspect them. George noticed their look of disdain as they moved along the line checking each convict's name against a list. Occasionally they stopped to ask further questions that seemed to be of a medical nature.

When they reached George, one of them he presumed to be the hulk captain stopped. 'And your name young fellow?'

'White, Sir, George White'. His pulse quickened. As the pair prepared to move on, he took the opportunity to ask, 'may I have your permission to write a note to my family to tell them where I am?'

The hulk captain gave him a leer of contempt before turning to his associate. 'Do you hear that, doctor? The fellow claims to be literate.'

Both men gave a short laugh'. 'And where did you learn that ability?' the doctor asked with a sneer.

'My mother, Sir. She taught me to read and write, and do arithmetic.'

'And did she teach you to steal too, eh, eh?'

Both officers continued along the line of convicts, still rather amused at their little joke.

Having checked the group and passed it as correct, the hulk captain turned to address them. 'You bunch o' filthy scums need some cleanin' up. Now all of you strip off and get hosed down.'

Despite the cool morning air, the hulk captain's command raised George's spirits. During all his months in prison he never had any opportunity to wash. Clothing could not be removed over leg-irons, and he knew his prison garb to be full of lice. With their clothes off he noticed many of the convicts even more emaciated than he had imagined. Martin looked thin, but not as wasted as many of the others. Some appeared weak and depressed, and George wondered how they would fare on the hulks. When a guard directed the hose on to him for a short time he felt pure delight, but all too soon the full force of the stream turned to others.

'Now each of you take a turn in that tub o' lye water.'

Despite being cold water, the few moments he luxuriated in it were the most pleasant George could remember since his arrest.

When he looked for his clothes and money belt, the guards had replaced them with a set of slop clothing as he heard it called. While hardly a good fit it was at least clean and free of lice. But his white shirt had gone forever. When the group lined up again, their pall of misery had lifted just a little. Odd, thought George with a shrug, the loss of that white shirt that once meant so much to me means nothing to me now.

The doctor, who had been watching the proceedings, came forward and called out about half a dozen names of the more sickly-looking convicts, and instructed guards to escort them below deck to what George imagined to be a hospital ward. In fact, he later learned the merchantman they were on was the prison hospital ship.

As they all stood in line, George could tell the guards enjoyed their authority. He had no doubt they would respond with the birch at any suggestion of trouble.

'Now we's goin' t' iron you all up again,' one of the guards announced. The blacksmith reappeared with hammer and rivets, and banged their leg-irons into place.

'Now get down to your boat.'

George found descending the old wooden ladder more hazardous than going up, and hoped it would soon become a routine he could take in his stride. But over the next few weeks he realized he had much more to learn if he hoped to survive unsullied on the prison hulk.

After rowing a short journey from the merchantman, their new destination loomed out of the mists in front of them in the form of a dilapidated old man-o-war. George made out the name *Ganymede* in faded lettering near the stern. From the days when his mother read him stories of Greek mythology he remembered Ganymede as the handsome cupbearer to the god Zeus. What a fall from grace, he thought.

As the longboats approached the hulk he detected the same nauseating jail smell from more than a hundred yards away. Like the other hulk, its masts and rigging were long since removed, and the fo'csle replaced by a rickety wooden housing, obviously modified from time to time in a rather haphazard way.

If Newgate had been a shock to George, his arrival at the *Ganymede* filled him with despair. After struggling up the old wooden ladder attached to the side of the ship, another array of bearded ruffians met them with cutlasses drawn. The hulk captain came on deck accompanied by an overseer, a brute of a fellow, barrel-chested and taller than any of the guards.

'Line yourselfs up,' he yelled. 'An' be quick about it'.

Once again George and his group stood in a row to be checked. As the two officers passed, he had a close view of the captain: a short, thickset man with a prominent chin and receding forehead that glistened in the morning sun. George noted the captain's surly expression of cold command. The sight of them caused him to wonder if justice existed on the hulk.

'Get 'em below,' was all the captain said.

Despite his experience of jail life, George had never pictured the scene he found below deck, or the undercurrent of depravity he had to contend with. As the convicts edged their way down the hatchway, it seemed they were descending into nothing short of the infernal regions of hell.

George could barely stand upright in the gloomy flush deck. The only light filtering into the semidarkness came from the hatch and several portholes guarded by iron straps to prevent escape. Within the narrow confines he made out scores of men, many in double irons, and most occupying six to a cell. But most of all, it was the constant noise of rattling chains, the shouting of coarse oaths, the filth and vermin, the lack of ventilation, and the overpowering stench from the hordes of miserable inhabitants that filled him with a sense of despair. He learned there were two further decks below where conditions were even worse.

Guards immediately allotted the new arrivals, pushing George and Martin, who stood next to him, into a cell with four hapless occupants. One of them, a wretch in ragged clothing straightaway pulled off his shirt and confronted George.

'Here's your shirt,' he declared, waving it in front of George.

'Keep it,' George replied, 'I already have one.'

'Does you think I can't get it?'

'I doubt it,' said George. 'You look too frail to take it off me.'

'I'm boss in this here cell and you does as you's told.'

Remembering his successful skirmish at Newgate prison, George met the fellow's look of command with a challenging stare. 'Well, come and get it,' he said.

Within moments George found himself thrown to the floor, and held down by the other three inmates. Despite his struggles, they managed to remove his clean shirt, and leave him the convict's old verminous slop. For once he was glad of his fetters, as they could not remove his trousers over them. Martin quickly removed his shirt to avoid the same rough handling, and exchanged it with one of the old hands..

Once again George and Martin found themselves in filthy and verminous clothing that must have been worked and slept in for months. His fellow convicts would have taken more, but his empty money belt and clothes had already been taken that morning onboard the merchantman.

Now I'm here we are going to be all cooped up together in this cell for a long time, George thought. I'll have to make an effort to get along with these old hands, and hold no grudges.

'I'm George White, highwayman,' he announced with a grin. They laughed and slapped him on the back, and he hoped they would all get on well together.

His mood improved when he detected the smell of food being heated at the end of the corridor. Soon, a midday meal of barley soup with a little bread was slopped out in bowls, to be followed by a lump of the toughest meat he had ever encountered.

'That be bullock cheeks,' one of his new cellmates told him. George found it almost impossible to chew. Still, it was enough to take the edge off his hunger, and he felt just that little bit better for it.

All afternoon he heard groans from a nearby cell, and in the semidarkness made out somebody across the passageway chained to a sleeping pad. The man's repeated cries gradually wore George down prompting him to call out, 'What's the matter over there?'

'Old Bert slipped on the deck and broked 'is ankle,' one of the man's cellmates answered back.

'Doesn't the doctor do anything about it? George asked.

'No. The overseer reckons he's stubborn and fit for work,' the man replied. 'He had 'im chained to the bed. Says when Bert has finished shamming, his chains will be removed.'

'Is he really shamming?'

'No. His leg be all swelled up, and he says it keeps throbbing with pain. He can't get to the bucket 'cause he's chained down, and his bed is soaking wet. Now he's getting sores on his back.'

How bad can things get? George pondered. When first sentenced he often cheered himself by thinking seven years incarceration would be just a short span of his lifetime before being freed to pursue a career. Now, sitting wretchedly in the noise and evil-smelling semidarkness of his cell the same seven years had become a time of trial where every minute dragged. Freedom seemed so far away. He realized how unworldly he must have been when he left home and family. But he felt the hardships already suffered made him stronger, more resilient, and better able to face the future.

As day followed day, the constant stench and chaotic noise of clanking chains were a protracted ordeal for George, and a life-threatening horror for others. He learned many of the convicts with a more predatory character preyed on those less fortunate, and with no supervision below deck they exploited the weak in a most shameful way. Guards could have prevented many of the assaults and thefts, but they only patrolled the upper deck and had no inclination to bother with what went on below.

Slowly, in the midst of all the misery round him, gloomy feelings began to overtake George, threatening his last remnant of independence. Sitting all day in his cell, struggling to make sense of his situation, he feared that like the great man-o-war he too might be reduced to a mere shell of his former self. Finally, by constantly telling himself he would survive and inherit his grandfather's estate, he managed to rally and became more determined to remain positive.

Not so Martin. Sometimes George heard him muttering to himself, 'My poor wife and children. What's become of them?'

As the days passed, Martin remained withdrawn. He often sat on the floor with George; their backs against the cell wall and hands clasped round their up-drawn knees. With all the wretchedness about them, George asked Martin how he came to be in Newgate.

'I was a potter, and lived with me wife and three children in Lambeth. 'Tis a poor part of London,' he said. 'But when me employer died I lost me job. I walked the streets for weeks, but couldn't find no work. When me children woke at night crying with hunger I became desperate. I had to do something for their sake, and tried to steal some meat.'

'How did you do it?' George asked.

'I waited nearby in the street 'til I thought nobody was looking, and quickly snatched a lump o' steak. But the butcher saw me and ran out after me. 'Twas bad luck for both of us. His shouting attracted attention, and people came running. He almost reached me, but tripped and hit his head on the road. Bystanders grabbed me, and others hurried over to the butcher lying there unconscious. They called for a doctor, but the man died a few hours later. He left a wife and seven children. They said I caused his death, and sentenced me to hang. Later, witnesses came forward to say it was an accident, and I was reprieved: but for what?'

'At least you escaped the rope,' George said. 'Why be so sad?'

'I don't know what has happened to the butcher's family. They would have been poor like us if they lived in Lambeth. That one act of mine has wrecked the lives of a dozen people. Me wife is probably in a poorhouse. Perhaps the butcher's wife is there too. All the children will be scattered. God knows what's become of 'em all. I'll never see me wife and children again. 'Tis a tragedy. I might as well be dead.'

'Things may not have turned out as badly as you think,' George said, hoping to give some comfort to Martin.

Since his arrest George had never met anybody he felt so comfortable with as Martin, Drawn by his fatherly bearing, he told Martin of Aubrey Jones and the false evidence against him, and of his worry about what Jones might have done with the solicitor's letter. Martin in his turn encouraged George to keep up his hopes of the inheritance, and of eventually settling down in some quiet place away from people who made trouble for others.

From word that got round, George gathered the hulk jailers came from the lowest class of society and did not hesitate to take advantage of their authority by bullying the prisoners for the slightest reason. He suspected even the overseer seized every opportunity to profit by cutting down on rations. Clearly, the quality of their food varied, and George worried about the near absence of any fruit or vegetables in their diet. He remembered once reading a story about someone called Captain Cook and another individual named Banks who were at sea for years, and prevented scurvy with vegetables. Although many prisoners knew about the disease, when George heard complaints of painful gums that made eating difficult, it convinced him some of the prisoners must have scurvy. Where possible, he began to bargain and exchange his bread for other convicts' vegetables.

They ate every meal in their cells, and all the haggard faces showed him nobody ever had enough to eat. Occasionally someone sickened quite quickly, or even died from what was said to be nervous atrophy or mortification. Whenever George knew the man by sight, it troubled him, and after each death he lay awake at night worrying it could happen to him too.

Breakfast was a pint of barley soup with a little bread. On Sundays the lumps of almost unpalatable bullock cheeks and small helpings of vegetables were often replaced by salt pork or beef, and washed down by a modest ration of an almost alcohol free by-product of the brewery known as small beer.

'If you drink water, you'll go down with the trots,' his fellow convicts told him. George noted the advice, and kept to small beer.

Whenever meat stank through being kept too long and could not be eaten, each cell was allotted two pounds of cheese and an extra portion of oatmeal porridge, all to be shared between its six occupants. Supper was a pint of peas and barley soup alternating with a pint of oatmeal porridge known as burgou.

Each day George hunted for vermin in his clothing, and did his best to keep them to a minimum, but never managing to eliminate them. He slept more soundly than at Newgate, but with only one blanket, he suffered through the bitter winter nights.

Many times he watched as more assertive convicts bullied weaker men out of their blanket.

After several weeks George felt his toes becoming painful and noticed his toenails eroded back beyond the quick. For a while it puzzled him until one of his cellmates said, 'It's the cockroaches. They come out at night to feed, and toenails make a juicy meal for 'em. A dozen or more probably feeds off you every night. It happens to us all,' he assured him.

Although George had to live with rogues and scoundrels of all descriptions, he never saw any of the unnatural acts that everybody said took place on the lower decks. Bands of guards with cutlasses seldom went down to George's deck and never after dark. Perhaps because of the stench they never patrolled the lower deck or orlop either day or night. Convicts down there were the most hardened of the criminals and were left much to their own devices.

One afternoon as he lay in his cell George heard occasional cries and shouting from the other end of the corridor, and asked his cellmates what it could be.

'Oh, that's Charlie again,' one of them said. 'We do believe he's mad as a maggot, but the overseer says he be lazy. A couple o' months ago they caged him up to teach him a lesson. When he's no better, they take him upstairs and flog him.'

A few days later as a guard escorted George to the deck they passed the man's cell and he saw it really was a cage: one so small it had no room to stand. The poor wretch lay naked in pools of excrement, his back covered by scabs and blood from previous floggings. He returned George's nod of encouragement with a glazed look of helplessness. A swathe of the man's blood had congealed about his face, and when he tried to say something George could see his swollen gums and tongue. George felt a surge of helpless rage, and resentment against the establishment. Muttering to himself, he wondered how one human could torture another with such cruelty. Blind fury almost had him lashing out at the guard who accompanied him.

Later in the week George no longer heard the man's babbling and he learned guards had flogged the man again, but after twenty strokes of the birch he had choked to death on his vomit. It was a salutary lesson for George. He decided the best way to stay out of trouble would be to keep to himself as much as possible. He thought the fewer people who noticed his existence, the easier it would be for him.

After a couple of months, guards put him to work with a group of convicts maintaining a shipping channel by dredging the ever-changing river bottom. What with rats and cockroaches at night, and the maddening itch of lice all the time, he realized life was not going to get any easier.

Chapter 14

Dredging and Flogging

The sun had not yet risen when a jailer approached their cell swinging a bunch of keys, and unlocked the door.

'George White and Martin Williams, get out here,' he ordered.

After languishing in the company of his fellow convicts for several weeks it pleased George to respond to any change in his circumstances, whatever it might be.

'Yes sir, we're coming.'

'Get up on deck and join your working party.'

Martin looked at George and gave a shrug. 'I don't feel strong enough for hard work,' he said. 'After lying in the cell for so long I can hardly walk.'

George nodded. 'We'll just have to do our best, or be flogged.'

They hurriedly scrambled up the hatchway, emerging on the deck near several groups of convicts. A guard pointed to one of the working parties waiting to descend the ladder on the side of the ship.

'You two, get over with that lot,' he ordered.

George and Martin followed the group down into one of the longboats waiting below.

'Where are we going?' George asked the man next to him in the boat.

'Out to a ballast lighter moored downstream,' he said. 'Two of our gang was hurt bad yesterday, an' we don't believe they'll ever come back.' After a pause, while he appeared to be contemplating the fate of the injured convicts, the man gave a sigh. 'So I suppose you two be taking their places.'

George wondered what they expected him to do: clearly a dangerous job. At least to breathe fresh air again despite its chill gave him some relief. As the longboat approached the lighter, an overseer with cutlass drawn emerged from a small cabin on the deck to supervise their landing. Both George and Martin struggled in their leg-irons to get across the gap between the rocking longboat and the deck of the lighter, and once there they lined up with their fellows without delay. The overseer, a coarse-featured fellow, inspected the group. All but George and Martin knew their place and what to do.

'White, get up on the platform and crank up the ballast,' he ordered. 'And Williams, start shovelling.'

George and several others clambered up to a raised area equipped with windlass and bucket machinery worked by turning a handle to scrape silt from the bottom of the river. As the sludge came up, it tipped into a pile on the lighter. Although he was young and still reasonably fit, George, along with the others, strained to turn the handle. It was backbreaking work.

While they kept cranking, Martin and others shovelled the dredged mud and rubbish from the lighter and into boats. Further teams of convicts rowed their load to the shore and unloaded it into piles of mud. From there, other convicts barrowed the muck elsewhere for screening before spreading it. From the distance George made out men in shackles and chains on the shore, struggling with their loads.

By midmorning on that first day his back ached, and with every turn of the handle he felt the strength going from his arms. By mid-afternoon it had become almost unbearable agony. Still he kept working. He knew the overseer would notice any slackening of pace and respond with a taste of the birch. That would only make matters worse for him. He never imagined he would ever look forward to his prison cell, but on that first evening he arrived back at the hulk exhausted and aching, and more than ready to collapse onto his straw pad.

On winter days with its wind and occasional showers he cranked up mud from eight-thirty till three o'clock in the afternoon without a break before returning to the hulk. In wet weather the overseer cancelled all work, not because of any compassion for the convicts, but because of the difficulty in dredging the ballast, and barrowing it across softened ground. Firearms, too, became less dependable in the rain. Misty days reduced visibility and increased the chance of escapes. Attempts were not unknown, and many guards armed with cudgels patrolled the shore.

After a few days George could see he was a small cog in a well-regulated scheme. The convicts all worked as a large team; like ants, they distributed a constant supply of filling to wherever it was needed. Each time he went to and fro between hulk and lighter he could not help but see the huge piles of filling dredged up over the years, reminding him of the immensity of human suffering it represented.

Under their strict supervision, and constant dredging George found it difficult to notice, or even care what others were doing. Still, he gave an occasional glance towards Martin knowing him to be sickly. The man's strained expression told George of the difficulty he had with constant shovelling.

As spring merged into early summer, the morning mists that shrouded the river began to lift; the days lengthened and the heat of the sun made work on the lighter even more backbreaking. Each morning when he climbed up the hatchway George looked skyward hoping for an overcast day. In warm weather everybody worked without a break from seven in the morning till noon when the arrival of the midday meal brought a welcome hour's rest. At one o'clock, work began again and did not stop until six in the evening.

Despite constant supervision by armed guards with absolute authority there comes a breakpoint where the limits of endurance have been reached. On many occasions George thought he had almost reached that state, but forced himself to keep going despite the pain. Occasionally he saw others who could no longer carry on, and they slowed down either by choice or physical necessity. After several strokes of the birch, resentment and anger sometimes goaded a convict into answering back, or showing disrespect to an overseer. If a man did not respond to the light reminder of the birch, much worse lay in store for him.

One afternoon George noticed Martin slowing down with his shovelling. Quick to notice, the supervisor bellowed, 'you's slacking, Williams,' and struck Martin across the back with the birch. For a few minutes he increased his pace, but soon wilted with the effort.

Once again the supervisor struck. 'I'll teach you to slack,' he yelled with anger in his voice. This time it was six strokes.

Martin burst out, saying, 'leave me alone. I'm doing my best.'

This proved too much for the supervisor. 'You'll answer for this insubordination,' he shouted.

Shortly after returning to the hulk a guard approached their cell and unlocked the door. Seizing Martin, he half-dragged him out and pushed him to the companionway. That night he did not return to his cell.

George knew what to expect. Next morning as he emerged from the hatchway to join his gang of workers, he saw everybody lining up to watch a flogging: a drama always performed in front of the convicts to remind them the authorities meant business. But George wondered what good it ever did. Rather than being cowered by the spectacle about to be enacted, those round him seethed with resentment.

Soon, two guards brought Martin on deck. His wan face and wasted body convinced the assembled crowd of convicts, that like so many of them, he had been too ill to work as hard and long as was expected of him.

Without delay guards stripped him to the waist, exposing an emaciated torso that had come to be little more than a bag of bones inside a thin envelope of flesh. They proceeded to tie him to a pyramidal frame of three wooden poles about seven feet long. Guards spread his legs apart and strapped his ankles to its base. After binding his wrists together, they stretched his arms above his head and tied them to the apex.

One of the jailers produced a birch, and without delay lay into the helpless man with all the strength he could muster. Martin's skin soon ruptured under the force of the blows. At first the only sound from him was a grunt as each blow knocked some of the wind out of him. But later, as his back became a mass of blood and reddened flesh he gave cries of pain as blow followed blow. After thirty strokes, and Martin barely conscious, guards removed him from the breach and carried him from sight.

During the whole of Martin's ordeal George stood benumbed, and dwelling on what his wife and children would feel had they watched his agony. Beset by sadness, a trickle of unheeded tears exposed the depth of his passion. It prompted the convict next to him to say, 'come along lad, bear up.'

'Martin is my friend,' George replied in a voice trembling with shock. 'He is a good man, and would never hurt anybody. He was simply doing his best.'

''Tis something we all have to put up with,' the convict said.

'It's all barbaric,' said George. 'The jailer even seemed to enjoy what he was doing. He tried to shame Martin in front of us, but I reckon it's the jailer who acted shamefully.'

'So I suppose you ain't seed 'em wield the cat,' the man continued.

'No,' George said. 'And I'm not keen to.'

Martin remained in the hulk sick bay all day, but in the early evening guards returned him to his cell. Trembling, and with his back still oozing blood, he looked a pitiful sight.

'I have to go back to work on the lighter tomorrow morning,' he said in a voice full of anguish. 'It's agony to move. There is no way I can carry on shoveling. They'll flog me again. I'll finish up like Charlie.'

Full of rage, George and his cellmates knew they could do nothing to help. Later, as darkness invaded the 'tween decks the convicts settled down for the night. For a long time George lay awake with the sound of Martin's groans and laboured breathing, but eventually he drifted into a restless sleep. As the first fingers of light stirred him, he heard a shout.

'Bloody hell! Call the guard!'

George woke to see Martin hanging by the neck. At first glance he appeared to be sitting against the cell door with his legs stretched out in front of him. While everybody slept he had taken laces from his cellmates' boots and tied them together into a long cord. He had attached one end round the lintel above the low cell door, less than a man's height, and knotted the other end round his neck. He must have sat down, the cord taking his weight, and leaving him to suffocate while suspended with his buttocks only a few handbreadths above the deck.

His cellmates soon recovered from the shock, but the memory of Martin strangling himself continued to haunt George, making him even more determined to maintain his fortitude. He knew, in the end, his one trump card would be his inheritance to help him rise above the squalor of his circumstances.

As time went by George often had to watch other poor wretches flogged with the birch. He knew a few of the unfortunates were incorrigible rogues or murderers; others, clearly physically worn out, had simply gone off their head. Most of those flogged seemed to be less violent men who, like Martin, must have felt driven to breaking point, and had defied a jailer.

George could see those weakened by illnesses of all sorts suffered most from the punishments inflicted by guards. He sensed disease all round him, and every night he had to live with the sounds of coughing and spitting. There is no justice here, he decided.

Chapter 15
Failed Escape

After several months of gruelling work on the lighter, a jailer unlocked the cell door early one evening. 'Come with me, White,' he ordered, and escorted George up the hatchway and to a cabin near the fo'csle where an officer waited to question him.

'We understand you have a background in metalworking. What do you know about it, White?'

'My father and I worked at the mills in Birmingham, Sir, but I hadn't reached the stage of being a qualified tradesman. I stamped out metal shapes at the foundry, and saw men making cutlery and other household articles. My father showed me how to make various small metal containers and pots for use round our home.'

'Why did you not take the opportunity of honest employment in the mills?'

'I could read and write and do arithmetic. I thought I could better myself in London.'

'What a pity you went off the rails, White,' said the officer, with a smirk.

George knew it would be pointless to try and reason with him.

'Well, since you seem to have an inkling of metalworking we'll send you to the Warren tomorrow to work in the metal shop. You'll be allotted to the appropriate party in the morning.' Turning to the jailer, the officer then said, 'take him back to his cell.'

'Thank you, sir,' said George with some relief. He expected his new assignment would still be demanding, but he welcomed any change from the exhausting work on the lighter.

Each day as he went to and from the lighter he had seen the Warren, a collection of buildings of various shapes and sizes where the royal arsenal and other public buildings were situated. He knew hundreds of convicts from the hulks worked there under the vigilant eyes of numerous guards and overseers, all armed with large wooden clubs they did not hesitate to use. The convicts worked in various locations, some dirty and arduous, others, sites of frequent accidents.

Next morning as he emerged on to the deck, a guard shouted, 'George White, join that party over there,' and pointed to a group of about a dozen convicts.

George realized they must be the metal smiths, and on the order they all clambered down to a waiting longboat and set out to the arsenal metal workshop. Here, in an old brick building, George and his workmates spent their days making and repairing various tools and implements used on the Warren. They all worked in silence, the only sound coming from the hammering and scraping of metal as they repaired shovels, barrows, or wheels.

George found the guards brutal and cruel, devoid of compassion and ignorant in the extreme. Although his work was not physically demanding he soon learned to keep moving even although at times he might have little to do. The only occasion he slowed through shortage of new work he felt the full force of the overseer's club across the broad of his back.

'Their wages be even less than common labourers,' one of the metalworkers told him. George concluded their guards only reward came from the tyrannical power they possessed.

All the convicts at the Warren, including George, wore leg-irons, some with double fetters on one leg, making it difficult for them to walk. Most, like George, had their chains attached to a leather belt round the waist, but a few had a longer chain, its weight taken by a collar round the neck. Occasionally he saw a particular troublemaker not only leg-ironed, but also attached to a chain that dragged a large iron ball and others even harnessed together in pairs.

Each day, those who worked at the Warren or with the dredging crews, received a supplement of gruel and an extra three and a half pints of small beer from the nearby brewery. George found little things like that assumed great importance to them all, and helped to keep up what little morale they had.

He soon learned work in the metal shop had another bonus. 'We all gets a shilling a week,' one of the men told him. 'And half can be spent on extra food.'

Like others on the Warren, George often met with free citizens there on business. They usually sold bread and occasionally vegetables, an advantage he made use of at every opportunity, and soon learned tricks of bargaining. Naturally, it offered a chance to engage in a variety of scams that many of the convicts seemed drawn to as much for the distraction as any material gain.

As the days lengthened and summer warmth made life more tolerable, George noticed the improved conditions made little difference to his workmates. None were hardened criminals, but were good at heart and basically honest. George imagined, like Martin, they had fallen on hard times and committed some petty crime. They kept their thoughts to themselves, and had scant empathy with each other. George thought they always looked rather miserable, as well they might when condemned to live much of their lives in such appalling conditions. They lacked any sense of humour, and his jokes rarely raised a smile. The only activity to arouse their interest was bargaining for food.

Whenever he heard of convicts elsewhere on the Warren committing suicide rather than going on living their intolerable existence, his thoughts turned to Martin and to his own situation. It reminded him of the justice system and his hammer would smash down even harder as his anger boiled up again.

With the end of the year approaching little had changed; for George every day seemed the same. In time he came to terms with the inevitability of his predicament, and managed to fit in and be accepted as one of them by his workmates. He could stand up to bullies, and even ceased to wonder when, if ever, he would be boarding a ship bound for the antipodes.

The boring metakwork reminded him of his Birmingham days, and gave him the same feeling he had before leaving home. The only matter to attract his interest was a change in the behaviour of two of the metal smiths. He suspected they were in some form of communication by signs and expressions that passed between them at times. Whatever it was, they never spoke openly about it, and he began to wonder if they were concocting some sort of plan, perhaps to escape. He was soon to find the answer.

One evening, on returning to the hulk a guard approached George. 'Come with me, White,' he said, and took him to the fo'csle for questioning.

An officer scrutinized him before saying, 'George White, I believe you can read and write and do arithmetic.'

'Yes Sir,' he replied, pleased his original request for writing paper had not been dismissed as lightly as he had imagined.

'What is seven times eight?'

'Fifty-six,' George replied as quickly as possible.

'And nine times six?'

'Fifty-four.'

'Now write what I dictate to you,' the officer said, motioning George to sit at the desk and use the quill pen. '*I have the honour to be your most obedient servant.*'

George promptly did as told, taking care with his copperplate writing before handing it to the officer. He realized it was not only a test of his ability to use a pen, but also a check on his spelling. He watched the officer's expression as he studied it.

'Well, White,' the officer said at last. 'Start work here in the office tomorrow. You will file receipts and make a record of all the food and other merchandise used from day to day on board.'

George was delighted. At last he could prove himself capable of clerical work. He imagined it being what he would be doing if he had never been arrested, and he began his new work with enthusiasm. But after a week of writing entries in the accounts book he began to doubt if he was really any better off in the hulk office rather than on the Warren. He found his duties physically easy, but he had no escape from the hot summer air, heavy with the pungent stench of neglected humanity below deck. Foul vapours drifting from the hatchways irritated him constantly, and while working alone for most of the day he missed the activities on the Warren, and the company of his group of metalworkers.

However, some of his old workmates had not forgotten him. Scarcely a week passed before the two convicts who had taken his attention on the Warren approached him one evening when they arrived back at the hulk.

'We knows you've got the key to the storeroom,' one of them whispered. 'Leave the door unlocked tomorrow night.'

'I can't do that,' George answered. 'The guards will find out, and flog me.'

Glancing about as he spoke, the other said, ''tis important you 'elp us.'

'I suppose you are trying to escape.'

They looked uneasily at each other. 'We has a pair of pliers to cut off our irons,' one of them said. 'They's hidden at the Warren and haven't been missed yet.'

After a pause the other added, 'We knows how to get out of our cell, and after dark we'll float across the river on a couple o' straw pads from the store.'

'That's where you come in, and leave that door unlocked,' the other added.

'I won't do it,' said George. 'You'll just have to manage the best you can.'

'If we can't get pads from the store,' the first said, 'we'll have to sneak them from the orlop, and drag 'em all the way up the hatchways during the night.'

'That's a harebrained scheme,' George said in a serious tone of voice. 'Even if you manage to get past the guards on deck, the pads will sink.'

'We's better drowned than spending another day on this here hulk.'

'You will both be caught and flogged if you try to escape.'

George watched as the two men turned and slunk away obviously annoyed with him. But their desperate plan of escape had so many flaws George thought it would never succeed. It worried him as he couldn't help feeling some responsibility if they were caught. He tried to put them out of his mind, and next day did his best to carry on as if nothing was brewing.

That night the men made their break. George learned the two had freed themselves from their chains. Then, taking straw sleeping pads from the orlop, they managed to get them as far as the deck.

Unfortunately for them, just as they were about to descend the ladder on the side of the hulk and quietly launch their pads into the water, one of the guards came upon them. With a shout he grabbed the nearer convict, threw him to the deck, and held him secure. More guards came running, but arrived too late to seize the other man. In desperation he threw his pad overboard and leapt into the river after it. Before guards could do anything further, they saw him straddle the pad and try to paddle in the direction of the shore. Instead, the current took him downstream.

Guards watched as his pad began to lose its buoyancy leaving him floundering in the water. One of the guards threw a rope, but before the man could reach it his threshing ceased and he disappeared beneath the surface. Despite a thorough search of the area in a longboat the man could not be found, and being dark they called off the search. Next morning fishermen downstream found him floating face down in the water, and retrieved his body.

As for the other convict, punishment came swiftly and brutally. In the morning, George along with all able-bodied convicts once again lined up on deck to witness a flogging. But this occasion being something special, the poor fellow was about to be made an example of what lay in store for anybody caught escaping.

Guards brought the escapee out on deck, his face the colour of one condemned. They stripped him to the waist, and tied him to the triangle, but his flogging did not start immediately. They left the luckless man suspended with arms upstretched and his wrists tied at the apex of the triangle. Then, like a well-rehearsed play, the hulk captain emerged to harangue the assembled crowd, his invective spelling out the fate of any convict who would dare attempt an escape. Despite a nip in the air, George saw sweat on the victim's back glistening in the early morning sunshine.

As the hulk captain continued his tirade, George cast his eyes over others involved in the drama. Behind the victim a jailer stood, his feet apart and hands gripping a heavy cat-o-nine-tails. From time to time he fingered the wiry cords, and drew their knotted strands across his hand as if eager to discharge his grim task. The hulk doctor stood nearby, like an undertaker about to consign a corpse to the grave. The assembled convicts looked on, sullen and incensed at the flagellation about to be enacted.

When he finished speaking, the hulk captain turned to the jailer. In a voice for all to hear, he shouted, 'Give 'im seventy-five lashes.'

The jailer swung the cat round his head and brought the cords down on the convict's back with all his strength. Within seconds the wretch was striped by white weals that rapidly changed to an angry red. With each stroke the cords whistled and cracked. The fourth drew blood, and as stroke followed stroke, skin split under the force of the blows. Soon the man's back was a mass of raw flesh that with each stroke splattered the nearby rows of onlookers. Whenever the cords tangled or became stuck together with blood and gore, the jailer stopped to untangle them before he struck again.

All the time, the poor wretch on the triangle remained silent, much to the annoyance of the hulk captain. As stroke followed stroke, George could not imagine a sight more degrading of humanity. It appalled him to see a man being lacerated so severely in front of his fellows. After the sixtieth blow the convict gave a groan, his head sank forwards and he appeared to be unconscious.

'Revive him,' the captain shouted. One of the guards advanced with a bucket of salt water that he threw over the still figure. On raw flesh salt must have been agony. The man grunted, and with a weak movement of his head, his eyes opened momentarily.

'He's shamming,' cried the captain. 'Give 'im another twenty-five.'

Flogging continued for the full hundred strokes before the hulk captain appeared satisfied he had convinced the prisoners of the dire consequences of a failed escape.

Once they untied the victim's limbs the doctor came forward to give a cursory examination. He ordered convicts to lift the unconscious man on to a rough stretcher and carry him to the hulk sick room on the fo'csle.

Forced to witness the whole grisly event, George felt so tense and angry he realized his clenched fingers were still digging into his palms. He looked to see if his nails had drawn blood.

When the hulk captain heard the convicts muttering among themselves, and saw their disquiet, he rapidly ordered them into the longboats, and they dispersed to their workplaces. For him the entire spectacle had simply been an introduction to another beautiful summer's day.

Chapter 16

Outwitted

On this day Aubrey Jones was on his way to Black Eddie the forger, and in a buoyant mood about his clever scheme. In his possession he had a letter from Dunlley who had fallen into Aubrey's trap, and replied in his own hand. Eddie read the letter and studied the handwriting.

Dear Mr Brown,

I have read your letter with its preposterous suggestions.
  I discarded it into the rubbish where it rightfully belongs.

Yours faithfully,
Luke Dunlley

'Yes, 'tis very good Aubrey. It's got most o' the alphabet, and a signature. There'll be no trouble drafting a letter for you.'

Aubrey Jones gave a smirk of satisfaction.

'You've got one more problem, Mr Jones,' Black Eddie said.

'Have I?' said Aubrey.

'We doesn't know how long it will take Dunlley to die o' natural causes, does we. So when does I get me share o' the inheritance?'

Aubrey Jones gave a vacant stare.

'I reckon we speed up the event, if you gets my meaning,' Black Eddie added, fixing Aubrey in his gaze. 'Or I may lose my patience.'

A terrible thought came into Aubrey's mind. He knew what the forger suggested, and murder was not a contingency he had considered. For a few moments he thought he might faint. It suddenly occurred to him he had handed the forger all the information he needed to take over completely, and realized if he didn't agree to have Dunlley murdered his own life would be in danger. Black Eddie wouldn't take the risk of being blackmailed. The implications frightened Aubrey.

'Where do we go from here?' he whimpered.

'I knows of several who'd be willing to put Dunlley under the sod for a price; none of 'em would 'ave a problem going to Birmingham to do the job. Dunlley would be set upon after dark as he leaves his place o' work. The assassin could be back in London afore anyone knew he'd been gone.'

Aubrey Jones winced at the prospect of his involvement in murder and cleared his throat. Things were clearly out of his hands.

'Meantime,' the forger said, 'I'll write you this here letter from Dunlley, and backdate it about a decade. And I'll tell you when the event is to take place.'

Aubrey Jones was in a daze when he left the forger. I'm in over my depth, he thought. I see no clear way out. He returned to his lodgings too distraught to think of working. He tried to weigh up his options. If I give up now, the forger could take over and eliminate me. On the other hand, if I continue with the plan, I have a good chance of succeeding. I'll just have to go along with it.

Chapter 17

Voyage to Parts Beyond the Seas

George breathed more easily as summer turned to autumn, the cooler days bringing some relief as he continued to work in the stifling atmosphere of his confined office. In his solitude, his mind often strayed to thoughts of his legacy and the promise it held. He struggled with the thought of his missing document, and hoped Aubrey Jones had discarded it. In other times of doubt, he wondered if his grandfather was still working, or had already sold his business.

Always aloof, one of the hulk officers came several times a day to check his work, leaving the impression George would suffer some form of punishment if his efforts failed to meet their expectations.

For weeks, something kept nagging at the back of his mind. The body of the convict who drowned had not been accounted for in any report he dealt with in his office. The man had never been officially buried. So where was his body? Then, one day while sorting a pile of new correspondence, he came upon a receipt and letter from a London medical school thanking the doctor for 'goods' they had put to excellent use. George had only one conclusion. The doctor, probably with the connivance of the hulk captain, had sold the body for dissection: a crime that could lead to imprisonment. He decided to keep the information to himself in case he could make use of it later.

And so matters dragged on, until one March day he chanced upon a list of convicts scheduled for transportation at the next embarkation. After carefully scanning it he was devastated to find his name did not appear. It occurred to him that despite the officers' strict supervision and veiled threats, they did not want to part with him. I could be stuck on this stinking hulk forever, he thought. The ever-present stench and unwholesome atmosphere below deck made him feel sickly, and he worried it could be only a matter of time before he was overtaken by some ailment.

One cold and dank day he decided to risk doing something about it. That evening when the officer came to check his work he stood up and faced the man. Before the officer spoke, George looked straight at him, and putting on a concerned tone, announced, 'I can't find burial papers for that man who drowned when he tried to escape. Do you know where they could be?' Then he paused to watch the officer's reaction.

The man's face reddened. He cleared his throat and in a slightly strained voice, said, 'That has all been taken care of.'

For a few moments George continued to stare at him with a knowing look, and noticed the officer's embarrassment. Several weeks later, while working through a pile of new correspondence, he came across a revised embarkation schedule. His name had been added to the list. His ruse had worked.

The new schedule told George the time for embarkation must be drawing near, and he began to look forward to the long sea voyage with a sense of adventure. He knew of its dangers, but longed for some relief from his oppressive life on the hulk. I would rather die at sea than rot away in this hellhole, he thought.

His excitement grew with a rumour the convict ship, *George III*, had docked at Woolwich, and had begun loading provisions. Several days later guards lined up George and a group of his cellmates on the deck and took them ashore for a medical examination. It was a cursory affair.

'Strip to the waist and file past the doctor,' a guard ordered. A scrawny looking doctor glanced at each one before weeding out a few who would obviously never survive the voyage.

'Keep moving, keep moving,' the guard shouted.

The prisoners shambled across to a long table piled with clothing where other guards issued each convict with a jacket and waistcoat of cloth, duck trousers, two grey linen shirts, flannel underclothes, shoes, yarn stockings, and a woollen cap.

Soon, the day of embarkation arrived. George estimated over two hundred shackled convicts came on board with him, each with a number painted on their jacket and trousers. After languishing in the filthy hulk, the well-scrubbed decks of the *George III* were a welcome sight. The coiled ropes and tackle sat neatly in place, and the clean smell of tar and oil mixed with the unusual odour of furled canvas gave him relief from the stench of the hulk.

Once on board, guards hustled the horde of convicts through the prisoners' area: a part of the deck fenced off fore and aft. At each end a locked wooden gate in the stanchions, and guarded by militia, gave access to other parts of the ship. As George glanced about he could see sheep carcasses hanging high in the standing rigging, and reminding him of the Newgate gallows. Food for the ship's officers, he imagined. As he waited to file below, he watched several smartly dressed officers observing operations from the poop deck, and scrutinizing the convicts with some care. From where he was in the prisoners' compound George noticed them turn in conversation as brief remarks passed between them. Meantime, the military stood by with loaded rifles, watching and directing the prisoners down hatchways to the convict quarters 'tween decks.

George found the hatchways were simply ladders, no doubt able to be pulled up on to the deck at night before battening down to prevent any possibility of escape to the prison deck above. Added to this, strong wooden stanchions arranged vertically, and spiked with nails surrounded the hatchways on the convict deck. The only access from sleeping quarters to hatchway was by a single door in the stanchions, and locked by three padlocks. Even so, a sentry always guarded the door. The stanchions consisted of wide planks set less than three inches apart, the gaps between them being the only source of light and air to reach the prisoners. The stanchions not only blocked the light, but also hindered ventilation, leaving the whole atmosphere on the 'tween deck dark and gloomy, and the air oppressive and damp.

Once his eyes became accustomed to poor lighting in the confined space below George made out a double row of sleeping-berths lining each side of the ship. They were about six feet square, and arranged one above the other. Soldiers dressed in smart red jackets and white trousers patrolled a corridor that ran down the middle of the deck. A bandoleer with cartridge-loops hung over their shoulder, and each soldier carried a firearm. George thought they looked only a year or two older than him.

While some of the military strutted about with loaded weapons, others set about getting order into the milling crowd of prisoners. They assigned four convicts to each sleeping shelf, and chained them to ring bolts to prevent them moving about, or causing trouble. Later, as the convicts lay shackled in their berths, guards issued them with bedding and wooden eating utensils.

As soon as they allotted him, George greeted two men already shackled in the sleeping berth, knowing they would be close companions throughout the voyage. The older man had a sinister appearance with an opaque watery eye sitting in his orbit like a white marble, and half-hidden behind a drooping eyelid, evidence, George thought, of an injury long since healed. The other, a gaunt fellow, short and wiry, wore a sly expression on his deeply lined face. When George held out his hand in greeting, he noticed the man's veins standing out like blue cords running up his spindly arms. He learned they both came from the north, and had already been together for months in a Manchester jail. They seemed friendly enough despite their rough features.

When the fourth member was allotted, both old lags recognized him from previous news reports. He had been a ladies' man; a rake who seduced wealthy women and lived off their money, but finally meeting his match with the daughter of a wealthy businessman, a knight of the realm.

'Hello H.J., fancy meeting you here,' the older man said to him as the new arrival climbed on to the sleeping shelf.

The other convict looked at him, grinned. 'Where's your heiress, H.J.?'

H.J. ignored the slight and turned to George.

George looked at him with astonishment. He was the most handsome man he had ever seen. His tall, lithe frame stood out among his stunted companions, and a shock of unruly blond hair gave him an air of boyish charm. He appeared naturally friendly; probably well educated too, George thought. He looked at George, gave him a dazzling smile, and held out his hand in greeting, his soft grasp confirming a hand unaccustomed to manual work.

'John Bell,' he said in a flawless accent.

'Handsome John 'tis what the public called him,' one of the convicts said.

'H.J. for short,' the other added.

George noticed a fleeting frown before H.J. answered. 'That was then,' he said. 'I am one of you now.'

It soon became apparent to George that H.J. preferred his company to that of the two confirmed gamblers who shared their berth. After months of mixing with social outcasts, it occurred to George perhaps he might learn more socially acceptable behaviour from H.J. -- maybe even hear something about women other than the obscene opinions of his fellow convicts. At first he felt a little overawed by his distinguished looking companion, but hoped they might become better acquainted. If so, he imagined the journey would not be time wasted.

Once the convicts seemed to be settled, a ship's officer came down accompanied by two senior men from the militia. Standing by the doorway between hatchway and prison deck he straightaway had everyone's attention. 'You're to elect a mess captain from among you,' he shouted. 'That man will be responsible for drawin' rations, maintainin' tidiness and orderly conduct. I also want several prisoners to be assistant cooks, an' bring the meals down.'

After a discussion among the prisoners they nominated several of the older convicts to carry out these duties. The officer pulled a small notebook from a top pocket, made a note of their names and numbers with the stub of a pencil, and within moments he departed, leaving the prisoners to themselves in their dingy surroundings.

The day before sailing, family and friends came on board to say their pitiful farewells. They crowded the 'tween decks, bringing parcels and presents for their loved ones. Even street musicians were permitted to cram into the area. Adding to the clamour came sounds of grief from the convicts, and the weeping of wives and children.

Like George, many of the single convicts had nobody to say good-bye to them. Although they faced years of exile, rumours of ex-convicts who had made their fortune in Australia buoyed many, and they looked forward to the opportunity of doing likewise at the end of their sentence.

All night the ship lay at anchor waiting for a fair wind to take them down to the Channel. Sleep for the prisoners came fitfully in the novelty of their new surroundings, some through excitement, others with the depression of knowing they would never see family or friends ever again. Lying side by side with three others in his small berth, George had scarcely any room to turn, and already the atmosphere had a suggestion of the same foulness he had left behind on the hulk.

Shortly before dawn they woke to sounds of seamen going about the task of catching the early morning breeze; the clinching noise of the capstan as it hauled up the anchor and the frequent shouting of commands as sailors set the sails.

'Haul round the main tack.'

'Aye, aye, sir.' And the ship was under way, vibrating in the river currents.

Cramped below deck, the prisoners saw nothing of the action, nor where the ship headed, but a sense of motion left them in no doubt they were under way. All went pleasantly until afternoon when the vessel began to roll from side to side. Below, in the semidarkness, sounds of creaking and the flapping of sails confirmed they had reached the Channel.

Late in the day, a sentry standing at the hatchway in his smart red jacket announced if all went well they would pass Eastbourne during the hours of darkness, and the Isle of Wight next day.'

After nightfall the sounds of the ship seemed louder, keeping many of the convicts awake with the soughing of wind in the rigging and sails, and the constant creaking and rattling as the ship rolled and bucked in the swell. By this time most of the prisoners were seasick, but happy next morning to hear an officer ordering their leg-irons to be struck off. Once again the prisoners were a humorous sight. This time it was the sailors who laughed to see them staggering about, not only freed from the weight of their fetters, but also having to cope with the rolling of the ship.

Once over their instability, the captain allowed them on to the deck for fresh air and a little exercise. George emerged into the prison deck area, a confined space easy for the military to guard, and made his way through the crowd of prisoners to lean on the bulwarks. As the ship plied forward in a strong breeze he watched spray misting across the bow, and the sea below rushing past. A long track of foam in the vessel's wake reminded him that each moment took him further from his past and all he had once hoped for. From nearby he heard one of the militia talking to a group of convicts. 'In another two or three days you will have seen the last of Old England.'

In a sudden fit of nostalgia, his mind turned to his family. He pictured his father and brother busy, even at that moment, sweating in the mill while his sisters shopped and cleaned the house, or settled to their needlework. He wondered if his father thought of him, or hoped to hear from him, perhaps wondering if George had found a job with prospects in London and simply be too busy to communicate. Or, had he heard of his son's arrest, and did not know how to contact him? All these questions came to mind. How can I ever tell them of my misfortune? Even as memories echoed back to him, he knew these voices from the past would never become a reality for him again. As he thought about it, he felt his cheeks moist with tears.

Through his misty eyes the distant shoreline became a passing vision of little white houses dotted in a patchwork of greens above the cliff-lined coast, with the surf breaking on stony beaches below. He knew he had left his family forever, and would never grow old and sickly in the mills, or prosperous in London's fog. Even so, he sensed a shiver of excitement wrack through him at the thought his inheritance might one day make him a wealthy man.

The days went by comfortably enough as they tacked down the Channel, but an unfavorable breeze veered them towards France and then back towards the coast of England. Meanwhile, the prisoners settled into a routine they would become accustomed to over the coming months.

George heard ship's officers handing out strict discipline to the crew. From general rumours going round he learned some officers were so illiterate they could barely write their name, most having worked their way up from the fo'c'sle. During the voyage he found them a rough lot, at times drunk and brutal, and the crew even rougher. He imagined they must have been recruited from seaside taverns. It surprised him to hear their conditions on the ship were almost as bad as their cargo of convicts. He came to the conclusion it was only the most uncouth of seamen who were willing to risk a journey to the ends of the earth with a shipload of convicts.

At about four-thirty each morning, those convicts selected as cooks went up to prepare breakfast. Later, at sunrise, the crew placed a bathing tub on the prison deck, unlocked the hatch doors, and all the convicts filed up to have seawater thrown over them from buckets. After returning to the 'tween deck, and after dressing, they carried their bedding up the hatchways to be stowed for the day. Breakfast began at eight, and mess-men from their own ranks served them.

Following their morning meal, George joined the group sent up on deck to clean it with soft sandstone known as dry-holystone. While one of the convicts hosed the deck to keep it wet, others rolled up their trouser legs and shirtsleeves, and knelt in a row shoulder to shoulder. At the command of one of the militia they began rocking back and forward scouring the deck. After several days they learned it was best to move in unison, and together in a long line, the men stretched their arms forward with backs arched like a cat stretching, then sat back on their haunches. Although his hands and body usually ached with the effort, George enjoyed the exercise and felt better for it.

After the decks had been holystoned spotless, those wanting to learn to read and write assembled, and several of their more educated fellows gave them lessons. George and the remainder usually came up on deck to pick oakum. They sat in groups unravelling the ends of old rope to get loose fibre used for caulking. He learned it was a necessary occupation because sometimes cracks occurred in the hull or between the decking, and they used the teased-out rope to pack into cracks as they appeared. When deck tar melted in the tropics it sometimes dripped, and could burn anyone it fell on below deck.

Just before noon, dinner guards handed out a mixture of limejuice and sugar known as sherbet as a way of preventing the onset of scurvy. But because it could be used for gambling, it had to be drunk in front of the medical officer to prevent trafficking. During the afternoon, schooling became available again, while other prisoners could be up on deck. They served supper about four o'clock, after which the convicts entertained themselves with singing or playing games such as leapfrog. Later, they took their bedding below, and guards locked the prison at sunset. Crewmembers shaved the convicts twice a week, and cut their hair every two weeks.

As they left the Channel, a fierce wind sprang up during the night. It soon reached gale force, keeping the whole contingent of prisoners awake. Wind howled through the rigging, and smacked the sails. They heard the deafening roar of the sea as wave after wave tossed the vessel about, causing great anxiety among those who had never been to sea before. George, with all those around, became violently seasick, the acrid stench of vomit in the confined space between decks making the stale air even more foul. How everybody wished for daylight. When at last the prisoners came on deck they found the sea calm again with all hands busy attending to rigging and sails, and checking for any damage.

'T'was just a small blow last night,' George overheard one of the crew saying to a prisoner. 'A bit o' brass monkey weather takes the boredom out o' sailing. Wait till we get to the Bay of Biscay,' he added in a rather portentous tone of voice.

Still, rather than sailing into more bad weather, they woke next day to a beautiful morning. After a breakfast of gruel and bread a few prisoners came on deck again. By now his seasickness had improved and George felt better able to enjoy his surroundings. As the day warmed, he and H.J. emerged from the hatchway and made their way across the prison deck to lean on the bulwarks. They saw they were alone on an ocean that stretched all round to a horizon that gave no hint of land. The sea remained calm, the wind barely a breeze, and hardly a cloud in a bright cerulean sky. During their time together on deck, they spotted several small groups of dolphins cavorting about the ship. Several took up a position near the bow, water cascading from their bodies as they leaped and frolicked. All too soon guards ordered the prisoners below. Fortunately they did not clap them in irons, and for the rest of the voyage only those requiring discipline wore shackles.

But the sailor's predictions for the Bay of Biscay were about to materialize. Next morning, as the prisoners came on deck to be washed, H.J. pointed to the sky. Looking up, George saw that overnight nature had painted a tempestuous scene around them. Blue-black clouds obscured the horizon, and were rapidly darkening a sullen sky. The air hung heavy and still. Distant flashes of sheet lightning followed by the faint rumble of thunder signalled an ominous warning of what would soon come.

While the vessel continued to make its way under an increasing breeze, George heard an order to clew down. Crew loosened halyards, sails rose in preparation for furling, and militia escorted the prisoners below. Seamen battened down the hatches and bolted them in place. They said with a storm approaching the prisoners should tie down anything liable to be flung about.

Soon the wind increased in violence, and in the darkened atmosphere, a flash of lightning accompanied by a tremendous peal of thunder rattled the sky directly overhead, and shook the vessel. Mountainous seas soon pounded the ship from all sides. In the sunless air the crests of the waves seemed tipped with bright silver to be swept away by the wind in a fine white spray to shroud the ocean in a mantle of mist.

Swell after swell surged across the decks. Seas found their way down hatchways and swirled from side to side below. As seawater began to seep through seams in the ship's hull and dampen the walls of their berths, even the most resolute of the convicts could not control mounting terror. In the noise and confusion of the storm, each creak of the vessel gave George the impression every timber in her was about to shatter.

With each passing hour they heard the wind shriek as it tossed the vessel to and fro. It tore at the rigging and almost laid the ship on its side. In a scene of chaos, with the prison deck in turmoil, George felt his head hit the deck. With sudden pain and a taste of blood in his mouth he realized he had bitten his tongue. He reassured himself with the thought that the sailors had all been in seas like this many times before and knew what to do. He hoped their ordeal would be nothing more than a frustrating day for the crew.

With hatches battened down the atmosphere below rapidly became putrid with the stench of overcrowded humanity already reaching nauseating levels. Above the noise and chaos of the storm George heard the sounds of men vomiting and groaning in the darkness. As he, too, lay prostrate with fear and nausea it occurred to him H.J.s handsome face and figure were no help to him here, where he sprawled contorted by seasickness. None gave a passing thought for an evening meal. But as night approached the wind began to drop, and by morning the weather had improved considerably.

But nature continued to be against them through the Bay of Biscay. With a head sea, the ship continued to pitch and roll in an unpleasant way, making walking an unnerving experience. Later, as seas calmed, those prisoners who felt well enough were allowed on deck. When George emerged he saw all sail hoisted with the ship moving swiftly in a fair breeze. He could make out land about ten miles away on the larboard side, and one of the guards mentioned they had been skirting the shore of Spain for several hours.

As day followed day, George often joined other convicts on deck to spend time leaning on the bulwark and gazing into the deep green of the ocean. The soothing sounds of the sea as it slipped almost silently along the side of the ship brought a great calm to his troubled mind. At other times when the wind howled in the rigging, the thunderous power of the waves and the ominous forces of nature suggested a forerunner of turbulent years yet to come.

Despite its terrors, George felt a touch of romance about going to sea, and a sense of being on the threshold of new adventures far more exciting than being a clerk in foggy London. His past ambitions now out of mind, the ocean and the challenge of his destiny now lay ahead.

Chapter 18

The Forger's Letter

Aubrey Jones could barely concentrate on his work. Plagued by sleepless nights and confusing days, he hadn't realized how much his scheme would take out of him. If I'd known I would be party to a murder I would have burnt that document, he thought.

'You's becoming grumpy,' his landlady said during his evening meal.

'In my line of business I have problems you would never dream of,' Aubrey told her.

'I hopes you ain't done nothing agin the law,' she said.

'I can assure you of my honesty,' he replied. But during the meal he could tell his landlady was not convinced, and he returned to his room feeling she already suspected him of a crime he had not yet committed. Feeling slightly breathless and noticing his throat parched he reached for the port bottle and poured himself a stiff drink.

After pacing up and down he flung himself on to the bed and stared at the ceiling. Once again an old habit overtook him, and his hand found its way to his *Don Cypriano* already swelling in anticipation of comforting its possessor. He grasped the stem gently at first, simply to quell his anxiety, but in his tense state of mind, his actions became more urgent until a sudden rush of seed brought him back to reality. It left him lying there rather torpid, surveying his stained shirttails, and thinking I've been sucked into something I've lost control of. Slowly his mind settled and he drifted into sleep.

After two weeks of worry it was time for Aubrey to make his way back to Black Eddie, the forger. Still in an agitated state after sleepless nights, his hand shook when Eddie handed him the letter. As he read through it, and its message slowly sank in, he started to feel a little better.

> *My dear Aubrey,*
>
> *How pleasant to see you again. I'm eternally in your debt after all you have done for me, not least in saving my life in that terrible storm all those years ago. I would not be here to thank you if it had not been for your courage and bravery.*
>
> *You know how I have tried to thank you on many occasions. I know it is beneath your dignity to accept a financial reward, but rest assured, I am forever in your debt, and as you are fully conversant with my business, I will repay you handsomely in my will.*
>
> *With my eternal gratitude for your friendship and help.*
>
> *My kindest regards,*
> *Luke Dunlley.*

'Excellent. It looks genuine,' Aubrey said. 'When I present it with the other document I'm sure the solicitors will believe it.'

'Now let us be clear about our little arrangement,' Black Eddie added, giving Aubrey a cold stare. 'Good quality assassins be expensive. With all the work we put into this, 'tis fair half be shared 'tween t'other person and me. You take t'other half o' the proceeds.'

With no escape from the hand of the forger, Aubrey saw his legacy shrinking even further. 'Draw up the agreement and I will sign it,' he said limply. 'I suppose half a loaf is better than no bread, as they say. I will wait for a certain event to take place and then come forward to claim the inheritance.'

Chapter 19

Fire and Pestilence

As day followed day the weather slowly warmed. With little if any breeze to ventilate the 'tween decks, life for George and the other prisoners became more uncomfortable, and they were always glad to be allowed on deck. Whenever George looked to the horizon, the ship always remained framed in the same unchanging scene as if the vessel lay trapped on a boundless ocean. Once a distant ship came into view, but was too far away to make out her flags or to attract attention. Madeira and the Canary Islands went by, but remained out of sight beyond the horizon.

During the hot and sultry hours of darkness, sleep for the prisoners became disturbed and fitful. As they lay about through the heat of the day conversations lagged. They all lived each day as it came, seemingly resigned to whatever lay ahead. George had not seen his face in a mirror for months, and wondered if his features had become as haggard and sun-tanned as those of his fellow convicts.

One hot morning after holystoning, George and H.J. took their turn on deck and, as usual, sauntered across to lean against the bulwarks. Resting their forearms on the railing each gazed in silence into the inky-blue glassiness of the ocean. For some time they remained deep in their own thoughts until George turned, and looking up to H.J.s handsome features, said, 'I've often wondered how you came to be involved with an heiress.'

H.J. closed his eyes, and his face took on a solemn expression. 'It's a long story, George. Do you really want to hear it?'

'We have the time, H.J.'

'Well, to start at the beginning, we lived in London where my father sold high quality goods in our well-to-do grocery shop near Westminster. Although we were not wealthy he could afford to give me a good education, and hoped I would eventually take over the business. After finishing schooling at seventeen he took me into the shop to teach me. But he soon noticed women would come in, buy something trivial and linger on to chat with me.'

'That doesn't surprise me,' said George.

'Girls my own age would giggle and blush and were often tongue-tied, but older women were the real trouble; some wealthy and more than twice my age would keep me in conversation. They would flush as they talked, and sometimes grab my arm, or want to touch me. At first it embarrassed me, but I soon learned how to say the right thing and add a little flattery, and I became quite comfortable chatting with them.'

'Were you leading them on?'

'No, George, at first I thought it was good for business, but my father saw trouble and warned me. Still, some women were persistent. They would come into the store, ignore him, and wait until I became free to serve them. He told me not to waste time, but I couldn't avoid their attentions. Finally he sent me to work in a less affluent area for another grocer. To save his business, he said. Unfortunately the same thing happened in that grocery, and after I drifted into a couple of affairs with married women the grocer returned me to my father.'

'But why did you do it, H.J.?'

'I was barely eighteen George. When attractive women gave subtle hints about their availability I found it hard to resist temptation. My face and figure were my downfall.'

'So what happened then?'

'My father decided I would never be a grocer, and arranged for me to go to Oxford University to study the Humanities, hopeful I would find my place in better things. Fortunately they accepted me, and I had a very pleasant year there away from women in the all male college.'

'So what went wrong?'

'I roomed with a chap a year or two older, and we became good friends. It turned out his father was a very wealthy knight of the realm with a country estate and all. My colleague invited me to spend a few days of my summer holidays with him and meet the family. We went horse riding together on several occasions until he suggested we take his sister along too: a charming and pretty little thing, younger than me. In retrospect, I think her mother mistook me for a wealthy marriage prospect because one morning my friend came to me rather piqued and told me he had an appointment elsewhere, and to go riding with his sister. Put up to it by his sister, or possibly by his mother.'

'I see your problem, H.J.'

'I could tell the girl was rather taken with me, but she had been raised a lady, and much too sophisticated to simply put herself in front of me. Rather, it is when somebody is nearby during the day you begin to see and hear little things about them that all add up, like the look in their eye, or the tender-hearted way they speak to you, and their little acts of kindness.'

'That would be hard to brush aside,' said George.

'Yes, but it got more difficult,' said H.J. 'On the day we went riding together, she led me to a small stream on the estate where she stopped and dismounted beside a shelving bank near the water. She stood there looking quite beautiful and so vulnerable. She seemed to want me to take her in my arms, which I did with a gentle caress. But I was careful to not overplay my hand. I could tell she was leading me on in a very elegant way. To be unresponsive to such feminine grace would have been humiliating for her, even showing scorn.'

'Her mother seemed to enjoy my company too, and on several occasions hinted in an oblique way of marriage, probably to sound me out. But a couple of days later my friend and I returned to Oxford leaving the girl clearly grieving. I sent a note of thanks to the mother, and hoping to finish the affair, implied I was not wealthy, but simply a grocer's son.'

'That should have finished the little escapade, H.J.'

'You're right, George, but about two weeks later the girl came down to Oxford supposedly to see her brother, but he left her alone with me, probably on purpose.'

'They surely must have considered you a prize worth having.'

'I guess so, George. She was obviously a girl accustomed to getting her own way. But in truth, I found her very attractive, and who wouldn't want to marry into a family with so much wealth.'

'I see your point, H.J., I would surely feel the same.'

'She was clearly suffering from love sickness,' H.J. went on. 'She said she didn't care if I was penniless. Then, with trembling fingers she handed me a pink envelope, which I opened to find a banker's order for five hundred guineas. It must surely have been arranged with her mother's connivance.'

'She said, "now you cannot claim to be poor." I could hardly believe it was all happening. Money was clearly no problem in that family, but I did not think my face and charm were worth that much to anybody. I made a weak attempt to return the envelope, but she easily persuaded me to keep it.'

'Sounds as if you were on a winner.'

'Not quite, because she said her father always hoped she would marry a man with firm prospects, and would be livid if he ever found out where the money came from. Because of her father she wanted to go with me to Gretna Green and be married on the spot.'

'But you did marry her there, didn't you H.J.?'

'Oh, yes, and for a little while it was the most wonderful time of our lives. But her father was unhappy at the lack of ceremony for his daughter's marriage, and soon became suspicious. If I were wealthy enough to marry his daughter, why would we sneak off to Gretna Green? He quickly discovered our secret, and accused me of deceit and initiating the whole affair. Being of the aristocracy he had the marriage annulled, and sent his daughter off to France. It seems I had committed a hanging offence, but fortunately the courts decided I should serve ten years penal servitude for my crime instead.'

'Well, when you become free again H.J., I'm sure you will have no trouble finding some rich land owner's daughter and become wealthy in your own right. Let me know if she has a sister, and I promise to be Best Man at your wedding.'

A smile passed between them and they continued to gaze in silence at the ocean.

While George and H.J. continued to enjoy each other's company, other men's cheerless thoughts never rose above the banal. A few like Martin must have left a wife and family behind, never to see them again. George found no enjoyment in listening to their daily grumblings. Nor did he ever hear anything from them that might be construed as nourishment for the soul. For them, everything was dismal, always the constant sameness of the ocean, or the stench of the convict deck. Still, George realized these men born and bred on neglect and vice taught him how deprived members of society survive, and also what little he knew of the outside world when he left home.

Accustomed to the grime and foggy atmosphere of slums where they grew up, the majority of his fellow prisoners found the clean, fresh air on the open seas a great attraction for them. Being illiterate, the tall tales seamen spun intrigued many of them. They spent hours scanning the horizon for mermaids, or worrying an albatross might swoop down and crack their skull with its beak.

'H.J., you knows about such things,' a skinny, jug-eared fellow said as he shaded his eyes to scan the ocean. 'Is mermaids human or fish? And what be their husbands?'

For a while H.J. continued to gaze out to sea as if deep in contemplation until turning from the horizon he leaned back, elbows resting on the bulwarks, and said, 'There are more wonders in the world than we can ever know.'

The old convict looked impressed with the answer, but no wiser.

Many found ways to relieve the tedium of being crowded together for weeks. Some went to great lengths looking for something they could bend into a hook, and spent hours leaning across the bulwarks fishing, usually without success. Whenever someone caught a fish a great shout came from the convicts, and they paraded it in triumph.

But the majority of prisoners developed a craze for gambling. It became such a passion the convicts gambled anything they could get their hands on: clothes, food, or whatever else took their fancy. They even bet on whether or not a certain wave would break before reaching the ship. By now, the few packs of cards in play had become floppy with use, limp as linen, and difficult to shuffle. George sometimes heard a shout of exasperation when somebody lost a prized possession. But to be caught cheating meant certain ostracism from ones companions.

One Sunday after their compulsory church service George and H.J. remained on the prison deck. Leaning on the bulwarks as usual, they idly watched the ocean as a keen wind raked spume from the crests of the waves. They often spent hours together, talking and watching the ocean, aloof from the blasphemous and obscene joviality of their comrades.

'The padre's sermons are a farce,' George mused in a vacant way, turning his gaze towards the horizon.

'Well,' said H.J., 'I suppose he has to make a point of outlining the certainty of a terrible damnation for all us sinners.'

'Yes, but does he always have to draw our attention to all the paths to hellfire and brimstone?' George added.

'Well, it's his job and we all nod in agreement,' said H.J.

'Still, whenever he's around everybody pretends to embrace a Christian way of life,' George said.

H.J. gave a nod. 'You can't blame us hoping for a good report from him, and perhaps a reduced sentence.'

'But behind his back there's all this thieving and gambling. They don't seem to care for friends who lose their rations on a turn of the dice.'

Whenever they discussed ideas, George listened carefully to H.J., especially his finer points about the opposite sex. On one such occasion a convict lounging nearby overheard their conversation. 'I don't believe a word of what you is saying about women, H.J.' he said with amusement. 'All women be evil and up to no good. Live with one,' the man said, 'and they'll send you mad with their chatter. 'Tis enough to drive a man out o' his own lodgings.'

'Aye,' said another coarse-featured ruffian who had sidled closer to listen. 'I've never knowed one what didn't pry and gossip. They can never keep quiet about what they knows. 'Tis dangerous in our trade.'

'You say women are up to no good,' H.J. exclaimed. 'But it is we who are the guilty ones, otherwise we would not be where we are.'

Others who had drifted closer to overhear the conversation seemed amused at H.J.'s assertions, and sniggered knowingly among themselves.

'If you think it is women who are wicked it means you despise them, and so you treat them badly,' H.J. went on. 'Or perhaps you have simply mixed with those of your own nature.'

George nodded in agreement. He remembered his mother telling him how she had bought food for unemployed workers in her younger days, and he thought of her working herself to an early death because of her family. It reminded him of all the other women who slaved for their families in his old neighbourhood. The memory encouraged him to say, 'it seems to me if you treat women badly they will do the same in return.'

'You are right, George,' said H.J. 'Respect them and show you honestly care about them. You will reap rewards.'

George looked at H.J.s handsome features, and thought of his ability to attract women of substance. It set him wondering if what H.J. said was really the whole story.

As weeks passed, a shortage of fresh fruit and vegetables became of serious concern to the prisoners. Together with their short rations and bland diet, food became a constant subject of discussion. 'Have you ever noticed when men are hungry, all they ever talk about is food,' H.J. remarked one day. 'But when everybody has a full stomach, conversations always turn to women and sex.' In passing their days talking about all manner of things, George began to feel more worldly-wise because of it.

George and H.J. used every opportunity to come on deck to escape the crowds of gamblers and foul air of the 'tween decks. Relaxing in the warmth of the sun under a clear blue sky, they enjoyed watching for flying fish that often broke the surface near the ship. It intrigued them to see fish leap into the air, bodies arched forward, and swoop in a long glide of many yards before dropping back into the ocean.

As they sailed on in tropical heat they sometimes passed through sudden squalls that seemed peculiar to those latitudes. Typical of these, as they skirted the nearby Cape Verde Islands, without warning a veil of darkness would descend across the ocean giving little time for guards to usher everybody below decks. Bare-footed sailors would run to reef the topsails and haul down the stud sails and royals. Within minutes a squall would hit, almost throwing the ship on her beam-ends and sending a tropical rainstorm of great intensity, drenching anybody still in the open. These cloudbursts usually passed quite quickly; the sun would reappear, and in no time nature would return to what it had been before the squall hit. These sudden downpours of tropical rain often made their plight worse. Bedding became saturated while being aired, and it seldom dried before the next cloudburst. Wet beds were uncomfortable to sleep on, and clothing was constantly damp.

As they neared the equator the atmosphere below decks became even more stifling. Temperatures rose, humidity increased, and they sometimes lay becalmed for days with sails hanging slack from all yards. With little wind to cause a draught through the convict deck, the air remained stagnant, evil smelling and oppressive, and left an acrid taste in the mouth. The deck blazed hot in the sun, and pitch stuck to whoever walked on it. Sometimes it melted and dropped from the seams to the 'tween decks below, burning anybody it happened to land on. The only thing everybody thought about was water: two pints of warm and half-putrid liquid, the daily ration for each person.

They had set sail with several cats with the run of the ship to keep rats at bay. Now grown fat, the cats were less active, and the prisoners enjoyed their company. The cats often lay on their backs to be stroked and fussed over, or would rub themselves against the rough material of the convict trousers. With eyes half-closed they would curl up in the shade, licking their fur with a rough tongue, or running a front paw over one side of their head. Even the bullies and murderers enjoyed stroking and tickling their glossy coats.

Despite prowling cats; rats, cockroaches and other vermin continued to infest the ship. In the overcrowded prison area the air had the irritating stench of stale bilge water and the smells of mouldering provisions, all mingling with the odour of perspiring humanity. Many of the prisoners had become frail, and the all-consuming heat only added to their miseries.

It had been a routine since the beginning of the voyage to issue the prisoners with a small amount of spirits each week. On a particularly hot and humid morning, with the ship in the vicinity of the equator, George and H.J. came up onto the hot prison deck with others to take advantage of the open air. They casually watched as two seamen crossed the prison deck, and heard them speak to a soldier guarding the gateway in the stanchions. He opened the gate, and both seamen went down a hatchway to the ship's storeroom.

'They're probably drawing our weekly ration of rum,' H.J. said, and he and George turned back to watch for more flying fish.

After several minutes H.J. sniffed and said, 'I smell something.' They turned to see wisps of whitish smoke billowing out of a hatchway and across the deck. In seconds it became a brownish-yellow cloud, pungent and thick.

'Fire. Pumps,' somebody yelled.

Several sailors already running towards the hatchway, shouted, 'come on. Give a hand.'

Guards allowed George and H.J. with several other convicts through the gateway, and they followed the seamen down the hatchway into a storeroom. Yellow smoke mingled with the smell of burning food and smouldering canvas met them. It swirled through the area filling George's throat with pungent fumes that irritated with every breath. In the smoke and chaos the hazy scene turned frantic seamen to shadowy figures beating at flames with sacks or anything else they could find. Pumps had not yet arrived.

In the dim light, George noticed the blaze spreading rapidly to an adjacent area where food was stored, and saw it start to burn their provisions. Through the smoke haze he saw flames threatening to engulf two casks labelled *gunpowder*. He grabbed H.J.s arm and pointed. Both rushed to remove the copper casks, but found them almost too hot to hold.

'They could blow any second,' H.J. cried out in despair.

George had his shirt off in a moment, and wrapped it round one of the casks, but found the container heavy to lift. H.J. grabbed the other, but released his hold as heat scorched his hands and arms. Two other convicts dashed forward with strips of thick canvas, and it became a desperate effort of willpower for them to carry the casks. The two wiry men strained and heaved the casks through the doorway and into the narrow corridor. George and

H.J. stood aside watching intently as the men struggled step by step up the hatchway and on to the deck.

'If the casks blow the whole ship will go up,' George cried.

'At least it will be so sudden we'll never know it,' said H.J.

By this time seamen had pumps working, and seeing the danger, began to hose the casks of gunpowder with seawater. The crisis was over.

'Those two men have saved the ship,' said H.J. in a croaky voice as he and George continued beating at the flames. With aid from more prisoners, the crew finally managed to extinguish the fire, but not before the ship suffered extensive damage. Everybody agreed that without the two convicts' efforts, the ship would have exploded in flames with the loss of all aboard.

When questioned, the two seamen said they had gone aft to the storeroom to collect the weekly ration of rum, and while one drew off the spirits the other struck a match to light his pipe. A bright flash followed, setting the storeroom ablaze before they could control it.

A grim-faced captain rushed to the scene to find the fire had consumed a large quantity of provisions. Clearly, food would be in shorter supply from now on. There was much talk among the crew and convicts concerning the ship possibly stopping at Rio or the Cape to replenish supplies, but the captain had other ideas. He decided any stop would be costly and a waste of precious sailing time, and elected to sail on; a risky gamble since all on board would have to be on short rations for the rest of the voyage. This callous disregard for the prisoners' welfare soon led to more problems.

A week of inclement weather confined the prisoners below deck, and while all those around them talked about the fire and their lucky escape, George and H.J. sat miserably in the semidarkness and foul air of their quarters while their burns healed. The sympathetic ship's surgeon visited them on several occasions and ordered oil to be applied. 'Your burns are superficial and will soon heal,' he reassured them. 'But there is little I can do to lessen the pain.' By the time the weather cleared George and H.J. felt able to go up on deck again with the others.

As the days dragged by, George sensed his energy, and that of his fellow prisoners, slowly waning. One day he heard groans coming from various places on the prison deck. Soon, men started to run for the toilet buckets, some not reaching them in time. Clearly they had the beginnings of an epidemic of dysentery, and before long fever wracked the whole convict deck.

George, too, became seized with sharp pains of abdominal colic that doubled him up. Within moments he felt a sudden urge to run for the commodes, but before he reached them a rush of bloody evacuations overtook him and splattered across the already fetid deck. Most of his weaker fellows were soon prostrated in the same way, and they could only lie in their bunks, resigned to their plight. The surgeon came down to assess the situation, worried to see the state of so many of the convicts. He could do nothing for them except give words of encouragement, and order the worst cases to be carried to the ship's hospital near the fo'c'sle. Within days two of them were buried at sea.

The epidemic raged for almost two weeks as conditions on the convict deck escalated to worse than awful. The smells, the groans, the sudden rushes to the toilets all in the gloom of the prison deck made life for the prisoners unbearable. They could only lie and suffer while they waited it out. Later, word went round that the surgeon-superintendent claimed it had been caused by the heat and miasmic dampness of the prison quarters. He had done all he could for the men, but found no evidence of a contagious nature.

While George and his fellow convicts remained weak and frail after their illness, the ship continued on its lonely way across seas devoid of all other human existence. It seemed to George the ocean was infinite enough to stretch on forever. He imagined it must have remained unchanged for eons, and they had reached a place where time had no meaning. Alone on the ocean, and with every day seeming the same, he often wondered where they were on the map, and how much longer their journey would take. He could not help but sense an ever-present threat of hidden dangers lurking in the primordial depths, and determined the sea could never be taken at face value.

As they sailed further south it was a joy for him to see Cape hens: beautiful birds that flew about the ship in great abundance. They often hovered close enough to float on breezes reflected from the sails, or folding their wings back, dived like an arrow into the sea after small fish. On other occasions George shaded his eyes to watch albatross soaring and gliding close above the waves with barely a movement of their wings. The first one he saw astonished him. He guessed it must have stretched almost fourteen feet from tip to tip of its wings. As he watched, it would occasionally dip a wing and circle the masts before returning to follow the wake of the ship.

At last they rounded the Cape of Good Hope, but without stopping to replenish their supplies. The ship sailed on, soon making good time in the roaring forties. But they found their thin clothing issued at Woolwich, and already threadbare, of little help in the cold of the Southern Ocean. The prisoners did not spend much time on deck. But in fine weather, George and H.J. usually went up for a short time, mainly to escape the atmosphere of the 'tween decks. But frigid gusts always hit them, and snapped and crackled at the rigging and sails. If they turned to face the wind, it seemed to force its way into their mouth and down their throat.

Storms sometimes sent shards of hail ricocheting off the sails to settle into drifts in corners of the deck. The wind often blew with such force the crew had the ship scudding bare masted with all sails furled, and making sleep for most prisoners out of the question. In lighter winds the ship bowled along with sails squared and spray flying from the bows. But gales often swept waves across the deck to find their way down hatchways and adding to the discomfort of those below. The rolling and pitching of the ship made it difficult to stand, or even sit. It became impossible to wash, and difficult to eat meals. The ship and everything on it was always wet, cold and dismal. Many of the prisoners took tumbles on the slippery deck to a round of cheers: the only cause for amusement among their fellows.

At other times the ship scurried along in inclement weather, often with masts bare but for main and foretopsails, both doubly reefed. They seemed to rush headlong down into a valley between the rollers, and mount the other side to reach the top of a mountainous hill of water. George could only wonder at the agility, and at times the downright bravery of the seamen who scaled the rigging in all weathers. He found it difficult enough to retain his footing on the deck, let alone imagining what it would be like for seamen high up on the swaying masts and yards in icy wind and rain. At times the ship rolled heavily, the tilt so steep it seemed only the wind forcing the sailors against the ratlines kept them from falling. When masts angled low over the seas he watched seamen clinging to the swaying yards, the ends often only a few feet above the waves.

Throughout the voyage, George and his fellow prisoners suffered from health problems of all sorts, not least from lack of nourishing food. For a reason nobody understood, from the very first day at sea, the captain replaced oatmeal in the diet with cocoa. But most of the prisoners refused to drink it claiming its vile taste always made them sick. Now, with short rations and a dearth of fresh vegetables, all the prisoners were in low spirits, and whispered among themselves that it could be a recipe for an outbreak of scurvy.

Several weeks after the dysentery epidemic, George noticed some of his rather depressed cellmates becoming more and more lethargic, and losing interest in their surroundings. Some of them stopped eating the tough salt beef because of painful gums. Every now and then one of them spat up a little blood.

Word soon spread and the surgeon came below to examine several of the convicts. He found one man's tongue and gums swollen, and his body showed several bruises he could not account for. The doctor decided the man had scurvy, and came across others with similar problems. He sent the worst cases to the ship's hospital, but could do little for the remainder except to give a few extra drams of limejuice. Guards, who usually passed on any rumours or tidbits of information to the prisoners, told them the doctor and captain agreed they should have taken on more vegetables at Rio or the Cape.

Below decks the ever-present fear of scurvy dominated conversation, and as the next few weeks passed, more prisoners fell victim to the scourge. Teeth loosened and many suffered the excruciating pain of toothache, the agony even worse when teeth had to be extracted from inflamed gums. Soon, the hospital held fifty seriously ill patients. Inevitably, deaths followed.

The minister cast twelve prisoners into the deep before the Australian coast came into sight. On each occasion, the convicts lined up on deck while the dour-faced minister read the burial service. Some had been friends or gambling partners of the deceased. A climate of fear took hold throughout the prison deck, and many stood with tears in their eyes as they watched the pitiful bundles of remains sent over the side to float away and sink beneath the waves. The ship's surgeon, clearly upset with the outbreak, did as much as he could to calm the prisoners.

As the ship sailed on through squalls and hailstorms, the crew twice sighted icebergs. The prisoners became very troubled by this new danger, especially during the long hours of darkness, and they muttered in fearful terms among themselves. But the surgeon had further problems. Both he and the captain were paid by the number of convicts delivered at the end of the journey. The more who died, the less their pay when they reached port, and there had already been too many deaths: almost one every other day. Guards told the prisoners they overheard the surgeon talking with the captain, encouraging him to reach port as soon as possible.

Chapter 20
Night of terror

By now it was more than a year since George had been wrongfully convicted, and he had already spent 120 days at sea. But they still found the rolling swells of the Great Australian Bight made movement about the ship a difficult feat. Now, with good speed, a following wind, and the end of the voyage in view, the crew began to get the ship ready for port. Some scraped from fore to aft while others began tarring the rigging.

On the morning of that fateful day George came on deck to exercise with H.J. and a group of convicts. While some remained lethargic and despondent, accepting whatever fate had in store for them, others, like George and H.J., became more cheerful and active, frequently scanning the ocean in the hope of sighting a shoreline. About eleven o'clock a shout from the lookout announced land in sight. George and H.J. joined the crowd milling about the bulwarks and peering towards the horizon. By early afternoon they could make out a low line of hills like a long shadow under a mass of dark clouds, and causing a general sense of excitement to spread though the ship. Even the militia had a smile. At lunchtime George heard the first mate say their vessel was in the vicinity of Port Davey on the western coast of Van Diemen's Land.

Later, they rounded the southernmost Capes and entered much calmer waters. As the ship turned northeast up the eastern side of the coast the weather remained mild. In the early evening guards said they could make out land on the larboard side quite clearly in the moonlight.

Despite the prospects of a successful arrival in Hobart Town, the surgeon-superintendent, still concerned for his patients, decided to speak to the captain again in his cabin.

'Sir,' he began. 'As you know, twelve prisoners have already died. I have a further sixty on the sick list. Fifty of them are confined to bed with scurvy. More will die if we do not get to port quickly. May I suggest we take the shorter route through D'Entrecasteaux Channel? This route will save us a day or two and several lives.'

'But doctor, that is a very unpredictable passage,' the captain replied. 'We could be struck by one of its sudden squalls. It would prevent us carrying sail. That's a potentially disastrous situation.'

'I mention it because men's lives are at stake.'

'Very well, doctor,' the captain said. 'The weather is fine. I'll study the charts and official sailing directions again.'

He took a chart from its drawer, and spread it out across the cabin table. For some minutes he sat studying its bearings and the hourly calculations of their progress, all carefully marked. He looked up from the chart as if in deep thought, and with one elbow on the table, cupped his chin in his hand and contemplated. Suddenly he stood up, walked across the cabin and reached for a thick book which he pulled from a shelf and flipped the pages. The doctor saw it was the sailing directions laid down by Captain John Horsburg, a recognized authority.

The captain returned to the charts, and after further thought, looked up at the doctor. 'The seas are calm,' he said. 'And the map shows good anchoring ground along the new route. I'll give instructions to alter course'

'Thank God,' said the doctor.

'As a precaution, I'll have a leadsman placed forward to take regular soundings,' the captain said. Together they left the cabin, happy with their decision.

The vessel moved cautiously at less than two knots, and with fifty feet of water beneath them the way ahead seemed clear. In the darkness they proceeded at a steady two or three miles off shore, and the soundings continued to show good depth under the ship. But the captain remained cautious. He kept the vessel under double-reefed topsails, and was ready to drop anchor at any suggestion of danger.

At about nine-thirty in the evening their optimism shattered when the leadsman suddenly shouted, 'Quarter less four.'

'Hard-a-port,' the captain yelled to the helmsman. Almost at the same time the ship scraped along an uncharted submerged rock, and came to a grinding stop.

The captain quickly assessed the situation, and realized they were in danger of sinking. But as the sea was still calm, he summonsed the third mate, shouting to him, 'Lower the jollyboat and take soundings.' It revealed the ship had foundered on a sunken rock with deeper water all round.

Unfortunately for all those on board, nature chose that moment to cause a swell to rise. Soon, large waves whipped up by the wind began to pound against the ship causing it to lurch from side to side so violently it flung to the deck all those standing.

Earlier in the evening guards locked the convicts on the prison deck as usual at sunset. George, keyed up in anticipation of arriving in Hobart Town, wondered what adventures he would have in this new and unknown country. There was much talk and the glee of obscene merriment from the ruffians round him as they made fun of what each other would be doing once back on land, especially in relation to the 'ladies'.

As the hours passed, conversations slowly quietened, and they began to drift off to sleep. But about nine-thirty in the evening they were startled to hear a loud grating noise followed by a sudden jolt that shook the ship from stem to stern. The prisoners were instantly awake, and at once perceived their peril. As the ship began to lurch from side to side they heard the splintering of wood as the rock holding it fast tore a large hole in the hull. Within minutes water began flooding into the prison deck.

Blind panic spread when all the prisoners locked below deck realized they were in grave danger of drowning. Springing out of bed they rushed to the hatchways begging to be released. Above the chaos and noise, George distinctly heard an order shouted down the hatchway.

'Don't let any of the prisoners escape on to the deck. They'll rush the longboat and swamp it.'

Sentries refused to open the doorway and threatened to shoot any convict who tried to break out. When the ship's officers heard prisoners screaming, the surgeon-superintendent went down, hopeful of being of some assistance. Throughout the voyage he had won the convicts respect through his kindness and willingness to be their advocate. George saw him come and stand at the locked prison door, and several prisoners managed to thrust their hands between the stanchions to seize hold of his arms and clothing.

'For God's sake do what you can to save us,' they pleaded.

'You promised to stand by us,' others shouted out to him.

'And so I shall,' he answered.

As he spoke, some of the prisoners managed to prize off a couple of stanchions, allowing enough space for two of them to squeeze through the opening and cling to his knees.

There were further cries of 'mercy, mercy,' from those trapped.

At that moment, another terrifying noise of grating and crashing added to the prisoners' fears as the rock continued to splinter the bottom of the ship. This new threat persuaded the surgeon to retreat up the hatchway taking the two prisoners with him.

As the ship continued to lurch from side to side several prisoners produced hammers, even a saw they had hidden for just such an emergency, and set about tearing down more stanchions. As they did so, other sentries from among the military rushed to the scene to form a compact guard round the hatchway. In scenes of panic they leveled their muskets at the prisoners.

'We'll shoot any who try to escape,' one of them shouted.

Caught like rats in a trap, the prisoners continued their frantic efforts to break free. In the confusion, George saw the militia fire several shots at them leaving two dead. In the noise and turmoil, the numbers of prisoners managing to break free caused the military guard to retreat, possibly in the hope of saving themselves. But some of them remained at the hatchway up to their waist in water, still trying to prevent prisoners from reaching the deck. Nevertheless, their efforts were not entirely successful.

From the first indication of danger George and H.J. were aware of their predicament, and rushed to the stanchions with others to plead for their release. When prisoners tore down nearby stanchions, George took the risk of being shot trying to escape, and managed to squeeze through with H.J. close behind him. As he reached the hatchway ladder he looked back for H.J., but saw his large frame wedged in the opening. He grabbed H.J. by the arm and pulled with all his strength. Screaming prisoners on the other side pushed, and soon freed him.

The two found themselves in the forefront of prisoners escaping up the hatchway. On reaching the deck, they looked back in horror, watching as seas welled up from below, slowly filling the ship with water, and drowning less fortunate cellmates trapped on the prison deck.

With the vessel rocking wildly back and forth in rough seas, George feared they were still in great danger. Barely able to stand, and unable to swim, he felt near to panic as he watched in dread as waves swept some of those round him overboard. Yet barely ten minutes had passed since the first warning of trouble.

George and H.J. clung to shattered bulwarks for support, imagining at any minute waves might sweep them into the sea. George noticed the commander of the guard among a crowd of sailors clinging nearby. At that moment the doctor forced his way from the poop deck to join the commander. 'Where are the prisoners?' He yelled.

'I fear they are mostly drowned,' the doctor shouted. In anguish he grasped the commander's hand, saying, 'Major, God bless you. In five minutes we will all be in eternity.'

In the darkness of evening, and with decks awash, George still clung to the bulwarks in a scene of utter confusion all round him. Amid all the noise, a loud grating sound startled him. Looking up he watched in dread as the mainmast crashed over the starboard side, smashing the nearby bulwarks in its path, and taking the mizen topmast with it. Seamen scrambled to cut away bulwarks on the opposite side in an attempt to launch the gig while crowds of soldiers and seamen rushed for spaces in it. In the commotion, as the crew lowered the boat, it became swamped and sank stern first, throwing all in it into the sea. Now the foremast went over the bow in a tangle of ropes and spars.

Sailors who had been taking soundings in the jollyboat managed to pick up most of those floundering in the water, but

George watched the jollyboat pull away from the ship leaving others still struggled in the sea. He thought the waves probably made it too dangerous for the boat to come alongside in any attempt to rescue them. Above the frightful noise of wind and waves he heard the captain shout orders to the third mate in the jollyboat. 'Find a landing place on the shore, disembark those on board, and return to the ship as soon as possible.'

At the time, the mate believed Hobart Town lay only fifteen miles distant and decided, instead, to seek help there. Unfortunately, it was over sixty miles away, and the jollyboat did not arrive there to alert a rescue until late the next day.

In little more than a quarter of an hour the vessel began to list even further, and in the midst of scenes of confusion the captain ordered the longboat to be launched. It rapidly filled with crew and militia eager to save themselves. But as seas kept surging across the rolling ship, each swell swept the longboat from one side of the deck to the other with the danger of it being staved in. As the ship rolled, the longboat slipped and slid, scattering the milling crowd already struggling to keep on their feet. One moment the longboat would be motionless, the next a battering ram

'Come on H.J.,' George shouted. 'Help to steady the longboat.'

They waited for a moment when it became stationary and scrambled across to hold it. Other convicts rushed to their assistance, and despite the disorder around them, they all somehow managed to restrain it. With the longboat fully loaded, the convicts helped get it into the water and to a short distance from the ship. But in mounting seas it became tangled among the broken rigging and debris in the water.

In desperation, the captain leaned from the longboat to push aside ropes and sails and splintered wood floating around and under them. But in no time he became wedged between boat and flotsam. It was only with frantic efforts by others aboard the longboat they finally freed him. At that moment, George saw the surgeon-superintendent, who had been anxiously watching from the deck, take the opportunity to leap into the longboat before a broiling flood of water swept it away into the darkness.

As seas continued to surge across the deck the ship began to cant badly to one side. The only part above water was the portside where all those aboard hung on frantically. George and H.J. grabbed a splintered part of the bulwarks, while those in the water clung to spars, or anything else they could find to support themselves in the tangled mass of flotsam round the ship. In the wind and cold sea some of the more fragile and sickly prisoners could no longer maintain their hold, and George watched as surging seas swept them away.

The moon rose, and in its faint light George watched as long rolling waves capped with foam kept coming silently out of the darkness. With each the ship rose, streaming spume and water from its deck, and from the top of the wave the ship would slide down a long incline to face the next onslaught. And so the waves kept coming; after surmounting one, there was always another wall of water behind it to add to their misery.

'Think we've got much show of seeing morning?' George rasped out.

'Morning's a long way off,' came H.J.s grim reply.

During the night they heard a loud grating sound, and watched as the mizzen mast broke off and fell overboard, allowing the ship to right itself a little. This exposed more of the deck, making things slightly easier for those still clinging on. But the survivors could tell the ship was gradually sinking. George felt so cold he had difficulty keeping his grip on the splintered woodwork. His hands were ice, and his fingers so stiff he could hardly move them. Waves kept sweeping over him, and gusts of cold wind added to his misery. With little sign of the longboat returning, he had no relief from his torment. Overcome by weariness, at times he thought how easy it would be to relax his hold and float off into oblivion. But something drove him to fight against taking a coward's way out, and he held on with added determination.

As the hours passed, George noticed H.J. straining to keep his grip.

'Can't hold on much longer,' he gasped. 'Strength's gone.'

'Keep it up, H.J.' George muttered. But even as he spoke he saw his friend start to tremble with the cold, his handsome face white as marble and devoid of expression. George saw H.J's grip loosen, and watched helplessly as he slipped into the sea and disappeared into the night.

Losing the only real friend he ever had, and facing imminent drowning, George felt at the lowest point in his life, and forced himself to keep clinging to the wreckage with all his strength. He kept telling himself, I've come this far and suffered so much injustice, and with all my hopes for the future I won't let providence destroy me now.

All night he heard the boom of surf, and wondered how close they were to the shore. But as dawn lightened the sky, all he could make out in the grey hue of sea and sky were white tipped waves pounding a rocky shoreline a little more than two miles away, and nobody there to notice their plight, or sound the alarm. The longboat had set out before ten o'clock the night before. By six o'clock next morning George wondered if it would ever come back. The strained faces of men around him desperately clinging to their lives gave him an extra urge to keep his hold. Numb with cold and barely conscious, only dogged determination kept him from giving up at this late stage.

In the morning light, gulls began to rankle the survivors with their shrill cries of joy as the birds rode the air currents, or swooped round the sinking vessel. George couldn't help feeling the mountainous waves that threatened their existence were little more than home to gulls sitting comfortably in groups on seas that meant no more to them than a handy place to rest.

As George continued clinging in desperation to the bulwark he heard a shout, and as the ship rose on a wave, he saw the longboat loom out of the morning haze. It had finally returned under the command of the ship's captain, and quickly picked up a further forty souls, bur George noticed it was mainly the remaining crew and militia. They left him and about fifty exhausted convicts still clinging to the wreckage. Two hours later, their spirits rose again on seeing the longboat returning in the distance. By now it was eight o'clock in the morning. They had been almost eleven hours in the wind and waves.

Then, to everybody's relief they sighted a schooner heading their way, and it soon came alongside. Many of the prisoners, weakened by the frigid temperature, had to be lifted aboard. After transferring all the survivors, the schooner headed for Southport beach where it picked up the longboat survivors. Finally, late in the day, they set out for Hobart Town.

The schooner had covered about thirty miles, and by four o'clock next morning she came upon three vessels with welcome provisions and dry clothing sent from Hobart Town to the shipwreck. Later in the morning the rescue boats arrived at Hobart Town with their cargo of bedraggled survivors. Without delay helpers rowed the ship's crew and militia ashore to be greeted by a great crowd of cheering onlookers lining the beach. George watched from the schooner as well wishers carried them up to the grounds of the governor's residence for a grand welcome. He heard a band playing in the distance.

The difference between free men and convicts was never clearer to George than in the manner of their arrival. The authorities simply considered them another group of convicts who had arrived to be placed in custody. If he had drowned, nobody would have cared. Probably his family would never know.

Later, after a roll call and inspection, armed guards accompanied the prisoners and rowed them ashore. On the beach more guards surrounded them and marched them to the nearby prison barracks. As they approached this austere group of buildings they could all see gallows protruding above the wall. George thought they must have been set in the prison yard as a gruesome warning not only to the inmates, but also to all passers-by.

At the court of inquiry that followed, George learned that of 220 prisoners aboard when the ship left the Downs, only 81 landed at Hobart Town. Of the 139 deaths, twelve died of scurvy or dysentery during the voyage. All the other 125, including fifty-eight bedridden hospital patients perished when the ship foundered.

The surgeon came out badly at the inquiry. It revealed he forgot his duty to the sixty hospital patients under his care when he sprang into the longboat as it pulled away from the ship. The court also criticized him for failing to remain with the prisoners as promised, having won their respect during the voyage. On the other hand, the court exonerated the captain and all the officers, saying they had taken every precaution before the ship foundered. Later, they did all they could to save those on board after the ship struck. Nevertheless, it was never explained why all the military guards and all but two of the crew survived, while of the 127 who drowned, all but two were prisoners.

Chapter 21

The False Claim

When Aubrey Jones returned to London he could not get to the forger quickly enough to learn what had happened.

'Tis good you are here, Aubrey,' Black Eddie said. 'I have a man for the job. The nights be dark at present. We'll go ahead with the arrangements afore you leave.'

Aubrey's breath quickened. 'Let me know when the deed is done,' he said as evenly as he could. He returned to his lodgings still unsure of the outcome, and more fearful of his involvement.

Several days later he found an unsigned note waiting for him at his address.

The matter we discussed has been took care of.
Present the document and letter in about two weeks.

Aubrey had a sleepless night knowing he had been a party to murder. Next day he rearranged his timetable to arrive in Birmingham after a decent interval of time, and took lodgings in his usual inn. In the quiet of his room he studied the documents again, and rehearsed everything he wanted to say. Next morning he set out for the firm of solicitors that had drawn up George's document.

'Well, this is a complete surprise for us, Mister Jones,' the solicitor said after reading the letter and document Aubrey showed him. 'We had no idea Mr Dunlley had such a good friend as you. It's important to us that all the details be known, because the family will be most concerned with the outcome.'

Aubrey sat back in his chair to make himself look as relaxed as possible. Extending his legs, he crossed his ankles and stroked his beard as if contemplating. 'It happened years ago,' he began. 'In fact, Luke's appreciation embarrassed me. I wondered if I should let it all pass, and simply burn his letter and your document. But after thinking about it, I considered it only right to show them to you for your expert opinion concerning my legal rights.'

'Normally an inheritance goes to the nearest male relative,' the solicitor said. 'But it appears your long-standing claim may have some merit.'

Aubrey put on a modest and humble expression: one he had often used in his acting days. He thought the solicitor was duly taken in by his performance.

'Can you tell me about the terrible storm mentioned in Dunlley's letter, and how you came to save his life?'

Aubrey expected this question and had his answer ready. 'It was more than twenty-five years ago. Luke and I were already well acquainted. As a young travelling salesman I often called upon him at his place of business in Navigation Street, and for reasons best known to him, he took a liking to me.' Aubrey gazed into the distance as if recalling those nostalgic times. Had he been more astute he may have noticed a momentary look of disbelief cross the solicitor's expression.

'Yes. Go on,' the solicitor murmured.

'On the day in question I was travelling by brig from the Downs to Hull on business when, by chance, Luke Dunlley happened to be on the same vessel. We conversed pleasantly until bad weather set in. A sudden storm and high seas struck us, and the vessel foundered just north of the Wash. In the turmoil a falling mast struck Dunlley a glancing blow and he fell overboard. He appeared to be unconscious and in danger of drowning in the rough seas. But we were near to the shore. I dived in and dragged him to safety.' Aubrey glanced to the solicitor, anticipating words of praise.

Instead, the solicitor said, 'I need a few days to discuss the consequences for Dunlley's family. I know them very well, and the matter should be resolved quickly. You will understand we must make suitable arrangements for all parties. Kindly see us again in two weeks when I hope the matters can be resolved satisfactorily.'

Later, two solicitors were seated in the same office.

'I would welcome your opinion about this fellow Jones who is making claim to the Dunlley estate,' one of them said. 'He did not impress me. I have handled their affairs for years and know the family well. Jones is a fraud. First, he claimed to have visited Dunlley on frequent occasions twenty-five years ago at Navigation Street. That is eight years before he moved to that address.'

'Surely that is enough to have him arrested,' the other answered.

'But there is more. He produced this document supposedly signed by me. You see it is dated 1822 when I was only a junior clerk. But the forger has made a damn good job of my signature.'

The other solicitor took the document and read it through. 'It's unlikely a junior law clerk would have signed a document of this nature,' he said.

'We would find that hard to disprove in a court of law.'

'What about the wording of the document?' his associate asked.

'I remember drafting something similar several years ago for a young lad named George White.'

'Where does he fit in?'

'His mother is Dunlley's daughter, but he disinherited her because she married beneath her station. She came to see me because her son is the male heir to the Dunlley estate. I drafted a similar document for her to this effect.'

'The plot thickens!'

'Later, Dunlley told me he had met the lad, a mill worker, and was impressed by his demeanour. He was waiting to see how he developed before taking him into his business. Over the years he never mentioned Jones, or put him in his will.'

'Even more reason to have Jones arrested,' the other said.

'I agree. But we have another problem if it comes to court. This letter supposedly from Dunlley is obviously a forgery, too.'

The other took it and studied it. 'The language is a bit flowery, but it could pass as genuine.'

'And hard to disprove too,' the first added. 'I have checked, and a brig was indeed wrecked about the time Jones claims.'

'That's a difficulty.'

'I have spoken to Mrs Dunlley, and she said her husband had never been to Hull. Although he owned several vessels, he always vowed he would never travel anywhere by boat. She believed his fears came from an early age, and were not due to the near drowning incident mentioned in the letter. I know Mrs Dunlley well, and believe her.'

'So, with a clever lawyer everything Jones has on paper would be difficult to disprove,' the other said. 'The only evidence we have against him was saying he visited Dunlley at Navigation St. And in court he could deny he ever said it.'

'So we must prevent Jones from bringing a claim through the courts.

'You'll have to call his bluff,' the other solicitor said.

In due course Aubrey Jones arrived back at the firm of solicitors, hopeful of finalizing his claim. Seating himself comfortably, he crossed his legs with an air of confidence.

'Mr Jones,' the solicitor began. 'We have made wide inquiries, and interviewed the Dunlley family. It is clear to us your claim on the estate has several inconsistencies that need explaining.'

Aubrey Jones flushed and sat forward. 'Sir,' he said with a show of indignity, 'are you accusing me of fraud?'

'Not for the moment, Mr Jones. But Mrs Dunlley says her husband never travelled on ships. He hated the sea.'

'Of course, she would say that if she thought her inheritance was being threatened. Dunlley's fears must have begun after I rescued him from the shipwreck.'

'Quite so, Mr Jones, but Mrs Dunlley said her husband had never been to Hull.'

'How would she know?' Aubrey replied, with a hint of disquiet. 'I would strenuously challenge this.'

'Then again,' the solicitor said, as he continued to put pressure on Aubrey, 'you say you often used to call on Dunlley at Navigation Street, but nobody remembers your visits.'

Aubrey dismissed it with a wave of his hand. 'Staff changes, and it was a long time ago. Twenty-five years to be exact.'

'But Dunlley did not move to Navigation Street until eight years after your stated visits?'

Aubrey Jones blanched, and for a moment was lost for words. 'Ah,' he spluttered, 'I... aah, must have been confused. Of course it was not Navigation Street.'

'Then where did you visited him?'

Aubrey pushed several fingers under his collar as if to release the pressure. Bewildered and ashen-faced, he mumbled, 'Mmm... I've forgotten. So many years ago.'

As he sat squirming in his chair, beads of sweat formed on his brow. Trapped and in a quandary, Aubrey Jones was beginning to crack. The solicitor judged it time to apply a final squeeze.

'Mr Jones,' he said, 'There is no doubt your document has been forged. It carries my alleged signature. But it is dated years before I was part of this firm. Indeed, even before I was a solicitor. Present this in a court of law and you will hang.'

Aubrey Jones sprang to his feet, his face white as chalk. He seemed about to say something, but gave a groan and sank to the floor in a dead faint.

Chapter 22

Assignment

George and the group of bedraggled prisoners shuffled into the Hobart prison yard, and after a warm meal of gruel and another roll call, guards issued them with fresh convict clothes and allowed them to rest overnight. While happy to have survived, a pall of sadness descended every time he thought of H.J. He had looked forward to a lifetime of friendship bonded by their sufferings. What a waste of a life, he thought.

After their ordeal most of the survivors remained shaking and withdrawn, and in a pitiful state of shock. But as they began to appreciate the sheer luck of their survival, old personalities slowly emerged and they became more settled. After resting for several days, most began taking an interest in their new surroundings. Meantime, they waited to have their futures assessed by the local prison authorities.

When one of the guards produced a small mirror George saw himself for the first time in months. He barely recognized his face, so tanned and gaunt under a moustache and stubble of beard. He rapidly handed the mirror to the next in line, glad his family could not see him now.

But he recognized his year of incarceration had given him a more muscular frame. Cranking up silt on the lighter and working in the metal shop had added to his strength and stamina, and had changed him from a callow youth to a maturity capable of meeting the challenges of prison life, and coping with any work expected of him now.

One morning, attired in fresh and presentable clothing, the newly arrived convicts lined up for inspection by Sir George Arthur, the Lieutenant-governor. Accompanied by the Colonial Surgeon and several clerks, Arthur addressed the group by reminding them of their degraded state, and went on to say they would be closely watched from now on.

'If you continue to act in a depraved way,' he warned them, 'you will be severely punished by working in chain gangs, or sent to a penal settlement.' He paused to make sure his words had sunk in. 'On the other hand, those who behave well and show repentance will earn their ticket-of-leave in due course. They will eventually be eligible for a conditional pardon. This will give the right to move freely within the colony.' At this point, George discerned a fleeting smile from the great man before he added, 'if your conduct continues to remain satisfactory it will open the way for a free pardon. This will enable you to return to England if you so desire.'

Having delivered his address, the Governor moved along the line of convicts, pausing here and there to ask an occasional question. He said nothing as he passed George, but in the brief moment their eyes met, George noticed a look of compassion despite his haughty bearing. Within minutes he had gone.

Next to inspect was the Colonial Surgeon who examined each of them with more care than George remembered had been taken before they left Woolwich. Finding several convicts showing signs of scurvy or other illnesses he had them removed to the prison hospital for treatment. This cleared the way for the Port Health Officer to issue a clean bill of health for the remainder.

The Principal Superintendent of Convicts arrived next, accompanied by his array of officials. They questioned each of the convicts, and dealt with all the paperwork. However, as they moved along the line, George saw they had problems assessing many of them since their records had been lost in the shipwreck. In those cases, any request for new indent papers would take many months to reach England. Several years might pass before the British authorities returned them. This forced the clerks to make their assessments by what each prisoner told them of their offences, and how long they had already served. Only then could a date for their release be determined.

Finally, another official came forward, announcing, 'the present interview is your only opportunity to lodge a complaint about your treatment during the voyage.' But the convicts were reluctant to make any allegations in case it antagonized somebody with influence in deciding their date of release, or to whom they were assigned.

With the assessments completed, clerks assigned each convict to a master who would control their lives until they earned a ticket-of-leave – a sort of parole. George understood the authorities believed this to be the best way to manage the convicts since they would have the discipline of a daily routine, yet remain under constant supervision.

On the Hobart streets of the 1830s, ragged assigned and ticket-of-leave convicts mingled with smartly dressed free settlers, though the two did not mix socially. Each morning and night in the town, convicts in chains marched to and from their workplaces where they spent all day with pick and shovel constructing new roads. But the authorities sent most convicts into the country to work on farms, even if they had never lived outside a city before. While their master had the benefit of their labour, the convicts had a chance to live in the community. George heard some particularly brutal masters worked their convicts hard and long with threats, and by inflicting severe punishments for minor offences. Other masters, hoping for a good response, offered excessive rewards for labour. Clearly, it was a lottery where you were assigned. When they read out George's name they had assigned him along with several others to a free settler at Launceston. This, he learned, was a small and recently settled town somewhere to the north.

A few days later the authorities assembled a small group of assignees, including George, in the prison yard. Under sharp eyes, the militia marched them down to the port where they boarded a two-masted brig. While it concerned George to see how small the vessel was, he became even more perturbed when guards ordered them below and ignored their request to be allowed on deck. Once again the terror of their shipwreck returned to haunt George and his companions. When he heard six armed militia guarded them, clearly the authorities feared the convicts might try to take over the ship and attempt to sail to some overseas port. Soon, the flapping of sails and creaking from the hull, announced they were under way.

Below deck the prisoners had no idea where they were going, or how long the journey would take. Several days passed before guards allowed them up on deck to find they were sailing up a wide river under a deep-blue sky devoid of clouds. In the still, dry air, harsh birdcalls from the bush-lined shore disturbed the silence around them, and a flock of white cockatoos flew overhead. As the brig made its way up the river the prisoners watched, intrigued by smaller multicoloured birds flitting about the brig. George had never seen birds as large or so beautiful; an omen, he hoped, of a more pleasant future.

The ship berthed at a small settlement, which he learned was George Town. Later in the day guards removed several convicts to work on an adjacent property owned by the Port Master and local magistrate. Next morning they transferred George and the remaining convicts to a smaller vessel to continue their journey up the river. He estimated they must have sailed about seventy miles before reaching Launceston where they disembarked.

As they filed ashore armed guards met them and marched them to the town barracks. Once again George found himself scrutinized by 'old hands' with every intention of filching whatever they could from the new arrivals. But by now he knew most of their tricks and threats, and apart from his fresher clothes he had little to bargain with.

It was the newcomers' first experience of mixing with these long-term 'government men' as they preferred to be called. When he first saw their toil-worn features, George wondered what might become of him. Many looked prematurely aged; due, he imagined, to their tedious and often dangerous work in the heat of a glaring sun. He learned some of his new associates cleared trees from surrounding properties. Others dug postholes in the hard ground and erected fences. A further group made bricks for some of the public buildings and fine mansions of the town.

'This is not a prison,' the overseer told them. 'But you have to earn your ticket-of-leave. If you misbehave you stay as long as it takes to be considered fit for release.'

The overseer gave the group of new arrivals little time to settle in before allotting them to their new gangs. Next day he sent George to a family of settlers living in a large and newly built residence near the banks of the Tamar River. Here he worked as a gardener and general handyman. At first it pleased him to have such light work until it became obvious some of his fellow convicts appeared jealous and aggressive towards him.

'Who did you suck up to, to get that job?' was the first question aimed at him.

'The luck of the draw,' he replied, doing his best to treat the implied threat lightly, but knowing henceforth he would have to steer a middle path between meeting the standards of the settler he worked for, while at the same time not being over zealous, and falling out with his fellow workers.

Glad to be away from the rough company in the barracks, George shared a wooden hut on the property with several other convicts, but he saw little of them as they left early each day for tree felling. He found them friendly enough, but once again he had little in common with his new companions who spent their free time gambling, or talking about when they hoped to get their ticket-of-leave.

After the damp coldness of Birmingham, George found it a new experience to work in the dry air and heat of Australia, and soon began to appreciate his newfound freedom. Despite being treated as a convict, he found the warm days more pleasant than they had ever been at the mill. For six days a week he worked in the sun, forming paths in the russet-coloured earth, or building stone walls to edge the many gardens round the house. Sometimes the cook asked him to gather vegetables from the garden and bring them into the kitchen for preparation, but he was unaware of being scrutinized and assessed by the family.

The owner of the property, a man in his late thirties, and of austere appearance, always looked well tailored. Of moderate height, thick set, and with wavy hair brushed loosely across his forehead, he always seemed to be on the move. George often saw him coming and going about his business, but the man never gave any sign of recognition.

At other times, one of his young daughters would come out to sit in the shade of the veranda. Carefully groomed and dressed in white muslin, she sometimes spent an hour or more reading a book, but never glanced in his direction, or gave any indication she was aware of his presence working close at hand. Each lived in their own world, and there seemed no common ground.

One morning before the heat of day began to sap his energy, George was working in the garden digging carrots and picking leaves of silver beet for the family. With his full basket he set out along the path towards the kitchen when he was startled to hear sounds of music coming from the house. Somebody was playing a piano. Unaccustomed to music of this quality he became gripped by what he heard, and he stopped to listen. Never had he experienced sounds of such beauty. In moments, it revealed a purity he had found nowhere else. The music, so different from the simple and banal ditties he commonly heard, was a revelation that wakened something in the subtlest depths of his being, and drew him away from the limits of his everyday experience. His present pleasure seemed to blend with all his past misfortunes, and a great calm possessed him. It reminded him again of the wide gulf between convict and free settler.

Enchanted by the experience he returned to his work with added zest. His thoughts turned to the time when his term of imprisonment would be served and he joined the world of free men again. Since he could never return to England, he often thought of what he might do with his inheritance. After working in the outdoors he toyed with the idea of purchasing a country property to farm. He saw great wealth from raising sheep in the area, and the idea appealed to him. But sometimes he worried his grandfather may have already passed away or sold his business, and the wealth had gone elsewhere.

Most of the old hands had their day of release worked out almost to the hour, and it encouraged him to hear that well-behaved prisoners usually had their seven-year sentence reduced to four. It meant he could be free in less than three years. He knew he could easily endure the time if his present conditions continued.

He wondered if he should write to his grandfather to let him know of his whereabouts. But he knew it took almost six months for letters to reach their destination, and perhaps as long again for a reply. Second thoughts convinced him to wait until nearer his release. Then he would be a free man when his letter arrived, and so he need not mention anything about penal servitude.

Every Sunday morning he lined up in the ragged company of his fellow convicts for a compulsory church service, to be reminded once again of the wages of sin. To be late for the roll call would mean certain flogging. Even the appearance of dozing on the hard wooden pew would earn twenty lashes for a tired and worn out body. Hard work and repentance was the only pathway to freedom. Sunday afternoons were free for relaxation. In these few hours George mixed with other government men, but everybody had to be back under supervision by six in the evening.

On just such an afternoon, as usual, he headed for the riverside to relax in the shade of ancient gum trees that lined the banks. As he began to cross the street; suddenly, and without warning, two horsemen rounded the corner at full gallop. Before he could jump clear one of the horses struck him with a glancing blow that threw him to the ground. His head hit the road with a crack. Flashes of light burst across his vision, and darkness closed in about him.

Chapter 23

Lovers' tryst

As George slowly regained his senses, he realized his head was cradled in the arms of a young woman. When his vision cleared he saw her genuine concern, and as he took in his surroundings he noticed she wore convict dress, and looked about twenty years old.

'Are you all right, sir?' she asked in an anxious tone.

It was the first time George remembered being addressed as 'sir'. 'Apart from a splitting headache I should recover,' he reassured her with the trace of a smile.

As he scrambled to his feet he saw other people about, but none of the free settlers came to his aid, and the horsemen had failed to stop. Clearly a convict's life meant little to them.

'I'm George White, a class two government man hoping for a ticket-of-leave,' he announced for her benefit.

'I'm Elizabeth Allen, a class one needle woman, hoping for a ticket-of-leave too,' she replied, as George noticed her worried look change to one of slight amusement at their mutual introductions.

Although he had often heard convicts discussing women and what they did with them, George had never had an opportunity to befriend one. This could be my chance, he thought, but I must not give the wrong impression. I wonder what H.J. would do.

'I really appreciate your concern for me, and after meeting in this rather unexpected way I think we should get to know each other a little better,' he began rather naively. 'There are still several hours before I have to be back at the barracks. Would you have a few minutes to spare for us to walk along the riverside together?'

Even as the words tumbled out he sensed them sounding stilted and naïve, exposing his inexperience with girls. He noticed her lips give the suggestion of an ambiguous smile that in a moment had gone. Did it come from her experience at the hands of the type of men he had listened to, he wondered. But her expression soon changed, and he thought she looked rather touched by what he had said.

'Yes, why not?' she said. 'I still have plenty of time to get back to my workplace.'

It delighted him to think she seemed willing enough to walk with him, and they strolled down to the riverside. In the brief time they spent together they began to learn a little about each other.

'I'm housemaid to a family in Paterson Street,' she said. 'The master is an official on government business from Hobart Town. He is here with his wife for several months. I came with them but I don't know how much longer they will stay.'

At the time, this was about all George knew of her, and he realized their offences would keep for other occasions. It reminded him of H.J. and their times together. George had never mentioned his false arrest to him, and assumed H.J. accepted him without question. For all he knew, I could have been a murderer. He put it down to H.J.'s inherent politeness, an attitude George respected, and adopted.

'I hope you will still be here next Sunday,' George said, hopeful she would want to meet him again.

'We must be careful; the mistress is very observant,' Elizabeth said. 'People think we are the wicked ones, but I'm sure there are as many villains among the free settlers as there are in the prisons.'

As she spoke her voice held an exciting allure for him. He wished he could listen to her forever. Delighted that she seemed agreeable to meet again, it encouraged him to ask one more question. 'Where do you come from?'

'From Churchill,' she said. 'It's near Birmingham.'

Their reminiscences of the city soon united them in a bond of common interest. For some of the time they simply sat side by side watching the river slip by, enjoying the pleasure of each other's company. George, desperate to say something appropriate, was mostly unable to find the words.

The hour for their return came all too soon, and they promised to meet again the following Sunday. As George walked back to his barracks he had never felt so close to anybody before, and their afternoon together left him restless.

During the following week he could scarcely concentrate on his work. Every day seemed to last forever, and each night he lay dreaming of their meeting, reliving each single minute of their time together. Her youthful face and kindly eyes filled him with new and strange yearnings, but he saw her poor emaciated frame being worn out by constant work and inadequate nutrition. He realized his plans for the future had suddenly changed. Now, his greatest wish was to be with her and care for her always.

Regardless of what crime might have led to her present state, he longed for the time when he could take her in his arms and tell her he would protect her and always love her. But what did she think of him? He was tortured to know if she would be able to meet him again as she had promised, or if she had changed her mind. He worried he might never see her again.

As the week passed, Elizabeth felt compassion for the injured young man, and hoped he had recovered from his nasty accident. She could tell from the way he spoke he was a decent person at heart. The brief hours she spent with him gave her an acquaintance with a happiness she had long ago consigned to the past. She felt contentment sensing he simply enjoyed her company without trying to take advantage of her in their secluded spot. She could tell he was different from the coarse types of convicts women talked about. Now, moved by so many misfortunes, she felt drawn to him, and a whispering voice in the depths of her being encouraged her to keep their appointment.

After waiting on tenterhooks all week, the hour rapidly approached when she would meet George again. At that first meeting, she had felt strangely at ease with him. Rather than be wary of him she trusted him. But for days, unbidden thoughts for him kept coming into her mind as she worked. What if he failed to arrive? Maybe he would be unable to get away or, heaven forbid, perhaps he had second thoughts and did not want to keep their appointment. As she hurried to their meeting she felt her limbs trembling. Would he be there to meet her?

But her concerns melted at the sight of George waiting for her by the river's edge. Their joy at meeting once again overwhelmed them, and for a few moments they stood mute, unable to speak, simply looking at each other. When she saw his face illuminate with a smile, Elizabeth could tell it was for herself alone he had come, and not to take advantage of her vulnerability. In her heart she confirmed her new understanding and returned a gentle smile.

George saw her welcoming smile and incredibly viridescent eyes, full of trust. Captivated, his heart thumped, and deep emotions left him speechless. They continued to gaze at one another as if mesmerized, and George saw a light flush begin to permeate her neck and cheeks. As they stood locked in a prolonged moment of silence, they each knew something tremendous was happening between them.

Somehow, words seemed clumsy and out of place, but at last George managed to burst out saying, 'I've waited all week for this moment. We must make the most of the next few hours. There is so much to discover about each other. Let's stroll along the river bank.'

Later, as they sat together he thought once again of his legacy, and the promise it held for their future. He did not refer to it, or even hint of it. Instead, he mentioned the possibility of raising sheep in the north, only to worry she may have thought him a boaster.

Each Sunday they met at their favourite spot on the riverbank where an old eucalypt, huge and spreading, gave a protective arch of interwoven greens against the ruthless glare of the sun. As far as the eye could reach, the land lay silent and empty. Elizabeth had come nearby on previous Sunday afternoons to escape the activities of her busy household duties, and enjoy a short respite where others did not trespass on her solitude, and it reminded her of happier childhood days.

Now, life for them held no more than these quiet afternoons and the few hours they spent in each other's company. With Elizabeth, the first girl he had ever had to himself, and with her presence so close, George's spirits rose. Until they met, girls had not been high in his thoughts; he had been content to wait until his prospects improved. As they sat engrossed in each other, ordinary things about him took on magical hues: the waters of the Tamar gliding silently by, the grass, the trees. He fancied the faint sound of a breeze stirring the leaves to be whispers of their secret love.

Sitting together and sharing gentle caresses, they watched the river flow quietly by. No sound reached them. Nothing stirred; the stillness of the warm spring air a soothing balm in their troubled lives. Just to be together was fulfillment enough. When Elizabeth moved in his arms he would bend and kiss her hair. The light caress of his lips on her skin communicated more than words. The touch of her fingers brought him new rapture, and he would lean across and gently kiss her fingertips. He had never felt as close to anybody or communicated as deeply.

For the pitiable few hours they shared, they talked of the future with its unspoken inference of a life together. But there were lighter sides, too.

'Whatever will become of us?' Elizabeth asked.

'Ah,' said George remembering one of H.J.s wiles. 'The answer is in your palm.'

'It is?'

'Yes,' said George, gently taking her hands in his. 'I see it all.'

'You do?'

'I see a handsome man, prepared to devote his life to you.'

'He will?'

'It's all here in your palm.'

'Wherever can I find such a man?'

'Look no further.'

For a few moments they gazed into each other's eyes before bursting into laughter.

For several weeks they lived for their time together. George knew he would be free to marry in less than three years. When his inheritance became available he would buy into a farm in the lush north and take Elizabeth there. Life promised richer prospects than he had ever hoped for before.

Chapter 24
Assignment Goes Wrong

One Saturday George saw the overseer approaching with the intention of speaking to him. 'The family will be hosting a number of important visitors tomorrow,' he said. 'You's needed to work in the kitchen from four o'clock on Sunday afternoon.'

Having delivered his message, the man turned to go on his way before pausing for a moment as if in thought. Looking back, he said, 'You must've made a good impression on somebody.'

It delighted George to think his work and thoughtful attention to their needs met with the family's approval. But his afternoon with Elizabeth would be cut short.

On Sunday morning he attended the church parade with all the other convicts as usual. However, word of mouth travels fast. During the lunchtime meal at the barracks he had to fend off occasional banter about his 'family ties' and four o'clock appointment. As he finished his meal he looked up to see several government men, all ruffians of a rather unsavoury type approaching him.

'Join us for the afternoon, George,' one of them said in a voice oozing cordiality.

Although they all appeared friendly, knowing convict behaviour, he immediately suspected their motives.

'You's new here, George. We'll show you round the town,' said one little man, wiry and dry as a chip from the constant sunshine.

'Yes,' said another. 'Perhaps you'll learn a few tips from us as well.'

'I'm sorry, but count me out. I have an appointment to keep.'

'No excuses, George,' one of them said with a wink. 'We knows all about your appointments.'

When they crowded round him he saw no easy way out, and was forced to reluctantly join them. He thought he would slip away once they were out on the street. But with their first stop being the nearby local inn, they clearly had other things in mind.

'Come on George, join us in a glass or two of ale,' the felon next to him said, putting his arm round George's shoulder.

'You's a good man, George,' one of the group declared, giving a jovial wink to the others.

'Here's to George,' said another, raising his glass, and pouring the contents down his throat.

The more they drank the more genial they became. With all their blasphemous merriment and good-natured friendliness directed towards him, George saw no escape from their antics. He found it impossible to refuse to drink, several even accompanying him on a bogus trip to the toilet in case he attempted to slip away. He had no doubt they would turn nasty if he tried to leave. That would invite certain assault, and he could never defend himself against so many.

Unaccustomed to the effects of alcohol he began to lose track of time, although somewhere at the back of his mind he knew he had to report to the kitchen at four o'clock. George knew his comrades had deliberately targeted him, and had no intention of allowing him to get away until he was late for work. If I'm to get back on time I will have to fight my way out of this setup, he decided, and began to walk to the door.

'Come on, George, where are you going?' one of the group said.

'I've got an appointment to keep.'

Another put his arm round George's shoulder in an attempt to stop him, but George gave the man a push and continued towards the door. Immediately the other felons crowded close round him to stop him leaving. That's when the fracas began. George started punching his way through his former drinking mates, managing to land several good blows. As the fight spilled out onto the street he left several felons lying bleeding, but numbers were against him. After his initial good showing they managed to knock him to the ground to be kicked and pummelled. His erstwhile companions finally stumbled off leaving him to struggle to his feet and limp away. It was almost five o'clock before he arrived back at the kitchen in a disheveled and somewhat inebriated state to be met with a tirade of abuse from the overseer.

From another room he heard a woman's voice say, 'I'm so disappointed in him. He always seemed such a nice lad.'

'Well, I've told you,' came the voice of her husband. 'You can't trust any of them. After all, they're criminals, and heaven knows what terrible crimes he may be guilty of. I'll see he gets his dues tomorrow.'

George crawled off to his bunk, angry with himself, aching and sick in the stomach. He thought of Elizabeth waiting for him by the river, and wondering what kept him. He had let her down, and there was no way he could explain to her. His only hope would be to meet her again the following Sunday. Sleep evaded him for hours as he lay staring into the darkness, fearful of what the new day would bring.

He awoke bruised and dejected, his thoughts far from the bright and sunny dawn. He took no notice of the white cockatoos wheeling overhead. Nor did he listen to the high-pitched chattering of rainbow lorikeets as they clambered along blossom-laden branches seeking nectar. He didn't see friendly crimson rosellas making bright flashes of colour among the trees, or flocks of them taking advantage of crumbs tossed to them from the house. None of it registered with George.

He had barely finished a plate of gruel when two constables approached dangling a pair of handcuffs. He immediately sprang to his feet and went out to meet them.

One of them came forward saying, 'George White, you're under arrest. Come with us.'

George held out his hands and the handcuffs snapped into place. With one constable on each side, the trio set off for town and the courthouse. His legs felt weak, and his misery grew with the sight of fellow convicts along the way. When he saw the occasional smile or wink that passed between them he knew they would all be laughing at him behind his back.

It was a usual Monday morning session at the courthouse. Several convicts who had offended during the weekend waited to be brought before the magistrate. George learned the man seated behind the bench and handing out the punishments was Lieutenant Friend, the Port Officer -- a stocky man with short sandy hair. He wasted no time with each case. Within a few minutes George stood in the dock.

'George White, last night you reported late for your work. Since this is your first offence you will receive twenty lashes, and be transferred to the brickmaking team. If you manage to learn this trade, perhaps you will see the error of your ways and, I hope, eventually become a useful citizen.'

Without delay guards took him into a walled courtyard where he saw the wooden triangle already prepared for his thrashing. During the past year he had witnessed many floggings, and seen men diminished by its spectacle. Now, it was his turn, and he trembled. Sounds of the cat greeted his entrance as a jailer swished it about in anticipation of using it. It unnerved him, and his face twitched. He kept saying over and over to himself, I won't cry out. No matter how much it hurts, I won't give them the satisfaction of thinking they have conquered my spirit. I won't cry out.

A jailer removed his handcuffs, bared his body down to the waist, tied his wrists together, and attached him to the triangle. Knowing what was to come, George clenched his teeth and braced himself for the shock of the first blow. When it came, the force almost knocked the breath out of him. He felt as if a thousand bees had stung him. After the second lash his back was on fire, and steady pain began to spread deeper into his flesh. As blow followed blow tears of agony welled up, but it made him even more determined not to utter a sound. By the final lash, pain throbbed though his whole body; his head felt as if it would burst.

The jailer roughly untied his limbs, and with George shocked and barely able to stand, made him walk back to the barracks where he lay all day, bleeding and in pain. Too exhausted even to think, he tried in vain to sleep, aware that next day he would have to pull a rough prison shirt over his lacerated back, and march to the brickfields.

His pain brought memories of Martin. But for George, no fellow convict came to comfort him. No friend gave sympathy or cared for his welfare. Each time he recalled how he had been tricked, his mind filled with bitterness. So often he had seen good men become brutish after the lash, and he began to understand why hardened convicts came to resent the brutality of the system so much that they defied the authorities, and continued to offend regardless of the punishment.

Chapter 25

Disaster Strikes

After a restless night George woke early. Stiff and aching, he struggled out of bed to dress, his rough shirt irritating mercilessly with every movement. At breakfast, the first sight of his gruel sent a wave of nausea through him. He felt like vomiting, but knew he had to have food of sorts in his stomach if he was to survive the day. With an effort of will he managed to swallow the insipid mess, and wash it down with several mouthfuls of water.

He had barely finished his meal when an overseer approached saying, 'George White, join the brickmaking gang outside on the street.'

George stood up slowly to lessen the irritation of the rough shirt on his back, and set out marching with them to their workplace. That long march, and his first day on the pick and shovel were agony. He cursed his shirt and the felons who had led him to this state, and he despised the system that had done this to him.

'You'll have to keep moving, or they'll thrash you again,' one of his companions said. 'The overseer be an ex-convict hiself, and can tell if any of his workers is slacking.'

When others stripped to the waist in the heat of the day it astonished George to see how many of them had scars across their back. His own lacerations and stories of his prowess as a fighter against huge odds soon led to greater acceptance, and his status increased among his new companions.

By Sunday he had not seen Elizabeth for two weeks, and his back still ached. He made his way to the riverside hoping Elizabeth would come. But after waiting for more than an hour he became impatient and walked to Paterson Street in the hope of seeing her. The house where she worked lay empty. With a sinking feeling he concluded the family had returned to Hobart Town and taken Elizabeth with them. George slowly returned to the riverside where he sat forlornly at the spot they had once shared, and continued to brood about his lost love.

In days of dark despair his thoughts always turned to Elizabeth. Through the sleepless hours of darkness he pictured her face, alert and expressive, yet so pale against her thick black hair in endless movement about her cheeks and neck. For George, her most striking feature was her eyes. They always seemed wonderfully large and bright, gazing at him so frank and full of trust. A hint of resoluteness in her chin gave him the impression she could also be forthright and honest. He saw a kind of uniqueness about her: a sense of confidence in her intimidating world. Despite her plight she had not been cowered into a submissive state. He must find her again.

As the days went by, a sense of loneliness continued to engulf him in a pall of depression. He remained embittered with those who had cheated him out of his assignment, resentful of the establishment and its brutality, but most of all angry with himself. He missed Elizabeth so deeply he lost interest in his surroundings. He had been given a tantalizing glimpse of a better life, and allowed it to slip from his grasp.

As a beginner, he had to learn the steps needed to make bricks. But kneading clay all day wore the skin of his hands and fingers, and small cracks appeared. Every movement became painful, but he knew there would always be a few strokes of the birch across his back if the overseer thought he was slacking. Slowly over the weeks the skin of his hands thickened and healed, and as his misery improved, he began to mix more freely with his fellow prisoners. Being naturally of a jovial turn of mind he was often at the forefront with an anecdote for their enjoyment, occasionally even making the overseer laugh.

Still, as weeks stretched into months, he found it increasingly difficult to resist becoming more like the rogues and miscreants he had to mix with and listen to all day. Although he refrained from alcohol whenever possible, he could not avoid drifting into fraternizing with his workmates through their constant close association. He soon swore as well as those around him, and he learned how to gamble at cards, becoming successful when he bet only when the odds appeared to be in his favour.

After spending his days in the heat of the sun, and digging out clay from a large bank, he could sense his body becoming stronger. Sun bronzed his skin, and his muscles rippled as he worked. Although he became accustomed to summer heat, he welcomed the cooler days of autumn that made life more bearable. But when the chill winds of winter began to sweep through the site, the only way to keep warm was to work even harder.

By now, new convicts arriving at the diggings considered George an 'old hand.' Despite the wretchedness of his confinement, as months turned to years, George became expert at brick making. It pleased him to see his bricks used in so many fine Launceston buildings, and he found satisfaction in thinking they would remain a legacy to be admired, possibly for centuries to come. Now, having served four of his seven-year sentence, he began to look forward to the time when he would be a ticket-of-leave man, and freer to search for Elizabeth.

While he gained satisfaction from a sense of achievement in his work, others appeared less happy. Some of his fellow convicts continued to grumble and take easy offence. But a smaller number never gave up their evil ways. They constantly plotted to steal whenever the opportunity arose, or planned attempts to escape. Some even managed to keep in touch with bushrangers who terrorized the countryside from time to time. These convicts sometimes acted as go-betweens to dispose of loot, since bushrangers could not go into settlements to trade on their own behalf.

One day several of these felons approached George.

'We has to get rid o' some goods,' one of them said rather furtively. 'There's a lot of it. So we has to spread it round. Hide a bag for us, George.'

'No, try some of the others,' he replied. 'You know I'm due for my ticket-of-leave.'

'Come on man, nobody would suspect you. Even the overseer has a good word for you.'

'No. I can't risk it,' George answered as firmly as he could.

'In that case,' one of them said, 'Accidents happen, and I reckon you won't never get to be a free man.'

George shrugged his shoulders. The threat came as no surprise because he knew the type of felon he was dealing with. Still, it was a difficult decision to make without careful thought, and he tossed the alternatives in his mind. Refusing to cooperate singled him out. From now on he would be a marked man. They would get him sooner or later. On the other hand he was less likely to be caught receiving stolen goods. He weighed up his chances, and the odds seemed to favour co-operation.

'All right,' he said. 'How big is the bag?'

'Small enough to hide in your kit; we'll bring it tonight.'

'How long do I have to keep it?'

'About two days; then we'll get rid of it. We'll give you a share o' the profits.'

Not likely, thought George, but he saw no other way round the impasse.

That evening after their meal, one of the felons came into the dormitory with a bulging jacket casually draped across his arm. After a brief glance round he placed it on George's bed. Nobody gave any indication of noticing what had taken place.

Next morning George heard rumours there had been a particularly brutal hold-up close to Launceston several days previously. He realized the authorities would now be on the lookout for any suspicious behaviour among the convicts because he knew the constabulary were aware bushrangers often needed inside help to dispose of their loot, and would search any convict they suspected of receiving. On tenterhooks all day, he found it difficult to concentrate on his work.

What excuse could I give, he kept asking himself. What story can I concoct to explain it away? Would they believe it? Whenever he thought about it, he trembled. He had little appetite for his midday meal, and as the day progressed he feared the overseer might notice the change in him and report it.

The hours dragged by so slowly the day seemed never ending. Yet he knew he had to keep hiding the bag for at least another day. He struggled to keep up with his work without drawing attention to himself, and at last the brick gang all lined up as usual to march back to the barracks. Along the way nothing seemed changed. His companions still talked and laughed. The setting sun still gave out its usual warmth, but with his mind blank with apprehension, he noticed little of it.

His anxiety grew as they approached the barracks, especially when he saw several constables standing in a group near the entrance. As he passed by he thought two of them fixed him in their gaze. Had they found the bag, he wondered, or was it just his imagination and a guilty conscience on his part? When his group entered the dormitory, two more constables watched them closely.

'Stand by your beds,' one of them commanded.

All but George seemed happy to oblige, many having been through similar inspections in the past. Several constables and overseers worked their way along the line of convicts making each in turn empty their gear onto the floor in front of them.

When they reached George he tried to remain nonchalant. Forcing a smile, he upended his kit of clothes. The contents hit the floor with a loud clatter as the bag of silverware spilled out. It immediately had everybody's attention.

'What's that?' he spluttered, assuming a look of complete surprise and bewilderment. 'How did that get there?'

'You are under arrest, White.' one of the constables ordered.

'He's taking the blame for others,' somebody shouted in his defense as they led him from the dormitory. The constables gave no heed to the remark.

At the jail they thrust him into a bare room and subjected him to intense questioning. 'Who gave you the silverware?' one of the constables asked.

'Nobody.'

They shouted the question at him again and again, each time with the same answer. 'Nobody.'

'What did you intend doing with it?'

'I know nothing about it,' he kept repeating every time they shouted the question at him. 'With rumours of a search the real thief must have planted it on me,' he would add.

George thought they were inclined to believe him, but having found stolen goods in his possession, he knew they would not bother to look further for another person. That night they locked him in a cold cell. Overcome with a surge of helpless rage he paced the floor, every now and again kicking the wall in a fit of fury. Sleep was out of the question. Next morning guards took him to a blacksmith to have leg-irons riveted on. As the smith hammered them into place he told George his companions all agreed he was innocent of any crime, but had doubts about the outcome of his trial.

Later, guards marched George together with several other hobbled convicts to the wharf, and put them on a boat bound for Hobart Town. At his trial George had no convincing defense. Although the overseer put in a good word for him, a guilty verdict was inevitable.

The stern-faced judge glared down at George. 'For your crime, you are condemned to serve a further seven years penal servitude at Port Arthur.

Chapter 26

Life in Port Arthur

Although George remained angry with himself for the loss of his gardening assignment and for his thrashing, the sentence of a further seven years completely devastated him. Groaning in despair he kept thinking, I was so close to receiving my ticket-of-leave and finding Elizabeth. I've always tried to act honestly and do the decent thing by others, but fate seems to work against me. At night he would lie awake mulling over how his search for a better life had led to a hell not always of his own making. Now all I have to cling to is the possibility of an inheritance, and a vain hope of finding Elizabeth in the years ahead.

Seeing himself branded a hardened criminal, a further change began to take its hold. With nobody expecting anything better of him, he drifted into thinking and acting more like those convicts sentenced to serve out their time at Port Arthur. As his resentment grew, his attitude to authority became defiant.

After his trial he languished in the Hobart Town barracks for several weeks until enough convicts for the journey to Port Arthur had assembled. Eventually, one morning after breakfast, a guard entered the mess room and called out a series of names, including that of George.

'Get yerselfs outside an' be quick about it.'

George and the small group of convicts hurriedly did as ordered. Other guards appeared and marched them to the quayside where a two-masted brig awaited them. They filed on board, and within an hour the square sails caught a freshening breeze and they were on their way to Port Arthur.

As the brig swung out into the Derwent waters the river remained calm, and George's impression of the area was of the sheer beauty of the landscape. But after rounding the outermost cape, towering grey pillars of basalt rock appeared. They stood out dark and ominous from the cliff face with their bases lashed by ocean rollers that sent spume and spray high into the air. George remembered feeling intimidated by the entrance to Newgate prison, but here, these huge fluted columns standing like towering sentinels at the gateway to Port Arthur completely overawed him. But once they reached the calm bay of the prison settlement his ill boding had faded.

They came ashore on a busy waterfront, and overseers immediately lined them up. After another roll call guards marched the group to the blacksmith to have their leg-irons removed. Along the way they passed a row of workshops where George saw convicts busy working in trades of all sorts, and everyone going about their work in silence. It was clear to George they were all under strict surveillance.

While his group waited at the foundry to have their leg-irons struck off, he noticed the wide variety of work done there. A furnace and several forges blazed in action, reminding him of his days in the Birmingham workshop. Convicts worked at their benches and anvils making all manner of pots and other household metal goods. But as they worked they did not give even the briefest of glances at the newcomers. No doubt any appearance of slacking would be met with a few strokes of the birch.

Freed from their irons, his group lined up again and guards escorted them to their new quarters. On the way they passed other workshops that astonished George with the amount of industry taking place: shoemaking, tailors, coopers among many other trades. Further along the street they passed a series of depressing looking stone-breaking stalls, giving the group their first lesson into the brutality dealt out to troublemakers. These stalls were compartments separated from each other by a low brick wall, and open to the street. In each of them a miserable looking felon in heavy leg-irons stood day long, chained to the wall like a shackled beast of burden. All were engaged in breaking up stones with a hammer in a life of mindless purgatory; a sobering sight for George, and he wondered how long it would take him to go mad if they ever sent him there.

A little further on, the group of newcomers turned up a long slope beside a narrow stream to reach the barracks that would be their home until they earned their release. As they approached, George saw a cluster of buildings surrounded by a high log wall a little way up the hill. They entered the compound through an open gateway and came to a halt in a large yard surrounded by huts that appeared to be offices.

A person of military bearing whom George took to be Captain Booth, the Commandant, emerged to inspect them. As he passed along the line he paused to study each man with some care, but said nothing before returning inside.

A few moments later a clerk came out and proceeded to read them the rules of the settlement. The message George got from this harangue meant they could expect to remain imprisoned here until they showed themselves responsible enough to be released into the community. Good behaviour would be rewarded, bad behaviour severely punished. A ticket-of-leave would come only through hard work and adherence to Christian principles. If they misbehaved they could expect to remain in custody for as long as it took them to reform.

The clerk then called out each name, and tension mounted as he allotted work. He assigned some to the sawpits to cut timber by hand for export, and gave others equally strenuous work. But to George's relief, the clerk placed him in a brickmaking gang; grueling enough he knew from experience, but not such exhausting work as the hard labour most of the others received.

Then a barber appeared from one of the doorways, scissors in hand, and proceeded to cut their hair. It was hardly a professional job. He simply grabbed hair by the handful and cut it off. Guards then issued each man with eating utensils, a blanket, a straw pad for sleeping, and a convict suit of yellow and black.

Having gathered all their gear, guards shepherded the line of convicts through another gateway and into a larger courtyard surrounded by more than a dozen large huts. The group stopped in front of one with enough accommodation for all of them. Its outer walls were clean and whitewashed, and the inside spotless. Two well-scrubbed tables for meals stood at the centre, and two tiers of narrow bunks about half a metre wide lined the back wall, and were separated from each other by a board about eighteen inches high. George, with a shrug, thought it hardly enough to give privacy during the night.

Being late in the day, the overseer told the new arrivals to change into their new prison garb and wait for the evening meal. Soon, gangs of convicts began returning for the night, and George found the old hands generally well organized in their activities. In the early evening most went to another yard to have lessons in reading and writing or other pursuits, while a few remained in the hut to gamble.

Chapter 27
Port Arthur Assignment

Early next morning, as the first cold fingers of dawn crept into the sky, George woke to the tolling of a bell. In the half-light he barely made out his surroundings still illuminated by the feeble glow of a lantern that burned all night on the table. Within minutes the hut became alive with men tumbling out of bed and dressing. Soon, a breakfast of gruel and bread arrived to be gulped down before the whole barracks assembled in the yard for work. It was still barely light when George and his gang of brick makers marched over the hill to their place of work.

The overseer placed George, being a new arrival, with the mixers, the least desirable work of all. From five-thirty in the morning until six at night he mixed clay and water to the right consistency with his hands. Within days the coarser clay at Port Arthur began to abrade the skin on his hands, and within a week painful cracks opened on his fingers and palms, making kneading almost unbearable.

Although the overseer seemed quiet and inoffensive, when he noticed George had very painful hands he gave no mercy. He had to keep up the rate of work, or face a thrashing on the triangle in the flagellation yard. But word had spread that the Commandant had recently begun introducing less violent forms of discipline. Instead of ordering thrashings, he had sent a few convicts to solitary confinement for minor offences. To heal his hands, George decided there was only one thing for him to do: take a gamble. He considered it a logical bet, as the odds appeared to be in his favour.

One morning he refused to work, and showed his hands. He knew flogging was still a possibility, but, as he hoped, the

Commandant sentenced him to a week's solitary confinement. His gamble had paid off.

Guards marched him to a long wooden building near the barracks, and thrust him into a gloomy cell little more than two yards long and a yard and a half wide. The door slammed shut behind him, leaving him in complete silence. Trapped in the dim light and dank air in the little cell, a sudden sense of panic overtook him with an impression of being buried alive. Although the feeling lingered most of the day he slowly grew accustomed to the silence of his isolation, and with nothing else to do, he simply sat on the cold stone floor. From time to time he stood up, or exercised for a while, but in the half-light of the cell each minute seemed to last for an hour. No sound reached his ears, he saw nobody, the only break in his solitude coming when a guard pushed a ration of bread and water through a slot in the heavy wooden door. Normally, this treatment had a punitive effect on even the most wayward convicts, and George soon understood how some prisoners confined for a month or two came out so deranged they would commit murder.

After several days of isolation, he became aware of strange dark shadows that from time to time would suddenly appear and dart about in front and around him. Later, during that night he awoke to see the frightening figure of a man dressed in black standing over him, his ugly face glaring down at him with a fearsome expression. George let out an involuntary cry, and as he did so, the menacing apparition disintegrated above him, leaving the face glowering at him for a further second or two before it, too, floated away to disappear into the gloom of the cell. For some time the shock of the encounter left him breathless and with a pounding heart. That night further sleep came only fitfully.

George realized these sensations must come from his own mind, and when a similar spectre appeared the following night, after a brief moment of consternation, instead of becoming overawed, he simply shrugged his shoulders and watched the ugly figure dissipate above him. But the shock of his encounter with these apparitions made him wonder if his sanity was about to fail, and he, too, could go mad.

He recalled hearing eerie convict stories about spirits of the dead who had once occupied a cell, and that these phantasms sometimes returned at night. He had laughed them off as old wives' tales. Now, their presence made him glad his stay would be only for a week. Still, although time dragged, it served its purpose by giving him the opportunity he sought for his hands to heal.

When he emerged from isolation and returned to brickmaking, the same quiet overseer, named Bickley, remained in charge. But some of the brickmaking gang looked on him with disdain. George had always been wary of some of this group, especially of a man named Shaw whose unpredictable behaviour could be quite violent at times for no apparent reason.

Several weeks later a new supervisor took charge, and George heard the story going round that during the night Shaw had crept up on Bickley who lived about a mile from the barracks. Shaw hit the overseer on the head, and strangled him in revenge for some imagined slight. He did not try to escape, but stayed in the vicinity of his crime. Guards easily caught him the next day, and later hanged him at Hobart Town. George thought Shaw must have preferred death to his ongoing life of misery and suffering in prison.

Throughout the months that followed, George continued to resent his term at Port Arthur. He missed Elizabeth, and found difficulty in resigning himself to his undeserved conviction. Within a year he became so frustrated he absented himself from work. The next day guards arraigned him before the Commandant who had little sympathy for a shirker. This time George received six weeks hard labour. Straightaway, guards took him to the blacksmith to be riveted back into leg-irons, and they assigned him to a timber gang that kept working to the limits of their physical endurance.

All day George cursed his fetters as the gang struggled back and forth for almost a mile, carrying logs weighing more than an hundred pounds. The convicts picked them up at the sawpits, carried them to the port and stacked them ready for export. The overseer expected them all to keep up with him, but he walked as fast as he could, shouting threats of the triangle for any slackers. Half way, he allowed the gang to rest for a few minutes before going the final distance. No sooner had they stacked their load in the lumberyard than he would be yelling for them to hurry back for the next log. Any who could no longer carry his load, or even keep up with the pace, he had flogged within an hour. By the end of each day George collapsed exhausted on to his bed.

For the final two weeks of his sentence they transferred him to the *centipede*. Most of its gangs consisted of obstinate men like George, who continued to offend in some way, and had been sent to the *centipede* as punishment in an attempt to make them conform. George had already heard rumours of its terrors and hardships, but had never seen it in action.

On the first morning an overseer arrived just as George finished his breakfast. 'Come with me,' he said, and escorted him to a nearby block to join a group of silent convicts gathering in the courtyard and waiting to be chained together. They all ignored George's casual greeting, unnerving him with their silence. He sensed it was not the silence of men consumed by private thoughts, but the silence of minds gone blank, like the silence of men about to be led to the gallows. Their silence warned George this day would be a challenge to his fortitude.

Guards marched George in leg-irons with more than fifty others to begin their day. Then, to his dismay, he saw what he had to do. Several huge tree trunks roughly trimmed into beams up to twelve yards long and half a yard square lay on the ground.

The first order came. Ten convicts lined up on each side of the first log. George, among the group, heard the crack of a supervisor's birch followed by an order.

'Lift.'

All twenty men stooped and heaved the great log onto their shoulders.

'March.'

Although of different heights, the men, were forbidden to bend their knees. George found carrying the load for almost a mile to be backbreaking work, and more strenuous than carrying logs had been in the previous weeks. The roughhewn beams bit into the flesh of his shoulder with each step. His arms ached. His back ached. His legs ached, and his ankles twisted in his leg-irons as he struggled over uneven ground. Added to his pain, fear of the log escaping from his grasp kept him from any show of slacking. He knew beams sometimes slipped, crushing men to death under the weight. It was a continual worry. Nobody let up. None of the men wanted to be crushed or die a slow agonizing death.

Common sense at last convinced George antagonism gained him nothing; he could never beat the system. If he offended again it would only prolong his time at Port Arthur. The *centipede* finally persuaded him to become a model prisoner, and conform to whatever they expected of him.

After his six weeks of hard labour, and now with leg-irons struck off, he returned to the brickmaking gang. For another two years George followed the rules, and life went along day by day without any adverse incident. With this good record behind him he became a class two convict, meaning he could work for himself all day Saturday, and earn a few shillings.

At last, prison authorities transferred him to Hobart Town where he lived in barracks near New Town Road, and worked at the local brickfields. For the first time in more than a decade he began to save a little money that he placed in a bank for the time of his release.

Now, nearing the end of his sentence George decided to write to his grandfather. One sunny Sunday afternoon he sat down and drafted a letter with sentences he had thought about for years. He knew it would be prudent to let his grandfather know where he was, and tell him he enjoyed life in the colonies, but wondered if his grandfather still rejected him. He hoped to be a free man by the time the letter arrived. His grandfather need never know of his convict years. George knew almost another year would go by before he could expect a reply.

Being a second-class convict he had to attend the service at St John Church on every Sunday along with all the other convicts in the barracks. As he emerged from the convict gallery on the morning of his first attendance he caught a momentary glimpse of Elizabeth before she vanished among the crowd of women convicts leaving the church. He wondered if his sight deceived him, but he rushed to follow and located her, as she was about to leave. When he saw the blush rise in Elizabeth's cheeks he knew she had not forgotten him. With free settlers all around, the two dared not speak or show their feelings. So they simply walked their separate ways to the street in a manner that gave no hint of their association. Still, one tall, gaunt, hawk-nosed woman noticed the looks that passed between them and made a mental note of their bond.

Further along New Town Road they met where nobody disturbed their solitude. Overjoyed, they embraced and rejoiced in their newfound rapture. With their world restored so unexpectedly they exchanged experiences since they had last sat together on the banks of the Tamar River. Elizabeth said she had heard of his flogging and grieved for him. But within a few days the family she served returned to Hobart Town where she continued to work at their house in New Town Road. She imagined him still at Launceston and unable to contact her.

The hours passed swiftly, and they arranged to meet the following Sunday afternoon. They saw their future together suddenly before them, and Elizabeth promised to tell George of her past when next they met. He would have to know of her original crime, and the long trail of suffering it spawned: memories that remained like an apparition too painful for her to forget.

Chapter 28
Elizabeth's Story

Through all her hardships Elizabeth faced the gravest problems imaginable for any young woman. In her loneliness after losing George, her thoughts often returned to her carefree childhood days in the small village of Churchill. It had been a world where misfortune and anguish had no existence for her; it was simply a place of childhood happiness and dreams of the future. Fond memories and nostalgia carried her back to all the things that had special meaning to her.

She told George of her mother, always busy with her children, and doing needlework to help with the family's meagre finances. She remembered her father, a short thickset man with thinning hair, who seemed so wise in the ways of the world. She would listen to him and take his advice.

She saw their old kitchen again, with its beamed ceiling and worn flagstone floor showing the wear of centuries. She pictured the dishes and plates arranged in neat rows along the shelves, and several bright copper pots and pans hanging near the hearth, gleaming and twinkling in the reflected firelight. She remembered the large table where she often sat talking with her father while her mother, working at the bench, would join in and glance over her shoulder as she spoke.

Beyond the house, the wide-open spaces of meadows and rolling dales always appealed to her. In her dreaming she relived the days of her childhood when she ran free across the fields; the sky and the larks above her, the wind billowing her skirt as she ran, and her hair streaming behind her. From high up on an outcrop of rock she had a view across the meadows to a winding stream below, and her village in the distance. Out in the dales she had secret wild places known only to herself, where she felt the presence of primitive nature all round. Here, she would lie back in the long grass, look up into the deep vault of an afternoon sky and listen to skylarks high overhead. As she grew she loved the freedom and the stillness of the dales, always a brief change from her busy week of needlework and laundering. In summer she would sit in a bower of greenery where several old oaks gave a canopy of shade. In the cool days of winter she watched fine mist floating over the landscape to settle in the hollows.

On such a day, she happened to glance up, and noticed the distant figure of a man crouching and looking in her direction. At first it annoyed her that somebody intruded on her privacy, and she decided to ignore him. Within a few minutes curiosity made her glance again. It perturbed her to see he had come much closer. Suddenly she realized how alone she was. The solitude that had given her so much pleasure now frightened her.

At the sight of the stranger so near, she stood up with a feeling of apprehension and turned to leave. At that moment he sprang to his feet and ran towards her. She had little time to escape. Before she had gone more than a dozen steps in flight the man caught up with her. He grabbed her arm, exclaiming, 'my pretty little thing, don't struggle.'

She tried to shake him off, but his grip tightened and his fingers bit into her flesh. 'Please let me go, sir,' she said, squirming to face him as calmly as she could.

'Sir,' he laughed. 'Enchanted, I'm sure.'

With this, Elizabeth took the only action she had heard might protect a girl trapped in such circumstances. She brought her knee up with enough force to cause the man to double up with pain. As his grip loosened, she tore herself free and fled with a burst of speed that surprised her. She did not falter, her feet instinctively following the secret twists and turns of a path known only to her. Breathless, she reached the crest of a rise where she paused to gain her breath and looked back. The stranger appeared to have given up the chase, and she watched as he limped off. In the near distance the welcoming sight of her house with its smoking chimney brought a sense of relief. She ran down the long slope and reached her father working beside the door.

"What's the matter, girl,' he said. 'You look like you've seen a ghost.'

'Tis the last time I'll walk alone in the dales,' she said.

Her father shook his head, but asked no questions. 'Speak to your mother,' he said.

Inside, she collapsed onto a wooden armchair and told her all that had happened.

'I've said to you afore; at your age you should be thinking of marrying, not wandering about daydreaming in the open dales,' her mother replied. 'If you runs into trouble, 'twill not only be your own fault, but you could bring shame on our whole family.'

'How can I ever find a husband in tiny Churchill?' Elizabeth said.

'Well, young lady, I's been speaking with your aunt,' her mother said. 'She tells me she knows of a family in Birmingham what needs a housemaid. If Churchill be too small for you, perhaps the city will be more to your taste.'

Elizabeth went to her room and thought about it. It did not take her long to reach a decision. She emerged with a smile, and put her arms round her mother, saying, 'I will be very happy to go to Birmingham. 'Tis not far away. So I should be able to visit you from time to time.' And, adding with a blush, 'I'm sure to find a husband in such a large city.'

When arrangements had been made she set out from home with expectations of a new and happy life. She wondered if a prospective husband would even at that moment be thinking about his future wife, and she began to imagine what he might look like.

Despite her enthusiasm, she found her new job more onerous than expected. Working from five-thirty each morning, and often until late in the evening, she had little time to herself, and certainly no opportunity to make herself available to a prospective husband.

'These people were tyrants,' she said to George. 'They had no respect for me, or any appreciation of all I did for them. I wondered whatever would become of me.'

Chapter 29
Feminine Justice

As she told her story, George looked at Elizabeth with compassion, and waited for her to regain her composure before continuing her story. She paused as she thought back to her brush with the law on a cold November day in Birmingham.

Wondering how to begin, she hesitated before saying; 'It all came about after the mistress of the house sent me on an errand to the Birmingham Mail Coach Depot to collect a parcel.'

George saw tears well up in her eyes.

'Outside,' she said, 'I faced a cold wind blowing snow flurries that clung to me and melted, seeping through my thin clothing. As I hurried along the streets I kept mulling over what right the mistress had to demand I go out in such weather, knowing there was no particular urgency.'

George gave her a smile of encouragement.

'I felt cold and miserable, and thinking that the family who employed me had so little compassion or care for my welfare,' she said. 'Like so many women, my work was little short of slavery.'

'Some people can be such hard taskmasters,' George said.

'On my way to collect the parcel I had begun to feel angry and more and more resentful of the mistress when I happened to pass a clothing shop. A pile of pretty-coloured woollen scarves and other clothing lay stacked within easy reach.' Elizabeth paused again, considering how to go on, but she knew she had to be honest with George.

In a trembling voice, she said, 'I was shivering with the cold and feeling very angry with my mistress. I stopped for a few moments to handle a scarf and feel its warmth. It gave me a sudden urge to take it for protection. I glanced around, and could not see the shopkeeper or anybody else. I must have been out of my mind at the time because I knew the consequences if he caught me. But I was so cold and miserable I just couldn't bear to think about it. It was the first and only time I've ever been tempted to do anything illegal.'

George took her by the hand and held it to his lips.

She took a deep breath and said, 'I grabbed the scarf to protect my head and ran off. At that moment I heard a shout from the shopkeeper who must have been watching me from behind some of the merchandise. He rushed after me. Before I had gone more than a few yards he caught me and held me until the constabulary arrived.'

George had never seen her so upset, and taking her in his arms, held her in a warm hug.

'I could see my predicament, and began to cry. I offered to pay for the scarf when I received my wages, but the constable would not hear of it. The disturbance drew a crowd of onlookers, and the shopkeeper became embarrassed. He urged the constable to take me to the watchhouse. Again I offered to pay for the scarf, and begged the clerk to set me free, but he just laughed at me. The constable pushed me into a prison cell.'

George watched as tears welled up and trickled down her cheeks.

'It all happened so quickly,' she said. 'I've looked back so many times. I was so foolish. I've had such a wretched life ever since. Still, it is all my own fault.'

'Being so cold and wet, it would have been easy to fall into temptation,' George said, hoping to comfort her.

'Once inside the cell I found it full of women waiting trial. I had never mixed with such rough company, or seen such filth. The stench of bodies almost overpowered me. Cockroaches lived in the cracks and crevices in the walls, and after several days I began to itch from lice that had found their way into the seams of my clothing. But even worse, rats came out every night, and ran over me when I tried to sleep.'

'Yes,' George said. 'I know the feeling.'

'I had been employed in a fine house, and worked for people of so-called social class. It came as a shock to mix with whores and felons, and be seen as one of them. Now I am vulnerable to any free settler who cares to take advantage of me.'

She did not confide certain other problems to George, but having to use a bucket in the corner became a constant ordeal until she gradually overcame her self-consciousness. Then, after about two weeks, she woke one morning to find blood on her thighs, and already staining her dress, her only recourse being to tear strips from her underwear to absorb the flow. She learned these troubles were common to the other women, but they accepted everything without complaint, obviously being well used to it.

'After several weeks they arraigned me and about a dozen other women before the Birmingham Court of Quarter Sessions,' Elizabeth said.

'That must have been an ordeal for you,' George added, and continued to hold her close.

'With no change of clothing since my arrest, I looked as disreputable and dirty as the other women in front of the bewigged legal people,' she said. 'It was a frightening experience for a twenty year old, and I felt very threatened by the pomp and dignity of it all.' Elizabeth gave another deep sigh before going on. 'I never saw my parents among the crowd; they probably rejected me because of the shame I brought on them.'

George felt her trembling in his arms. 'It must have been very intimidating for you,' he said, as he continued to comfort her.

'After the judge sentenced me to transportation for ten years, I spent that night sobbing in my cell, and have cried a lot ever since.'

'Transportation for men is bad enough, but it is a cruel punishment for a girl as young as you,' George added.

'Yes,' said Elizabeth. 'They left me in the Birmingham jail all through the freezing winter months. It seems ships suitable to transport women convicts are few and far between.'

'For a young girl it is nothing short of inhuman,' George ground out.

'On one cold day my mother left my sewing kit and a bag of clothes at the jail, but she never asked to see me. I am clearly a thief in my family's eyes. I always thought we were a happy family, but my actions must have affected them badly in their small community. My thoughtless action has touched so many people. I still feel ashamed and deserted.'

George looked deeply into her eyes and reached to gently stroke her hair. 'I will never desert you, Elizabeth,' he said. 'You can depend on it.'

'At first I tried to block it all out by sleep, but that never came easily. I was a convicted felon, and rejected by all those I had depended on and loved. My family had always tried to do their best for me, but I betrayed their trust. I must have slowly fallen into some sort of torpor, and simply withdrew into myself.'

'It would have been so hard for you, suffering from the way they neglected you,' George said.

'I can understand my family's opinion of me,' she said. 'They've probably never mentioned my name again. It's as if I never existed. How I wish I could see my mother, cry on her shoulder and know she forgave me for my stupidity. It would give me peace of mind.'

'At least your family knows what has happened to you,' George said. 'But surely they don't look on you as being the type of woman you have to mix with all the time.'

'I hope not,' Elizabeth said. 'I used to hear a lot o' their gossip in the cell when they chattered among themselves. Now, I know many of those sentenced to transportation are simply girls who couldn't find work, but had decided against prostitution to survive. Their only way to keep from starving was to steal something they could either sell or eat.'

After a pause, Elizabeth went on to say, 'two of the girls told me they worked together to lure drunk men to a room and steal their watch, or take money from their pockets before running off. Another girl told me she found stealing was too difficult, and prostitution so much easier. She fancied she would never get caught.'

'Yes,' George said. 'My father warned me about girls like that.'

'I remember an older woman boasting how a shop owner caught her hiding material under her skirt, and then she laughed about it. And we also had a few hardened criminals among us,' Elizabeth said. 'They had been prostitutes who made a business of stealing from their clients and pawning their proceeds; I found their behavior the worst and most deceitful. Many of them had led lives of great hardship, competing for the necessities of life, and surviving by cunning and selfishness. I soon learned to protect myself against their thieving and lying.'

'There always seems to be a hard core of criminals among us,' said George. 'I try to avoid them.'

Elizabeth nodded. 'So do I, but sometimes 'tis not possible. Soon after I was sentenced, I noticed a woman I knew only as Betsy kept looking at me. Then she came across and folded her arms in front of me. "Now you's in jail," she said, "I suppose your boyfriend has gone off with somebody else." She was probably trying to stir me up.'

'Not a nice type,' George said.

'I told her I didn't have a boyfriend, but she kept on. "My, my! A pretty little thing like you, and no boyfriend? Perhaps 'tis the girls that takes your fancy."

'She disgusted me. I'd heard rumours from cellmates how some women like Betsy prefer the company of another woman rather than a man, and there were whispers of the things they would get up to together.'

'It's the same with a few of the men,' George added. 'But it's not common.'

'I told her in all innocence the family kept me too busy to have a boyfriend. Then one of the older women came to my aid and told Betsy to leave me alone, as I was only a lass.'

'It always helps to have somebody on your side,' George added.

'Yes, Betsy turned her attention to other girls, but in a crowded cell she was always nearby; I had to stay on my guard.'

'As time went by,' Elizabeth continued, 'I became more settled. Then early one miserable winter's morning in late January, guards ordered all us women for transportation to gather in the prison yard to be manacled in irons. Outside, in our thin clothing the frosty air soon had us shivering, and a threatening sky gave us the promise of snow and sleet later in the day.'

'Guards took us one at a time to the blacksmith,' Elizabeth told George. 'He riveted manacles on to our wrists, and lined us up in the yard again. I could scarcely move my arms from the sheer weight.'

George held her close to comfort her before she went on.

'Shortly afterwards an open deck prison wagon rumbled into the yard and stopped in front of us,' Elizabeth said. 'One of the guards shouted, "Now all youse ladies get aboard and we'll be agoing." The pain of our manacles made it difficult to climb on to the wagon, a problem we all had. It set some of the women cursing and yelling abuse at the guards who were hardly polite as they bundled us aboard and chained us together. An armed guard sat at each end of the tray, and we were on our way to London. It was a miserable journey.'

'You had a long way to go,' George said.

'It took us three days to reach the Downs on the lower Thames. All along the way we sat chained together in full view of anybody whose curiosity was aroused by the sight of us. Several light snowfalls left us wet and dejected, and with no chance to dry out. Next day the weather got even worse. A cold wind cut through our flimsy clothing like a knife.'

'What a terrible time for you.'

'Yes, we reached the Woolwich barracks all half-dead from cold and hunger. Even Betsy looked subdued and miserable. They removed our manacles, and in the next few days more groups of women convicts joined us. We all had a quick medical check, collected our clothing for the voyage, and waited for embarkation. Finally, they assembled us and marched us to the dock to file onto the ship.'

'I heard one woman burst out in disbelief. "We ain't going in a little tub like that, are we?" Like many of the others, it concerned me to see how small the ship really was,' Elizabeth said. 'I wondered how such a tiny vessel could ever reach our distant destination. As we filed on board, guards directed many of us to quarters on the bottom deck, but for once I was lucky. When I heard my name called, a guard directed me to a shelf to sleep on; it was on a higher deck said to be the 'tween decks.'

'Over 150 woebegone women, most in their late teens and early twenties, came on board. We shared the ship with poultry cages, cattle pens for the cows, goats, hogs, and a few sheep. We apparently had enough food to last us for the months it would take to reach Cape Town, said to be our first port of call. As we boarded, I noticed small animals being passed up from the dock, and cattle being hoisted aboard in canvas slings, and trample fresh manure into the decks.'

'I shared my sleeping cell with three older women,' Elizabeth went on to say. 'And glad to see Betsy allotted to a bed cell a long way from me. The day before departure was a sad time for one of the women in my cell. She told me ever since her husband had died, and her being illiterate, her only source of income had been prostitution. Her two daughters aged twelve and fourteen came aboard to say their farewells, and it concerned their mother that the two girls had to live on their own. She knew the same profession offered them their only chance of survival. They did a lot of crying, hugging and kissing. Later, one of the woman's cellmates tried to comfort her, saying, "don't be too sad. You'll surely all meet up again when your daughters be transported." Probably true,' Elizabeth said.

'I guess so,' George added. 'But the woman's sentiments seem a little misplaced.'

Chapter 30

Sea journey

'When all seemed ready to sail, guards ordered us women below decks,' Elizabeth said, as she continued her story. 'At the beginning of the voyage, down below we didn't know what was going on, and the noise frightened us. We could tell when we were on our way by the sounds of activity above us. We all heard the shouting of commands, but didn't understand all the running about, or the noise of the capstan hauling up the anchor and the crack of ropes and the flapping of sails when wind began to fill them.

'I know those sounds,' said George. 'On hearing them for the first time they could be quite scary.'

'Yes,' said Elizabeth. 'Some women found the racket too much, and became so terrified they collapsed in a faint. Others just lay around, unable to move for hours. Many of us had a feeling of helplessness; a sort of fear of the unknown that spread among us, and for a time I found myself caught up in the general alarm. It took a big effort to overcome my feelings of near panic. When we felt the deck start to heave, and heard the ship creaking, I knew we had left the Thames behind and had reached the Channel. Seamen opened the hatches, and along with other women suffering a bout of seasickness I scrambled on to the prison deck to vomit over the side.'

'It was much the same when we set sail,' said George.

'As for us,' Elizabeth went on, 'we had been under way only a couple of days when I learned that by some law of the sea, all the militia, seamen and ship's officers had the right to choose a mate for the duration of the voyage from the scores of women on board. When I looked at the rough mob sailing the ship, I wondered how any woman could enjoy a relationship forced on her in this way.'

'Quite a worry for you,' said George, with some apprehension for what she might be about to tell him.

'Yes, it was a worry', said Elizabeth. 'People sometimes called me a pretty young thing, and it concerned me to think one of the men might take a fancy to me. I would have no option but to live with him for the voyage. To avoid that possibility I put on a sour expression, and did my best to keep away from their gaze.'

'Quite a tricky situation,' said George.

'Still, many of the other women competed for the position of mistress to a sailor. I suppose after a life of hardship many of them had learned to struggle for anything they could get. Living with a member of the crew would kept them away from the cheating and bullying that went on after dark among the women below decks. They would have a man to look after their interests, and give them extra comforts and privileges.'

'I don't suppose you can blame them,' said George.

'Most of the crew seemed much the same age as the women, and very likely they had been raised in similar surroundings. So I presume sleeping with men would be normal for them. In fact, many of the women appeared to look on their relationship as a pleasant interlude between the squalor of their former life, and their probable future exploitation in Australia.'

'So I take it you escaped their attention,' said George with some relief.

'Yes,' said Elizabeth. And with that, she decided to change the subject. 'For discipline's sake, guards gave us a daily routine of work throughout the voyage. Ship's officers put us into groups of about eight headed by a trustee convict we named Matron. These women spoke for their group, and did their best to keep order. They also supervised cleaning activities, airing of bed linen, and the collection of rations for their group from the cook.'

'Much the same happened with us,' said George.

With a slight blush, Elizabeth went on to say, 'most of us felt embarrassed using the *heads*. At first we found it quite daunting to sit on open toilets in full view of the crew, or anybody who cared to look, but we soon got used to it.'

The memory sent her mind back to these platforms with holes cut in them, and lashed to the side of the ship near the bow. She remembered how effluent went straight into the sea, and everybody rinsed off with a bucket of seawater. But she could never forget how the distinctive odour of menstrual blood from the 150 women locked below deck at night always added to the stench of their commodes.

'Still,' Elizabeth said, 'Despite the annoyance of the atmosphere 'tween decks, I'm sure the ship was a cleaner place than many of the women had lived in before their arrest. We regularly scrubbed our quarters and aired our bedding; even scouring the boards we slept on, and we scraped and washed down the sides of our quarters. All this cleaning left our deck neat and tidy, and kept us busy.'

'We had to clean and scrub, too, but clearly not as much as you,' said George.

'Most of the women did all that was required of them,' Elizabeth said. 'Still, trouble soon flared up. A small group of troublemakers began to make life miserable for us with their thieving and bullying ways. Once we had settled into the voyage they went back to their old habits, and soon formed a hierarchy.'

'One night after battening down, I woke up with screaming nearby,' Elizabeth said. 'I heard somebody shout, "you thieving whore," followed by other curses that echoed round the 'tween decks. With the sounds of women struggling and punching in the dark, those of us close-at-hand hurried to the fighting and did our best to separate two women. Others joined in, and in the course of the uproar somebody turned on me, and I felt fingernails scratch across my cheek. The quarrelling soon settled and we went back to sleep. In the morning we found a girl of about sixteen lying bruised and miserable on her cot. Whenever anybody passed she would wail that Betsy had stolen her ring. I happened to know her, having often talked with her in the Birmingham jail.'

'We all felt sorry for her and tried to calm her, but when she kept on whimpering, I left her and went up to the deck. Among the crowd of women there I saw a small group pranced about with Betsy who kept showing her hand to anybody prepared to look. I recognized the girl's ruby ring on her finger: quite a windfall for her.'

'I asked a woman standing near me why young Laura didn't complain to the officers. She laughed at me, saying if she did that, she will get much worse from Betsy who is well-known for her bullying.'

'We had the same sort of bullies on board when I came out,' George said.

'Many of the women were angry with what Betsy had done to the girl,' Elizabeth said. 'I wished I could do something about it, but Betsy was a buxom woman in her middle thirties: somebody well used to bullying and theft. She was clearly bigger and stronger than me, and had a group of cronies around her. What chance would I have against her? Still, I felt I had to do something, but trembled at the thought.'

'Finally, I went across to Betsy, and she held out her ringed finger for me to see. But instead of congratulating her, I told her it was a mean trick to rob the poor girl.'

'You were taking a big risk,' George said.

'I suppose so,' said Elizabeth, 'Betsy looked at me with surprise; her expression hardened, and through clenched teeth she said, "Nobody talks to Betsy like that and gets away with it. I'll fix you tonight." '

'No doubt you could, I told her. You're bigger and stronger, but think again. She looked at me with a horrible glare and said, "I'll give you more than scratches on your face, you little miss too-good." But I stood my ground and told her she had robbed a young girl of more than her ring. I reminded her everybody knew it was a legacy from her grandmother, and had been in her family even before that.'

'Betsy looked daggers and said, "Don't you moralize with me," and continued to glare.'

'I hoped my trembling didn't show in my voice, but I reminded her the ring was the only bond the poor girl would ever have with her family. I told her she stole more than a ring. She had robbed a girl of her birthright. As I spoke, I saw a blush on Betsy's cheeks.'

'I went on to tell Betsy I was sure she was a decent person at heart. I told her to give the ring back and we will all know it. I gave her no chance to respond, but turned and walked away. To my relief nobody attacked me during the night. Next day I noticed the ring back on the girl's finger.'

'That was a daring thing to do,' said George. 'People like Betsy can be very unpredictable; she could still hold a grudge.'

'You are right, George,' Elizabeth said. 'Each time I saw Betsy she glared at me, and whenever we came close she sank her voice and whispered. "I'll get you one day little girlie, don't you fret." I knew Betsy was waiting her chance to get even, but an opportunity for something really nasty never arose. But I realize, even today, I still have to be on guard.'

'It wasn't long before other gangs began to appear, and at times vicious fighting broke out. They targeted weaker women and bullied them to get anything worth stealing. Most trouble flared up after we had been left to ourselves after being battened down for the night. Everybody knew it went on, but it was too dangerous to complain.

After a long pause, Elizabeth went on to say that few of the women had ever seen the ocean before they set sail. 'So each day became a new experience for us,' she said.. 'Once we left the rough seas and gales of the north behind, we came to calmer water where we could enjoy more gentle breezes, and warmer weather. It made our days pleasant, and the crew told us we were in the trade winds. Sailors took advantage of it to spend time checking the rigging and cutting out new sails in case we needed them later in the Southern Ocean.'

'By the time we reached the tropics we had never seen any other ship,' Elizabeth said. 'Often we would watch for fish that sometimes swam close to us. From time to time we saw large fish the sailors called *bonito*, and the crew would rush to fish for them. If a sailor caught one he shared it with his mistress: an added bonus for her.'

Elizabeth went on to say that as they got closer to the equator the winds dropped, and their little ship lay becalmed on an oily-smooth sea. She described how dead sails hung limply from the yards, and the ship vibrated and creaked from crosscurrents that brought on seasickness. She said they all felt exhausted by the heat, and wet with sweat, and their ration of three pints of water each day barely replaced what they lost naturally.'

'That tropical heat can certainly be exhausting,' George said.

'Yes.' said Elizabeth. 'Often during the day we lay limply under awnings on the deck. Even Betsy and the gangs of bullies looked washed out. Sailors spent several unpleasant hours in the heat of the day pumping water from one side of the deck to the other trying to cool the air below decks. But after battening down at night, we were left restless all night in the foul and sweltering atmosphere 'tween decks.'

'But what was even worse, effluent from the heads and refuse tossed overboard remained pooled round our ship,' Elizabeth said. 'It became home to a variety of plant life, growing long green fronds that floated round the ship, and trapping even more refuse that gave rise to a sickening stench. Each day we watched the crew launch boats and hack away as much as possible. It must have been exhausting and distasteful work for them.'

'Fortunately that didn't happen with us,' said George.

'Sailors told us the only way to make any progress in the doldrums, and get away from the reeking cesspool that surrounded us, was to tow the ship. So day and night, they spent two-hour shifts in the boats, rowing hour after hour, and slowly pulling the ship behind them. Now we could see the benefit of our little tub that at first had given us so much concern.'

'I think it would be almost impossible to tow a large vessel like ours loaded with hundreds of prisoners and stores,' said George.

'As for us, lookouts posted aloft spent several weeks watching for signs of a breeze, or even a brief gust of wind. Any suggestion of a ruffle on the water, and we saw the crew on watch up the mast signal those below to trim the sails accordingly. I continued to marvel at the work the crew did to keep the ship moving,' Elizabeth said. 'But like so many of us, I spent most of my days lying under the deck awnings quite overcome by the constant heat, and not feeling up to any strenuous duties.'

'At last, to our relief an occasional light air stream caught the studdingsails, and the ship began to slowly move forward,

Elizabeth said. 'From below we watched them fill and slacken, and fill again until one day, winds freshened and the main and foresails caught a puff of breeze and we saw them bellow forward. The ship creaked and gained speed on fresh swells, and we soon left the doldrums behind. But the sailors told us Cape Town still lay two thousand miles away: at least another three weeks' sailing.'

'About this time greens began to run low, and fresh water had an unpleasant taste,' Elizabeth said.

'I know that taste well,' said George. 'It makes the water so hard to drink at a time you really need it.'

'The crew told us that the captain was going to start us on potable soup,'

'I'll never forget that mixture of vegetables and offal,' said George. 'I remember the cook boiled it with a few greens while we still had them.'

'But we had a further problem,' Elizabeth said. 'I believe one of the unknowns for the ship's officers was the fear of scurvy. Although nobody knew what caused it, they told us it was more likely to affect those in low spirits or feeling miserable rather than contented people. So to keep us happy, or at least occupied, the captain started us dancing on deck and play-acting, or anything else that took our minds off personal worries.'

'I spent my time doing needlework. I had kept the material and sharp scissors my mother had left me, and also a sewing kit given by members of Elizabeth Fry's Quaker group who campaigned for prison reform in England. Although I had only a small amount of material, I hoped to earn a few shillings from my needlework when we reached Australia. I made friends with several girls who slept near me in the 'tween decks, and we formed a sewing circle. We spent our time chatting together working and comparing our embroidery.'

'I happened to be good at *Broderie Anglaise,* a name that impressed my friends when I first mentioned it, and I showed them how easily they could do it.' To impress George she added, ' They would crowd round to watch how I formed the small, details of round and oval eyelets in the material, and they admired its finely stitched edges joined by ladders of stems and scrolls to connect the various parts of the design. I worked mainly on dainty handkerchiefs and small tea trays, turning the all-white embroidery into fancy articles.'

'That's how the weeks passed as we slowly made our way down the coast of Africa until one morning the lookout shouted, 'Land ahead'. Soon all those on deck could make out distant hills and the flat top of Table Mountain like shadows on the distant horizon.'

Chapter 31
The Challenge of the Southern Ocean

'Our little ship sailed into Table Bay late in the afternoon,' Elizabeth said as she continued her story. 'It was a huge expanse of water where we could see many other vessels laying at anchor. Until the previous few weeks, none of us women had ever heard of Cape Town, or knew it was on a direct shipping route between Europe and all the countries of the Far East. After our long, lonely voyage it surprised most of us to come upon a harbour alive with so much activity. We crowded on to the deck and stared, fascinated, as sailors from many countries plied to and from the shore, loading or unloading goods and stores before sailing on.'

'We never stopped at Cape Town,' said George. 'We sailed right past and into the Southern Ocean.'

'We were luckier,' said Elizabeth. 'Our ship dropped anchor close to the shore, and we watched as seamen lowered a gig for the captain to be rowed ashore to pay his respects to the authorities. Being the first time any of us had seen a town outside England, the buildings seemed strange and unusual to us. We could make out many flat-roofed houses, and a huge five-sided structure the crew told us was the Castle of Good Hope.'

'From where the ship anchored we easily made out the place of execution. It lay exposed for all to see with its gallows, gibbet, poll for impalements, and wheels for breaking criminals. Officers who went ashore brought back grisly tales of body parts displayed at street corners to deter crime. We all muttered among ourselves that justice at the Cape seemed even more brutal than in England.'

'The officers and crew put the time at Cape Town to good use. For almost a month we cleaned the ship from stem to stern while the crew checked rigging and sails, and repaired any leaks or doubtful seams with oakum and tar. Meanwhile, the officers lived ashore in rented tenements, negotiating for food, buying fresh livestock and various supplies required before tackling the dangerous Southern Ocean. The sailors said the best time for this passage to be in late spring or summer. Now we would not leave before autumn, and we heard the crew say we may not arrive until July when winter seas with icebergs and gale force winds whipped up from the Antarctic could make the crossing hazardous. We all knew we had a long, cold, and perilous time ahead. If trouble struck there would be no handy port, or any passing ship to give aid.'

'Along with most of the women, I looked at the cheap clothing issued at Woolwich, and worried. It had already worn thin, and seams had begun to come apart. Now, after weeks of humid tropical weather we were already feeling the cold of Cape Town. Despite having a woollen jacket, I worried how I would cope with the freezing temperatures of the Southern Ocean.'

'At last they had the little ship in as good repair as possible. Stores had been loaded, animals were safe in their pens, and the crew seemed ready to tackle the long journey to Van Diemen's Land. Once again guards locked us women convicts below until the ship was under sail, but allowed us on deck again as soon as we left Table Bay and reached the open sea. As I came out from the hatchway a cold wind hit me. The wintery air irritated my throat with every breath, penetrating to my lungs. I worried it may be the beginning of future trouble.'

'After several days of easy sailing, the sky clouded over, the wind freshened, and soon huge seas battered the ship. Waves came at us like rolling hills. The howling wind whipped up spray from their crests, keeping the air in a constant mist. We pitched and tossed as the prow dug into each mountainous wave, sending water streaming across the deck and through hawser holes. Even with hatchways battened down, water found its way to the decks below, saturating our bedding and clothing, and with little hope of it drying out.

'I could hear the ship creaking with every onslaught, and felt the timber vibrate. While the sound of the elements concerned us, the amount of water coming into the ship frightened us even more. It alarmed me to see it seeping through cracks in the seams of the hull, and to hear it rumbling down below in the orlop deck. With each plunge of the bow the noise became thunderous as water sloshed to and fro. Although we saw seamen busy on the pumps, much of the time they never managed to remove all the water. We did not know what to expect and became fearful the ship may sink. On several occasions seas swamped the galley, and the stove could not be lit. Adding to all these worries a smell built up in the restricted area between decks. Since it was not safe for us to go on deck, commodes could not be emptied overboard, and the contents sometimes spilled across the 'tween decks as the ship rolled.'

'Foul weather lasted almost three days before clearing enough for the crew to open the hatches. To our great relief we could at last breathe fresh air again, and bring our straw bedding and clothes on to the deck to dry. The ship looked a strange sight with clothing hanging from every available rope, and the deck strewn with mattresses. But the chill wind was slow to dry, and left bedding damp. So we had further miserable nights.'

'As one dismal week followed another, the weather remained cold and blustery. No bird or passing ship gave relief or interest in the encircling horizon. Now and then a weak sun broke through the clouds but brought little warmth. We all felt miserable and could not help becoming downhearted and despondent. In this appalling climate I developed a hacking cough that failed to improve in the damp air. It sent my throat into spasms of irritation at times, but the surgeon had no treatment to help.'

'For over two months our tiny ship weathered frequent storms in the Southern Ocean. At times the wind dropped, and the sun made a brief appearance between scurrying clouds, but it was never calm sailing. The sea, usually a deep inky blue, kept rolling on relentlessly, and making it awkward for us to walk steadily. Adding to our misery, waves continued to send up clouds of spray, while misty weather always kept decks slippery. Sometimes one of us took a tumble, and as none wore knickerbockers, it always raised a cheer and a good laugh among the crew who were quick to notice any 'exhibition'.'

'At last the lookout's cry of "land ahead" sent a flurry of excitement throughout the ship. The news spread like wildfire, reducing many of us to tears of relief. After several hours there could be no doubt about it. Even those on deck made out a distant row of hills on the horizon. Despite the rolling seas, spontaneous dancing and singing erupted as spirits rose to the occasion. Women sang and twirled about the deck, and the crew needed no encouragement to join in the merriment. But darkness soon obscured any signs of land, and overnight the ship rounded the southern capes of Tasmania and turned nor-east well out to sea.'

'All day we remained out of sight of land, but early the following morning we came on deck to find we were quite close to the coast. For city bred women it was a depressing sight. Forested hills and steep mountainous terrain with mist-filled valleys gave us all the impression of a primitive and hostile land, untenanted and devoid of any welcome. It surprised us to find a landscape with so many different shades of green despite the onset of winter. Our memories of English winters were of trees looking lifeless, their bare boughs stark as if dead.'

'Two days later we entered a wide river with signs of cultivation here and there along the banks. By late afternoon we came in sight of Hobart Town and anchored in a small inlet the crew said was Sullivans Cove.'

'It filled us all with despair when we saw our new home. With memories of English cities still fresh in mind, the dismal little settlement seemed to be little more than a huddle of miscellaneous buildings set in muddy streets. We looked with dismay at the surrounding hills stretching back to a high mountain, barren and forbidding, and dominating the whole landscape under a sullen grey sky.'

'I wondered how I could ever become accustomed to life in such a godforsaken place.'

Chapter 32

Hobart Town

Elizabeth looked at George, saying, 'I hardly need to describe Hobart to you, but our arrival really lives in my memory.'

'I would still like to know all that happened to you after you arrived,' George said.

' Well, we did not go ashore at once,' Elizabeth continued. 'We stayed on the ship for another three days until the authorities completed all the formalities, and issued us with fresh clothing. Finally, small boats ferried us to the shore where we lined up to be marched under guard to the Female Factory at Cascades.'

'It was the same routine for us,' George said, 'Except we marched to the men's jail in town.'

'Anyway, I felt glad to be back on land again,' Elizabeth said. 'But Hobart Town gave me no pleasure. As we made our way up the street it was the first time we came across those swarms of flies that irritate wherever they land on your exposed skin. When we brushed them aside we soon learned they simply flew out of range before descending once again to the same spot. Sticky mud coated our shoes, and dirty water from numerous puddles splashed up our legs and soiled our skirts. Onlookers stopped to stare at this line of newly arrived whores as we trudged up the long slope. Some of the more vocal convict women greeted bystanders with cheeky remarks, but most walked in silence. It seemed hours before we reached a damp and sunless valley. In the distance I made out a grim-looking stonewalled compound that I imagined would be our new home.'

'We all filed into a large yard already occupied by such a crowd of women that I wondered how another hundred and fifty newcomers could possibly fit in. As soon as we arrived overseers assembled us in a large dormitory to be addressed by the matron who outlined what she expected of us. She classified us all as grade one convicts, and we were to await assignment to work either in Hobart Town or in the countryside. During the next few days I noticed our numbers getting less, but it was almost two weeks before they assigned me to domestic duties for a family living in New Town Road near the edge of town.'

'Early next morning guards bundled me onto a prison wagon going in that direction and the family's laundress, a pleasant woman in her late thirties, met me at the address. She helped with my bag and showed me up to a room we were to share in the attic. The laundress said she had been assigned to the family several years previously. I took an instant liking to her, and felt happy to be in the care of someone who would take an interest in me, and perhaps help with any problems. The laundress knew all the likes and dislikes of the master and mistress of the house, and said the master, whom she seldom saw, worked at the administration offices, and had some power in the colony.'

'Almost immediately, the mistress summoned me to the sitting room for assessment and instruction about my duties. The laundress accompanied me as far as the door, and told me to go in alone.'

'I gave a gentle knock and heard a voice say, "enter".'

'I closed the door behind me, and found myself in a large room overstuffed with dark furniture. Hunting pictures hung round the wall, and I noticed a small bookcase and a rack of guns just behind an oversized desk. A middle-aged woman, tall and gaunt, and with a hawk-like nose, stood behind the desk. I noticed her hair drawn back and tied into a bun, and framing an unsmiling face. For a few moments she simply stared at me with eyes that took in my appearance from head to foot.'

'Having gained her first impressions, the woman motioned me to stand beside the desk. "Before you were transported for theft," she said, "I understand you were a servant in an English household. So you will be aware of what we expect of you here". She certainly knows how to intimidate, I thought.'

"You will rise at five-thirty each morning and set a fire in the coal range for the cook to prepare breakfast," she said, and paused. I began to feel uncomfortable as the woman continued to scrutinize me. Then she told me all the things I had to do. "You will be responsible for cleanin' and dustin', scrubbin', helpin' the laundress with the washin', choppin' firewood, makin' up beds and any other work I decide you should do. My husband often has guests to dinner in the evenin'. On these occasions you will scour the pots, wash the dishes, and put them away carefully before retirin'." I knew such dinners often went on until late in the evening, and I would not get to bed until the early hours of the morning."'

'Without a trace of a smile, she added, "You will be paid seven pounds a year. This will be held in trust until you obtain a ticket-of-leave." It seemed to me I was once again little more than a slave leading a life of endless drudgery, always at the mercy of a mistress who could punish me for the slightest irregularity.'

'Finally she came to my reward for good service by saying, "We firmly believe in the importance of adherin' to Christian principles. You will be granted free time on Sundays when you are expected to attend church, and sit in the convict pew with the cook and laundress for the mornin' service. Never forget your salvation lies in repentance for your crimes." No doubt to be reminded once again about the wages of sin, I thought.'

'The woman continued to look at me with searching eyes before adding, "Now go to your duties, unless you have any questions about your work." No madam, I said. I understand all you have told me.'

'It seemed to me, my daily routine would be similar to that of my Birmingham days, except I hoped life in a sunnier climate would be more pleasant. I served the family for more than six months before going with them to Launceston.'

Here, her growing love for George gave her joy and hope for the future, only to be dashed so soon. On her return to Hobart Town she felt a great sadness, and in the years that followed she continued her duties with heavy heart.

Chapter 33

False Accusation

Now they had found each other again, Elizabeth and George continued to meet for a few short hours each Sunday afternoon after attending their church service. They would sit together at their favourite spot overlooking the distant Derwent River and talk of their future.

At their first meeting Elizabeth turned to George, saying, 'we must never lose each other again.'

'Yes,' said George. 'We'll have to settle on a plan to find each other if one of us doesn't arrive one Sunday.'

After a few moments of discussion Elizabeth suggested, 'apart from illness, the most likely place to find the other would be the Cascade Factory for me, or heaven forbid, Port Arthur for you.'

'How could I get a message to you at the Factory?'

'I've heard said there is an underground network getting messages and supplies to and from the outside world,' Elizabeth said. 'It's a matter of buying one's way into it.'

'In that case we'll have to keep a little money aside to bribe a messenger.'

'But we have to find a way to get it started,' said Elizabeth.

'I'll throw a message with some money over the wall if it ever becomes necessary,' said George. 'And we must have false names to avoid suspicion.'

'What names do you suggest?' Elizabeth asked.

' How about Mary and Joseph?'

'You are very irreligious,' she laughed. 'But those names should be easily remembered.'

And so they continued to meet for a few short hours until early in November when Elizabeth failed to arrive. George did not see her at church, and after waiting for most of the afternoon he made straight to the address where he knew Elizabeth worked. It was an act of desperation, as he could not be sure whom he might find to talk to. With the threat of being returned to Port Arthur, it was important he did not raise suspicion of any questionable activity.

He found the house: a spacious double storied villa set on a large block of land extending up a long slope. All seemed quiet. In the deserted street he walked briskly past the house, stopping further along at a sheltered spot where he could observe it in the hope somebody would emerge.

Eventually a woman in convict clothing came along the street. As she paused to open the gate, George rushed to ask about Elizabeth. She introduced herself as the cook, and was acquainted with all the facts. To allay suspicions, she suggested they walk separately and meet further along the street.

'Elizabeth has been returned to the Cascade Factory,' she said. ''Tis a long story. I'll start at the beginning.'

'Yes, please do,' said George in a tense voice.

'The mistress has a daughter who sometimes comes home at a weekend to see her parents. She usually stays for a day or two afore going back to Richmond. She is several years older than Elizabeth, and a bit spoiled. Sometimes she causes a scene with her mother.'

'Go on,' said George,

'She always treated Elizabeth and us with great contempt, and would often order us to do extra work. When it interfered with our schedule it usually brought us a reprimand from the mistress.'

'We all have to cope with these hard taskmasters,' George muttered.

'Elizabeth worked hard all through winter,' the cook said. 'But when the weather warmed in early spring, a cough she had on the voyage still bothered her.'

'Yes,' said George. 'She had mentioned it.'

'One morning, she woke ill and feverish. 'Twas hard for the lass to get out of bed and dress. So I went down to the kitchen early on her behalf, and set the fire in the coal range myself. Unfortunately the daughter came to hear of it.'

George frowned and shifted uneasily.

'She told Elizabeth she was lazy, and to dress and bring breakfast to her bedroom. Elizabeth did as ordered although she felt quite faint and sickly, but we heard the daughter shouting at her again and calling Elizabeth slothful, She would not hear of Elisabeth being ill.'

'What a bully,' said George.

'Shortly afterwards the daughter complained about Elizabeth to her mother. The mistress straightaway summonsed her to the study. When Elizabeth told her she was sick, the mistress would not believe her. She ordered her to get on with her work.'

'Poor Elizabeth.'

'A while later the daughter went to the study and told her mother she had discovered five shillings of her money missing from her room.'

'She was surely not accusing Elizabeth of theft, was she?'

'We all knew it was some sort of a ploy by the daughter.'

'Yes, go on,' said George.

'The mistress flew into a rage. We heard her shouting at Elizabeth, "I will put you in your place you young whore." Then she called the constabulary who took Elizabeth in charge.'

'What a terrible woman,' George ground out.

The cook nodded. 'As they led Elizabeth away the mistress shouted, "Have her strip searched, and her room thoroughly gone over." But they never found any money.'

'Elizabeth is no thief,' was all George managed to say

'T'was obvious the family could not keep her on after that. The magistrate, who always sides with free settlers, returned her to the Female Factory for misconduct.'

As the unfortunate story unfolded, George became almost speechless with bitterness and frustration. The cook listened to his angry outburst with great sympathy, standing silent while he kept deploring over and over how some of the free settlers would use their power to commit acts of great injustice, simply because they knew they could get away with it.

'What pleasure must they get from making poor people's lives even more miserable?' he muttered.

The cook fixed George in her gaze and said, 'Does you know what we think?'

George shook his head.

'The mistress must have suspected Elizabeth was meeting you. When we heard her call Elizabeth a young whore we think, to the mistress, it meant deviant behaviour. 'Twould be more than enough for her to send Elizabeth back to the Female Factory.'

The cook gave George what consolation she could, but at last left him to find his way back to the barracks in a distressed state.

He remembered one of the scenarios he had discussed with Elizabeth, and knew his next move would be to throw a message over the wall and make contact with her at the Female Factory. But before he could do this, he had a further week to wait while he fretted and fumed at the turn of events.

He knew Elizabeth would hope for some form of communication from him, and assume it would come on a Sunday afternoon. She once told him the Factory had three enclosed yards, but he had no way of knowing which one she occupied. In anticipation, he wrote out three identical messages during the week, and put each in a little cardboard box. He used her proper name of Elizabeth Allen to be as sure as he could of her getting the message. Then he tied each to a small stone for weight, ready to throw over the walls.

After the compulsory church service on the following Sunday he hurried to Cascades. Being a long walk up the valley, it took him until early afternoon to reach the slope beside the Female Factory. He found the hillside already crowded with a motley collection of men; ex-convicts, soldiers, sailors from the port, and a variety of riffraff, all vying for the women's attention. He heard shouting from the Factory, and made out women milling about inside the walls, but no matter how he tried he could not see Elizabeth.

At last he could bear it no longer, and came down the slope to the prison wall. It was higher than he had imagined, but he managed to throw each of the messages over the parapet before making his way up the hill again. But no return message came back. Finally, after waiting as long as possible, he gave a futile wave and slumped off to his barracks, intent on repeating his vigil the following Sunday. How happy he had been to find Elizabeth, only now to lose her.

Chapter 34

The Female Factory

After her arrest it was not just the loss of her assignment that troubled Elizabeth; her thoughts of George upset her even more. It saddened her to think of his concern for her, and she lived in the hope he would soon suspect her whereabouts and get a message to her.

The more she pondered about her return to the Factory, the more Elizabeth thought the woman may have heard rumours of her relationship with George. This would be enough to set about returning her to the Female Factory. She tried to resign herself to her situation and not dwell on it, but the dank valley of Cascades held nothing to raise her spirits. The early summer sun never shone long enough to warm the cold stonewalls of the Factory. Her thoughts were always with George, and in her despair she wondered if she would ever see him again.

On her arrival at the Factory guards took her to the ablution area and cut her long, wavy hair short. 'For the sake of cleanliness and health reasons,' they told her. In its place they issued her with a prison cap. A supervisor then escorted her to a bathroom, and ordered her to undress and give herself a good scrub in a bath under a watchful eye. After passing inspection, Elizabeth found her warm dress had been exchanged for rough prison garb.

Now attired in a coarse cotton dress and cap, a guard took her to the matron, Mrs Hutchinson, for questioning. Elizabeth knew her to be a woman widely criticized in the newspaper because of the high infant mortality at the Female Factory. A series of articles revealed how young women assigned to free settlers remained at the mercy of their masters. They had no rights, which left them vulnerable to sexual exploitation. If an overseer made a woman pregnant he simply returned her to the Factory for misconduct, and for her sin she received a sentence of a year's hard labour. This punishment did not start immediately, but after giving birth, babies remained at the Factory with their mothers. After two months they were weaned to an ordinary prison diet, and the mothers then began their year's hard labour breaking stones.

Later, Elizabeth met several of these women, one of them a girl of about sixteen with a small baby. The lass told her she had been assigned as housemaid to a middle-aged couple farming about twenty miles out of town. But on several occasions, while his wife was away during the day, the man took her to her bedroom and forcibly raped her. When he discovered she was pregnant, he returned her to the Factory for misconduct. Now, serving hard labour, and with her baby daughter weaned to gruel and burgou, she worried for the little girl's welfare.

With the death of scores of babies, and not a few mothers, it saddened Elizabeth to learn of so many little mounds of upturned dirt in surrounding paddocks where babies lay buried in unmarked graves. Overseers removed the few children reaching a year old, and transferred them to the orphanage at New Town. Mothers seldom saw their children again. All these newspaper reports made Elizabeth glad she had been assigned to a family that had not molested her in that way.

But despite adverse criticism of the matron, Elizabeth found her rather dignified, and giving the impression of being capable of maintaining strict discipline. She was not stern, but gave an air of authority as she spelt out the rules to Elizabeth on her arrival.

'Behaviour is the key to progress,' she began. 'At first you will be given a single cell at night to be away from the bad influences of some of our troublemakers. There, in solitude, your salvation will come about through self-reflection and repentance.'

Even from her own youthful experience, Elizabeth could have told the matron that good resolutions seldom succeed. She had seen people's habits change willy-nilly as they adapted to circumstances. She knew the same person could behave devoutly at church, badly in evil company, aggressively in a riotous crowd and cringe in the face of authority.

Rather than spending years cooped up at the Female Factory, Elizabeth considered it would be far better to allow women convicts to mix with decent people in society where they could gain self-respect. She believed nobody was a paragon, and was well aware custodians who looked after women prisoners were seldom models of probity and virtue. Later, she saw them use their authority to take advantage of defenseless women.

After her interview, an overseer gave Elizabeth a prison number and escorted her to a single cell of the same number in a long line of small stone cells, each a cold and miserable place. She shivered as she passed them. When the overseer opened the heavy wooden door of her cell she saw her bed was a raised block of stone with little space to move beside it. A straw pad and single blanket lay on top. She noticed the wet floor, and it hadn't rained for several weeks. Later, fellow inmates told her water constantly seeped in under the walls, compelling the authorities to raise the beds because the nearby stream sometimes flooded and poured water into the cells. To get out of bed each winter morning, women sometimes had to stand in several inches of freezing water to dress.

Nearby in the open yard, silent women went about their daily routine, many at tubs, and up to their elbows in soapsuds washing clothes. Elizabeth learned some of the laundry came from prison staff, but much arrived from free settlers and the military who routinely sent their dirty washing to the Factory.

Other women took advantage of the open air to do their needlework. Elizabeth wondered who would be wearing the beautifully decorated shirts and blouses the women worked on.

As the overseer conducted her through the yard, she noticed several convicts sitting about as if they had nothing to do. They stood out by being better dressed than those around them. Several younger women accompanied each of them, and seemed to be fawning about them. As the overseer escorted her past one of the groups, the woman at the centre of attention turned to look at Elizabeth.

The woman gave her a cold stare. 'Just look at who's come back,' she said in a mocking tone. 'I haven't forgotten you, little lassie.'

'Hello Betsy,' said Elizabeth. 'Fancy meeting you again.' And she wondered what revenge the woman might still have in mind.

During their long sea voyage the threat always worried her. Now she dismissed it with a shrug.

Elizabeth realized there was more to the groups' idleness than at first glance, and concluded the woman at the centre held some sort of power. She noticed them view her arrival with a certain interest, especially when they went into a huddle. She imagined them reaching a decision about her.

The overseer took her upstairs to a large workroom where dozens of women carded wool and flax in preparation for spinning. Others sat at spinning wheels and drew out long strands of wool for weaving into coarse tweed for prison dress. Further along the room women made a variety of hats, clothing, cushions, and even window blinds. Nobody hurried, but the workroom had an air of steady activity and little talking.

The overseer put Elizabeth into the charge of a woman to teach her to use a spinning wheel. She soon mastered the technique, but never settled to spinning from dawn till night for six days a week. At least her housework at New Town varied during the day. Here, under the constant eye of supervisors, the days became monotonous and irksome in the extreme. During her long hours of spinning, her thoughts would turn to George. How she longed to be enfolded in his arms. She would picture his smile, the way he walked, his gentle touch, and his kiss. Ah, his kiss. Her heart felt heavy in her loss, and she wondered if they would ever find each other again.

If she slowed in her work, the sharp tone of the supervisor's voice would bring he back to reality. Still, the occasional opportunity for conversation helped her to fit in with her fellow inmates, and into the general atmosphere of the workplace. Within a few days she recognized a widespread and generally warm feeling between the women. In the event of any trouble with the establishment she was sure they would all stick together. They certainly had in the past.

Most of the women had never been part of the criminal class, but had been transported for petty crimes like shoplifting, picking pockets, vagrancy and other minor offences brought about by economic need. Still, Elizabeth soon found herself back in a convict culture where some flourished and others suffered. In her workroom she became friendly with several women, otherwise illiterate, but expert in the rules of convict administration. She listened whenever they advised newcomers about the various prison procedures. The women knew details of a clandestine network that connected with the outside, and understood how to manipulate the system. They also gave excellent advice to those awaiting assignment, especially how to respond if victimized, and how to be returned to the Factory with the minimum of punishment. Elizabeth soon learned how to manipulate the Factory system, and twist the rules to her advantage. She wished she had known some of these ploys before being assigned herself.

She learned overseers were easily bribed, and convicts with a little cash could obtain almost anything. It only needed a compliant prison turnkey with access to keys, and any door could be opened. She soon learned some women communicated with friends outside the Factory, enabling them to bring in goods either for their own use or to barter, and in fact, do whatever they liked. They ate better food than others; drinking was common, and they had ready access to tobacco. These women always had cash, and used it to acquire tea, bread, meat, or sugar, some of which they bartered for clothing brought in by new arrivals. All this activity involved an underground of smuggling that entailed a complex organization of staff, or sometimes intimidation of fellow prisoners when necessary. Elizabeth learned this was how to contact George. To act without inside help was sure to lead to discovery, and further punishment. But the constabulary had confiscated the few shillings of her savings when they arrested her.

She knew if she could only get a letter to George and persuade him to send her some money, she would be able to use it to keep in contact with him. On the first Sunday afternoon she knew he would be waiting for her at their special spot, all the time unaware of her whereabouts. Even if he did come to the Female Factory, she wondered if he would be able to pick her out in the crowd when she looked like hundreds of others in identical prison garb and cap.

On the next Sunday, as she anxiously watched, she saw George arrive and stand on the low hillside opposite among others who kept trying to attract the women's attention. It gave her great joy to see him peering across to each yard in turn trying to pick her out before beginning to wave. But as most of the women milled about shouting and waving to the men, she could tell he had little hope of seeing her.

After a while she saw him leave the crowd and walk down the slope towards the Factory. She hoped he would throw something over the wall as they had arranged in case of such an emergency. Shortly afterwards she saw a small parcel come across, but it was immediately rushed by dozens of women. A few minutes later she saw him climb up the slope again and begin waving.

How she wished she could find out if he was the one who threw the parcel for her. In the end, the woman who snatched it was very good about it, although rather tardy in finding Elizabeth to hand it over.

She opened the small paper package with trembling fingers to find a small cake and a letter. It was addressed to Elizabeth but signed *Joseph* just as they had arranged. It poured out his devastation at the turn of events and wished her well, ending with his love for her. After his signature a further sentence read, 'Enjoy the Christmas cake,' a coded message to tell her it contained something. She found this was two shillings, a godsend under the circumstances. It enabled her to smuggle a return message to him through the underground network. In this way they were able to keep up their clandestine correspondence.

It did not surprise her that tensions and arguments commonly occurred among the hundreds of women crowded together in close confinement. In the midst of violence and intimidation between prisoners, and power struggles among a hierarchy of inmates, she did her best to remain as inconspicuous as possible, all the time wishing she could escape the cursing and swearing and obscenities around her.

She learned the women at the head of the inmates' hierarchy were known as the flash mob. They were easily recognized by their rings, silk handkerchiefs, by 'flash language' unintelligible to others, and by various symbols of status. She concluded Betsy must have been one of these. She imagined the admirers she had seen around Betsy and the other members of the flash mob were girls who had been introduced to their depraved habits. It was no secret the mob was interested in new arrivals and picked out easy prey, mainly young and modest women easily dominated and seduced into their lesbian ways.

At night in her damp cell Elizabeth remained remote from the shameless subculture that kept other inmates occupied after dark. Here, after finishing work, she spent her time all alone and engulfed in self-pity. She did a lot of crying. Finally, after several months, an overseer moved her to a dormitory containing more than sixty women.

Although prepared for what she might encounter, it came as a revelation to actually experience the scene. She watched as inmates spent their evenings making up bawdy songs about the male staff, their imagined sexual activities, and the size of their anatomical proportions. On some nights, Betsy and other members of the flash mob sang and danced naked, acting out all the references in the songs. Elizabeth soon became accustomed to their behavior and watched the fun.

She learned the women held in the highest esteem by their fellows were those who showed the most daring. Ones with the greatest prestige were the flash mob. They were ringleaders who could stir up trouble or lead riots. They had the power to unite inmates to resist anything that might disadvantage any of their number. Clearly, the authorities found the flash mob difficult to deal with. On occasions, the mob would assail a supervisor with obscene language, or even tear the shirt from his back if he tried to transfer a woman from their group. On one occasion Elizabeth saw firearms displayed.

Ever since her arrival at the Factory Elizabeth had noticed some women going round in pairs, and seldom seen apart. During the day the couple did little to attract attention, but simply sat together talking and giggling, and seemed interested only in each other. One Sunday morning after divine service in the chapel word quickly spread that while the minister preached morality and piety, two women were detected exciting each other's passions. While couples generally behaved with more decorum during the day, at night and away from the gaze of supervisors, they carried on in a most abandoned way, sharing a hammock during the hours of darkness to the disgust of other women.

While a few misbehaved, Elizabeth listened to others who spent their evenings talking about settlers they had once been assigned to. They advised new arrivals how best to pilfer, and how to avoid apprehension. If one of a pair became assigned to a settler, they would commit a crime to be returned to the Factory, and back to the arms of their paramour.

One evening soon after her transfer from the single cell, an inmate about her own age approached her. Elizabeth became wary when she recognized the woman as one of Betsy's paramours from the flash mob, and remained on her guard. After chatting in a friendly way for a few minutes the woman began to use the most foul and suggestive language. Within moments her hand was under Elizabeth's skirt and groping up her thigh. Elizabeth sprang to her feet shouting, 'Get away you filthy minded whore. I'll not have you destroy me.'

At first the woman looked surprised and not a little miffed, but soon took it in good part. Elizabeth did not think the woman had been acting on her own initiative. Rather, that Betsy must have sent the woman to test her. It left her wondering what revenge they might still have in store for her.

One day, while Elizabeth worked at her spinning wheel, a supervisor came into the room, shouting, 'all you single women get down to the yard.' As an air of excitement spread round the workplace, the women who seemed to know the reason wasted no time in rushing outside.

'What's going on?' Elizabeth asked as she hurried out with the others.

'Someone must have come here to chose a wife,' the girl beside her said. 'Any man, apart from a convict, can simply arrive here unannounced and pick someone to marry.'

How disgusting, Elizabeth thought. I hope he doesn't like the looks of me. 'Do you have to marry them if you don't want to?' she asked the girl.'

'Well, I suppose you could refuse if you had any real concerns about him,' she answered. 'But most of us would marry anybody who seems half all right. It gets us out of Cascades.'

As the excited women lined up in the courtyard, the matron appeared with a young soldier looking a little self-conscious, but doing his best to appear manly in the presence of so many eager women. Short and ungainly, he did not impress Elizabeth with his moon face, and crinkly hair. As he strutted along the line carefully scrutinizing each woman, she detected an arrogant expression on his face, suggesting he could be quite a bully. She made sure she gave him such a look of disdain that he glanced away as he passed. However, his appearance did not discourage other women who drew on all their feminine wiles to attract his attention.

After pacing up and down several times he finally selected a young well-proportioned girl with fair, wavy hair and pink cheeks. At first she appeared too overwhelmed to respond until suddenly, giving a whoop of joy, she began dancing up and down and clapping her hands with excitement.

When everybody joined in the fun, Elizabeth turned to one of the older women. 'What happens to her now?' She asked.

'Oh, she will be freed tomorrow to spend the day with him to get to know each other,' she answered. 'If he likes her they'll be married. If he doesn't like her he'll return her to the Factory and pick another.'

'It really is a man's world,' Elizabeth replied.

By now, more than six years had passed since she had first been arrested and sentenced. After being crammed into a tiny ship with a hundred and fifty women for almost six months she had learned a great deal about human nature, not least how to maintain self-respect in the midst of wantonness. Early in the voyage she remembered how her sense of common decency had been offended by licentiousness and unnatural practices. Now, in the overcrowded and undisciplined conditions of the Female Factory, the fiery temperaments and depraved behaviour of many of its incarcerated women meant little to her. Occasional messages from George continued to buoy her spirits. But she remained conscious of their vulnerability and did not want to draw attention to herself by communicating with him too often.

Chapter 35

Betrayal

While Elizabeth served her sentence in the Female Factory, George continued his brickmaking. Since finding Elizabeth again a great calm had brought him solace, and renewed his inner strength. After suffering so much injustice he was at last coming to terms with himself. But since Elizabeth's return to the Female Factory his old resentment of the law soon crept back.

While he understood how destructive it would be to continue his bitterness at the unjust treatment both he and Elizabeth had suffered across the years, he knew he had to keep thinking positively. He felt it was the only way to give him strength to cope with the disastrous events that had so recently overtaken them. How he longed to reach out again and touch Elizabeth, take her hand in his, caress her soft skin and tell her how much he cared.

Now, being a second-class convict able to work for himself all day Saturday, he had saved a little money for the time he received his ticket-of-leave. It pleased him to know Elizabeth had been able to buy her way into the Factory network with the help of the shillings he had tossed over the wall. In return she had told him how to connect with the network from the outside, and pass on other advice she gleaned from her fellow inmates. With this information he smuggled small amounts of cash into the Female Factory. It gave him great satisfaction in giving her a few shillings to make life more comfortable, and enable her to send messages back to him.

As part of the chain of communication he enlisted his friend, Henry Carpenter, who worked with him in the brickmaking team. But it was a risky business. If their messages were ever intercepted it would turn out badly for all of them.

The network worked well for almost nine months until George received no reply to his latest messages. He realized something serious must have happened to Elizabeth. Whenever he had communicated with her, he usually received a reply within a week. When she had not replied after several weeks he became uneasy. At first he thought it might be because she had been sent to a new assignment and could not yet arrange a message. But after a month he became desperate. Surely by now somebody should have got a message to him. Disturbing thoughts began to give him sleepless nights. Was she ill? As weeks passed, the very idea depressed him and began to affect his work.

'You's a slacker, White,' his supervisor said. 'If you don't get a move on you'll be back at Port Arthur.'

George forced himself to keep working to the supervisor's satisfaction, but as weeks turned into months with no communication he continued to worry for her welfare. With no way of discovering the truth, he could do nothing but wait.

Meanwhile, within the factory Elizabeth lived with the faith that one day, sometime in the indefinite future, she would be reunited with George. She resigned herself to wait out her time; hopeful it would all turn out for the best. Then, one morning as she sat at her spinning wheel a supervisor approached her.

'Come with me,' he said. 'You are summonsed to the matron's office.'

Elizabeth followed him perplexed, but worried in case of trouble, and tapped at the Matron's door.

'Word has reached me you have been communicating with somebody on the outside,' the Matron said.

Elizabeth flushed. 'Yes, matron, I was tempted to bargain for extra food at times.'

'What a shame you did not take my advice and pray for repentance in the solitude of your cell.'

'Oh, matron, I did pray, and tried so hard.'

'And who is this Joseph fellow you contact?'

'I know him only as Joseph. He sends me food at a price.'

'We will track him down, never fear.'

It terrified her to think what this would mean for George and Henry Carpenter if they were discovered. For all she knew, both would be returned to Port Arthur.

'You are reduced to a class four convict and transferred to yard one,' the Matron said. 'There, you will serve one year of hard labour. You will also be on bread and water for the first week.'

Elizabeth hung her head in despair.

The matron continued to glare at her. 'You will remain at the Factory until you learn what it means to be a good citizen.'

Elizabeth left the matron's office in a state of shock and barely able to walk. As the guard escorted her through the crowd of women in the open yard they passed close to Betsy and her group. Betsy turned, and Elizabeth saw her mocking smile.

'It doesn't pay to cross with Betsy, does it girlie,' she said.

Without warning Elizabeth leapt at Betsy. Both her fists shot out striking the woman's face with all the force of her body behind it. Taken by surprise, Betsy stumbled backwards. In falling, she struck her head on the rough courtyard where she lay in a daze with blood trickling from her nose and mouth. Before the guard could grab her, Elizabeth gave Betsy a good kick in the stomach, causing the woman to let out a squeal of pain before sinking back onto the ground.

The guard, accustomed to feminine disagreements, simply took Elizabeth by the arm and led her away as if nothing out of the ordinary had happened.

Chapter 36
BitterSweet Times

Elizabeth lived in deep despair. For months now, she had spent every day of her hard labour breaking up rocks in the company of the most recalcitrant and foul-mouthed women she had ever met. Each morning at dawn guards escorted her with the others to their place of work where a pile of large rocks had to be pounded into smaller pieces. As the heap of shattered stones grew, other convicts barrowed them away and replaced them with large, ill-shaped rocks waiting to be smashed. In all weathers Elizabeth stood exposed to the elements, and forced to work without pause. Her shoulders and back ached all day, and the jarring of the large hammer as it struck the rock sent shafts of pain up her arms.

With her mind full of self-pity she saw her emaciated body becoming thinner and more haggard, and she wondered if she had the strength to keep going for a whole year. In her despair, at first she hoped to get word from George through an alternative network. But she heard nothing, and worried he had been returned to Port Arthur. It would be all her fault, she thought. With her whole world collapsed around her, she saw no end to her misery, and doubted at times if her life was worth living.

***

While George forced himself to work, at times he felt so low in spirits he didn't care what they did to him. Towards the end of summer he went to the bank as usual to deposit his meagre earnings.

'A letter has arrived for you,' the teller said. 'Collect it from the other counter.'

At last a reply from my grandfather, he thought, and his body trembled at the prospects it might hold for him. When a clerk handed him the letter he noticed his address written in the copperplate script of an official scribe rather than that of his grandfather. He broke the seal and carefully unfolded the paper. His heart pounded when he saw a solicitor's letter.

Dear Sir

The letter you sent to your grandfather was handed to me to inform you he was cruelly murdered in the winter of 1836. All attempts to locate your whereabouts failed, and eventually your grandfather's legacy passed to your brother Alfred who, I must say, has proved an excellent recipient. He retains an interest in the business, which continues to prosper, and lives in the family home with his wife and children. He continues to care for your Aunt Maude and your one surviving sister, Emma.

One evening as your grandfather emerged from his office a footpad struck him down. At first he appeared to be the victim of a senseless attack. But several weeks later we, as his solicitors, received correspondence from a person by the name of Aubrey Jones who produced a document and letter, purportedly from your grandfather and supporting his claim to the inheritance.

He might have succeeded but for several small inconsistencies in his forged documents, one of which was a copy of a document given to your mother to hold on your behalf. It spelt out your inheritance. Jones had substituted his name for yours. He was arrested and under questioning finally broke down and confessed to an elaborate plan to defraud the estate. Because of his confession and naming of his accomplices, who were subsequently hanged, his death sentence was commuted to one of life imprisonment. At this time he languishes in Millbank Prison where he will remain till the end of his days.

I have the honour to be, Sir,

Your obedient servant,
J.W.Fellows.

The shock of the news sent his mind blank. He moved to a nearby chair and for a few minutes he sat as if in a trance before reading and rereading the letter. It saddened him to think of his father and sister, Mary; both were dead and he never knew. He continued to sit despondently, thinking I have lost Elizabeth and now have no inheritance.

For a long time he sat staring vacantly at the tellers and the people coming and going, but taking in nothing of the activity round him. He eventually walked out of the bank not knowing where he was going. He thought of the chimera of false expectations that had buoyed his spirits across the years, and as he wandered the streets his thoughts turned to Elizabeth. He pictured her tall, thin figure, and relived their secret times together when love brought them so much fulfillment and promise. He wondered if she was still alive.

Although the loss of his inheritance disappointed him, he realized in the end the legacy had served a double purpose. While his brother had the benefit of the inheritance, his own hopes of a better life had buoyed his spirits through troubled times. His expectation of a legacy had not been in vain, but he wondered what the future might hold for him now.

At last he knew Aubrey Jones was a thief. But while the letter gave him satisfaction that Jones had met his just deserts, he did not wish on him all the suffering the man had inflicted upon him.

But what had happened to Elizabeth? Sick with worry, as the months passed, he could do nothing to find out the truth. Why had nobody at the Factory sent him a message about her? Was she dead?

At last, in March 1845 he received his ticket-of-leave. In the past, being a convict, he was forbidden to ask for Elizabeth in marriage. Now he was free to marry. He planned to get information about her as soon as he could by legally applying to marry her. It was his only way to find out what had happened to her, or even if she was still living.

Without delay he sent a request for marriage to the Colonial Secretary who approved it in a matter of days. To his relief, this information confirmed she was at least alive. The Secretary's office in turn notified the Matron of the Female Factory of the arrangement. But for all George knew she might be seriously ill. It did not deter him, and he put this thought out of his mind. Now armed with the appropriate documents, he set out for St John's Church on New Town Road to discuss wedding bans with the Rev. Thomas Ewing, the Minister at that time.

***

One bleak morning, as Elizabeth stood in the cold compound breaking stones, a guard approached her. 'The matron wishes to see you,' he said. 'Come with me.'

What more could have happened, she wondered? If they want to interrogate me again I will never mention George's name whatever happens. She tried to look calm as she entered the matron's office.

'A ticket-of-leave government man by the name of George White has put in a request to marry you,' the matron said. 'Do you know him?'

The shock of the blunt question caught Elizabeth off guard. For a moment she hesitated, wondering if it was some sort of a trap. 'Yes, I remember him from the days before they sent me here,' she fimally stammered.

'You must have made a profound impression on him. I wonder why he suddenly remembers you when it was so long ago,' the matron replied with a knowing look.

Elizabeth blushed. It was clear to her by the way the matron spoke she must have known all along they had been keeping in touch. But why had she not tried to catch them earlier?

It suddenly occurred to her that the matron must have been using them as pawns to catch worse offenders. Only after Betsy betrayed her to the authorities would the matron then be obliged to sentence her to hard labour. It also explained why she had not reported George, too.

'If you are agreeable to marry him, arrangements will be made to assign you to his care,' the matron said. 'If you misbehave, or give him any cause to reject you, you will be returned to the Factory to serve out the remainder of your sentence.' The matron paused. 'Do you understand?'

'I do,' Elisabeth answered. 'And I agree to marry him.'

'Arrangements are already under way,' the matron added with the trace of a smile. 'But bans still have to be read. The earliest date available for the ceremony is the 28th of April. You will be discharged into the care of George White on the 26th. Meanwhile, your sentence of hard labour is suspended.'

Suddenly Elizabeth felt she stood on the threshold of a wondrous new life, free of shame and disrespect, and where her present existence would be only a grim memory. She realized her dreams of a better life had become an unexpected reality. Her days sprang into a fresh liveliness, and those around her quickly noticed her newfound happiness. Back at her old place at the spinning wheel, astonished companions plied her with questions.

'Why is you looking so pleased with yourself?' was their first question, as women keen for details gathered round her.

'I'm to be married in several weeks,' she burst out with excitement.

They met her announcement with gasps of surprise and encouragement to tell her story. Those working close to her suggested they make a wedding frock to sell her. Then everybody would gain, they said. Elizabeth agreed. She chose a dark woollen material as being practical, and in keeping with the fashion of the times. Women made the patterns, and within a week the dress took shape. Needlewomen decorated it with beautiful embroidery, and although they knew Elizabeth had no money at the time, they trusted her to pay them all once she became free.

The night before her release, she lay awake with a feeling of trepidation, knowing it would be the first time George had seen her for more than a year. She trembled at the thought, as she had become so thin and haggard she wondered how he would react on seeing her.

But at the first sight of each other all her doubts vanished. The Factory gate opened and she saw George waiting for her beside a small horse-drawn wagon ready to take her along the muddy streets. Although they could not show their true feelings in public, their eyes told each other of their deep abiding love. George helped her to scramble on to the wagon, and quickly joined her. For a few moments they simply sat gazing at each other, entranced. As they continued to look, George saw tears of happiness begin to well up and purl down her cheeks.

He took her hand with a gentle caress, and looking into her eyes, said, 'from now on the future is for us to share. It is a time of double happiness for us; a time of togetherness, and a time to say good-bye to the Female Factory, and this cold, bleak valley forever.'

With a shake of the reins the wagon began to move. She wondered where George was taking her, but this, he told her, was to be a surprise. Although she still wore prison garb, people on the streets barely gave them a glance. With a new sense of freedom they made their way down through Hobart Town and up the rise to New Town Road.

As they passed the house where she had been assigned, Elizabeth remembered the fateful day the mistress returned her to the Factory. Ever since that time, she had lived in misery and the unendurable grief the woman had caused her. Yet, it occurred to her it meant nothing to her now. Gone was the terrible darkness of despair when at times she had almost lost the will to live. She wondered how she could have ever survived without George.

Further along they turned a corner, and he stopped the wagon outside a small cottage set back from the road. George turned to her with a smile and said, 'we are home.'

She looked at him through tears of joy, and a smile illuminated her face with such happiness he leaned across and gently kissed her cheek, knowing any show of affection in public could have serious consequences for them. He opened the gate with a jaunty bow, and ushered her through the door and into the house. Its several small rooms had polished floors with dark matching furniture, and through a window she was delighted to glimpse a small garden at the back. It was a simple workman's cottage, but to Elizabeth it was more than a palace.

She scarcely had time to display her wedding frock when two people appeared at the door. 'Come in and meet the bride,' George called, and introduced Henry and Ann Carpenter who were to be best man and bridesmaid. Elizabeth found them a pleasant couple: Ann inclined to giggle with excitement, and the dour Henry, thickset and awkward. He explained that, like George, he was a brick maker and a ticket-of-leave government man. Ann confessed she had also been transported, and like Elizabeth, had been released in the charge of her new husband.

Elizabeth thanked Henry for the risks he took helping George communicate through the underground. She made him promise to give up these clandestine activities, as the matron probably knew of his involvement and may not be so considerate if he offended again.

After a cup of tea, they set off in their wagon to meet the Rev. Ewing for introductions, and final wedding arrangements. Elizabeth had attended St John's Church ever since her arrival in Hobart Town, and clapped her hands with joy. 'What a magnificent church and setting for us to be married in,' she exclaimed.

The approach between two imposing gatehouses on New Town Road led to the church, set on a rise at the end of a long driveway. The church, flanked by the Orphans' School, had always impressed her with its imposing bell tower and large clock near the top. She knew convicts built it, and she always enjoyed the view from the church, extending across the countryside to hills beyond the Derwent River.

Along with Elizabeth, George and the Carpenters also knew the church well, having regularly attended with their fellow convicts. Each Sunday they had climbed a narrow set of stairs to reach the convict gallery on one side of the church. Throughout the service they sat on hard, backless benches designed for convicts and their guards, with a partition separating men and women convicts to prevent distraction during the service. George remembered with a laugh that a few years earlier when the gallery had become overcrowded, the authorities allowed several selected convicts to sit in the body of the church. However, members of the congregation quickly objected to their presence, and complaints to the Colonial Secretary followed. To get rid of them, the free settlers accused the convicts of infesting the church with bugs!

During the service, the authorities always securely locked doors to the convict gallery to prevent any escape. The opposite gallery accommodated orphans who lived in the adjacent school.

George, always ready with a humorous tale, said that long before their time a screen had been paced to hide the orphans after the convicts were accused of leering at the older girls. Deprived of this little diversion during divine service, it left the convicts with no option but to pay attention to the sermon.

Since they had not yet received their pardon, George and Elizabeth still had to continue attending church every Sunday. From where she sat in the convict gallery, Elizabeth often saw the mistress who had returned her to the Female Factory. She sat with her husband in their family pew in the body of the church. Although Elizabeth had worked for the woman for several years, whenever they passed, she never gave Elizabeth any sign of recognition.

The morning of the wedding dawned one of those dull days when wet winds left the ground soggy and smelling of dead vegetation. Fortunately, George had the use of a horse and wagon as the access had become muddy, and would have been almost impassable on foot. But nothing dampened their excitement. They barely noticed the dreary day and steely-grey sky. All four arrived at the church with their thoughts on happier things.

The minister, waiting by the door to greet them, straightaway escorted them to the altar. In the absence of a congregation, George felt the body of the church empty and sombre. And because of the overcast day, and the gloomy atmosphere inside, he watched as the minister read the marriage service assisted by light from a nearby candle. The ceremony was quickly over, and the marriage register signed. Apart from the two Carpenters and the minister, nobody else came to wish them well.

They all simply clambered back on to their wagon and drove down the long driveway, giving little thought to the sound of the wheels squelching through the mud and puddles. George looked ecstatic. At last Elizabeth was his wife. He gazed at her and she smiled back. She looked so calm and yielding. He had never seen her so beautiful.

The newly weds had the rest of the day to themselves, remaining inside their little rented cottage, oblivious of the world around them. Their love had endured so much adversity and wrong, but at last had triumphed over a cruel justice system.

Chapter 37

Life Renewed

In the early evening five children lay asleep in one of the two bedrooms. Once they were quiet, George and Elizabeth relaxed in their sparsely furnished lounge room. Every day was always a long day for George. As the years passed, brick making became more and more strenuous for him, and he was glad to spend an hour or two in his rocker before turning in for the night. Nearby, Elizabeth sat mending by the light of an oil lamp set next to her. Tonight she had socks to darn, yesterday a smock torn in play. With a young family there was always work to be done after the children were in bed.

It was more than twenty years since George had first been arrested, in those days just a callow youth setting out to seek a better life. Across the years he had descended to the lowest depths of despair as day followed day bringing nothing but pain and anguish. But through it all he became a muscular and worldly wise man, still eager to lead a gainful life, and share the warm glow of his feelings with the woman he loved.

Each day he continued to work enthusiastically, and earned enough to support his family comfortably through the years. But it was not until 1848 that Elizabeth received her ticket-of-leave, followed by a conditional pardon several months later. Meanwhile, their family grew. Little more than a year after they married Joseph was born, and named in memory of their times of trial. In the years that followed, several brothers and sisters joined the little lad, as was the custom in those days.

As time passed, Elizabeth noticed George becoming quiet and pensive in the evenings. He seemed to have lost his natural sense of humour, and she began to suspect he harboured some kind of sadness. Then one evening he came home more cheerful, and she could not help but notice his smiles and look of happiness.

'You are in good cheer for a change,' she said.

'You know how gloomy I have been,' he replied. 'In the workplace I am constantly reminded of our convict past. In small ways the free settlers let it be known they still mistrust us. If we remain here we will have to live under a veil of suspicion for the rest of out lives.

'I have noticed it too, but it is something we have to accept. I try to ignore it,' Elizabeth said.

'But the stigma will last, and our children will suffer. We can't stay here.'

'After all this time, what has suddenly given you the inspiration to move?'

'I have been checking our savings, and at last we can afford to get away from Hobart Town for a fresh start. Our finances are good enough to go to where our past will never be questioned.

Elizabeth was all interest. 'Where can we possibly find such a place?'

'I have heard of a town that is about as far from penal servitude as we could ever get. It is across in New Zealand: a town called Dunedin. Gold has been discovered nearby and it's a growing region. They say there is ample work. Over there, nobody, and especially our young family, need ever know of our past. Once we are settled, I might even get to wear a white shirt at last.'

Elizabeth glowed with excitement. George saw a large tear form in her eye, and watched it slide down her cheek. In anticipation of a new life, she put down her mending, and going across to George, gave him a warm hug and the longest of kisses.

Printed in Great Britain
by Amazon